SO MUCH TO SAY
How to Help Your Child Learn to Talk

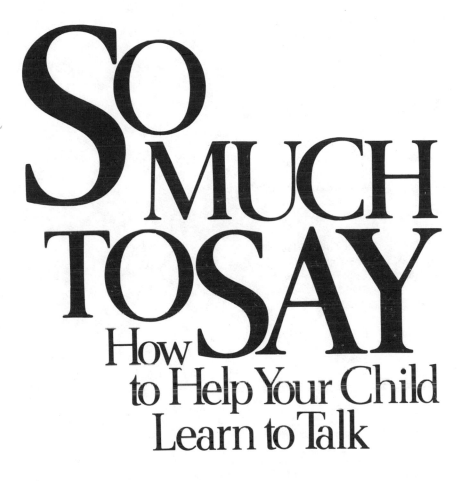

SO MUCH TO SAY
How to Help Your Child Learn to Talk

EDMUND BLAIR BOLLES

FOREWORD BY ANN C. NITZBURG

St. Martin's Press
New York

Copyright © 1982 by Edmund Blair Bolles

All rights reserved. For information, write:
St. Martin's Press, Inc., 175 Fifth Ave., New York, N.Y. 10010

Library of Congress Cataloging in Publication Data

Bolles, Edmund Blair, 1911–
  So much to say.
  1. Language acquisition—Popular works.
2. Child rearing—Popular works.   I. Title.
P118.B63   401'.9   81-16692
ISBN 0-312-73120-5   AACR2
ISBN 0-312-73121-3 (pbk.)

Manufactured in the United States of America

Dedicated to my own parents

BLAIR *and* MONA BOLLES

Probably I don't owe absolutely everything to them,
but most of me sure is a hand-me-down.

CONTENTS

Foreword

ONE OF THE JOYS of being a parent is your delight in your child's growth. The acquisition of language brings with it not only the opportunity to participate in a new area of your child's development, but also to further understand and share ideas and experiences from your child's perspective.

Traditionally, language has been defined as the entire communication system, encompassing gestures, body movements, crying, and other forms of communication, as well as listening, thought, and speech. Its roots lie deep in the warmth and trust of the preverbal parent-child relationship, where the initial communications centered around the child's needs and comfort and where the desire for communication and sharing was born. The child demonstrates this desire long before he acquires speech, but speech results in a new and different kind of development. With speech, the child is more precisely able to define and to communicate his needs, desires, and ideas. He also gains the ability to plan in a different way and to direct and regulate his own behavior toward long-term, less-immediate goals. Language helps a child to become—and to feel that he is—an effective, powerful learner who can affect both his immediate family environment and the larger world. Language provides a pivotal tool for self-control, self-direction, self-definition, and self-knowledge, as well as for active planning and the communication of thoughts and feelings.

Because language has so many different, overlapping dimensions, parents have difficulty knowing how best to help their children develop language abilities. This question is complicated by each child's individual style in learning. Each child approaches the same tasks in his own way at his own pace. As Edmund Blair Bolles points out, there is a range in normal development. This range relates not only to what is average for most children in our culture, but to what was average for other family members in the child's family. How then can parents differentiate between slow development and problem development?

In my experience, parents know their own children very well. Because parents often respond instinctively to their children's needs and individual styles, they can and should use themselves as sensitive barometers. Therefore, you should observe your own performance as well as your child's. Watch not only how your child responds to situations linguistically and to the language games which Edmund Blair Bolles suggests, but what you as a parent do naturally to support him. For instance, you may be concerned about your child's ability to listen and to understand what is said to him. Do you find that you automatically slow down your speech when you talk with him? Do you find yourself pausing after a question, or repeating the question a second time, in order to give him time to process the information? And do you add gestures to your language? Or almost always use shorter sentences? Your awareness of this interaction should enrich your appreciation of your child's strengths and unique style and what you are already doing to help him.

This book provides a good beginning point for the parent concerned with the issue of whether his child's speech is normal, as well as for the parent who wants to deepen his understanding of this aspect of his child's development. The book presents both the developmental path of language and descriptions of possible problems and idiosyncracies that can become evident at each stage of language growth. There is a wealth of specific information, much of which is highlighted in box format for clarity and easy reference. Strategies for stimulating language development, as well as specific games appropriate to each stage of language development are included in each chapter. Four chapters are devoted to questions of mispronunciation, hearing difficulty, and judging whether a language disorder exists. Finally, the language diary contained at the back of the book provides the opportunity for parents to record their child's process of language acquisition. This diary should also help parents formulate any specific concerns they have. It can become an invaluable referent in discussion with those professionals from whom the parent seeks help. When concerns are described in general terms, the worried parent is too often met with reassurances that "he'll outgrow it." These reassurances temporarily calm, then give way to nagging uncertainty or a secondary reaction of panic because the parent rightfully feels that he has not been taken seriously.

Despite the emphasis on the course of language development and desire to help parents pinpoint and enrich each stage of language development, this book is much more than a collection of milestones or ages and stages. Edmund Blair Bolles never loses touch with the complexity of language as a social tool nor underestimates the cultural forces embodied in language. He understands the primary power of language in personal expression and its potential for the creation of relationships and a social viewpoint. He is a writer in love with his subject, who conveys the awe and wonderment that the process of language acquisition and the power of language evoke.

—Ann C. Nitzburg

An Apology to Male Readers

HE, SHE, OR IT? A crisis has swept over English pronouns, and it is no longer acceptable to write sentences like, "When a child is one year old, *he* begins to talk." Offense is taken by many women over the way the pronoun *he* so cavalierly dismisses their sex. It does no good to point out that the use of *he* to mean any child is the result of a change in the sound patterns of Old English and has nothing to do with medieval chauvinism. The only real solution can be to coin a neutral set of pronouns that implies humanity but no gender. In the meantime, we are stuck with phony answers. Use of "he/she" is clumsy in a sentence and intolerable in a book. Alternating between "he" and "she" is contrary to the essence of language which calls for rules. To call a person "it" is barbaric, and I lack the gall necessary to invent a set of pronouns and then simply use them as though they were generally accepted. So, as a token of my good faith, I have chosen to use the pronoun "she" to indicate children of unspecified sex. Male readers have every right to protest that this solution is as outrageous as always using "he." I defend the decision only on the grounds that since I myself am a male, at least the language will not be taken as a sign that I am indifferent to the existence of half the population.

PART ONE
CHILDREN'S LANGUAGE

Here is that which will give language to you.
—W. SHAKESPEARE, *The Tempest*

Chapter 1
The Gift of Tongues

Mama. The word is ancient and everywhere. It is a baby's first word for mother in English, Swahili, French, Russian, Latin, Samoan, Swedish, and in many other languages. Indeed, its presence seems so widespread that we might wonder if it is really a natural cry rather than a word, but *mama* is not quite universal. We have to hunt a bit to find them, but some languages use different baby words for mother. In the South Pacific island of Tonga, the *m* has become a *b, bama.* In Albania, the first consonant has disappeared altogether, *ama.* Sanskrit used *nana,* the same word English children have for their governesses. And in the Australian outback lives a small tribe called the Njamal who do use the word *mama,* only it means father.

Obviously a baby's first word is in a special class. It is much more predictable than most words in a language, but it is not quite like the natural and truly universal sounds of an infant's first year. It is a word whose signification is set by society rather than by biology, and when a child first says it, she has made a firm step along the road toward becoming a member of a culture.

No wonder then that parents around the world are so

3

excited when their child begins to talk. It does not matter which language the parents speak; news that their baby has said her first word is always a cause for joy and a little bragging. It is a milestone as memorable as the first step. It is natural and expected, but when it finally comes, the event is so full of promise that instead of trying to find out what the baby means, parents frequently respond by running and congratulating her for being so clever and grown up. Not bad, thinks the child, and she speaks it again. *Mama.*

Uttering that first word is a uniquely human act. Other creatures have their ways of exchanging the bits of information that are necessary for survival, but none of them has a tool like language, a tool which permits them to share the contents of their heart. When we think of the uses of language in literature, drama, courtship, friendly conversation, disputation, sermonizing, sympathizing, and on and on, we admit quickly enough that language is not just another form of communication. Language is a keyhole peeking in on the mind, and, since the human mind can formulate so many new ambitions, sentiments, and attitudes, the keyhole has to be flexible and creative if it is to let us express what is in our minds. The first word promises that your child too will master language and be able to take her full place in the world of imagination and deliberate choice.

Naturally it will still be many years before the new talker can be told the things that are most important to a parent: ideas of right and wrong, good and evil, beauty and kindness. So a lot of the excitement about the baby's first word is excitement over what it promises for the future rather than for any immediate practical utility. Language is the tool which enables us to pass on the values and wisdom of the past. When a baby first cries *mama,* she has begun the long process of mastering the one thing which can bring her in touch with her parents' ideals, and with the whole culture that is to be her heritage. Most of this book will present a close look at the day-to-day details of how a child uses language, but the reason for all of these developments should be clear from the start. A person using language is able to give voice to the secrets of her inner self and to understand the thoughts of others.

The focus of this book, therefore, is on a double process: the use of new powers of language and the discovery of new things to say. The parents of a child who is beginning to talk will find a continuing delight in the way the appearance of language allows them to share in the development of their child's individual impressions and opinions of the world. This possession of private and unpredictable points of view is one of the most remarkable things about people, and alert parents can observe that individuality in their own child.

Traditionally it has been assumed that a parent's chief moral duty toward a child is to help mold and guide her attitudes. Nothing in any of the recent discoveries about children's language has challenged that assumption. On the contrary, the tradition has been reinforced.

We have learned, for example, that parents need not be especially concerned or nervous about their own understanding of grammar. Once the excitement of hearing a child's first word has dimmed a bit, parents can sometimes be troubled by an awareness of their own grammatical ignorance. None of us can fully explain the rules we use, and all of us occasionally have to hunt for the right word or the right way to put words together. Chances are the parents can remember being thoroughly puzzled by high-school grammar lessons. (I certainly can.) Honest parents are likely to admit to themselves that they may not be the most suitable language teachers a child could have. One of the points of this book is to insist that these concerns can be set aside. Your child is going to speak perfectly well, even if you flunked every grammar test you ever took. You should be more concerned about what your child has to say than whether she has said it perfectly.

Of course, I am not arguing that proper grammar is unimportant. The better one's grammar, the more likely the speaker will be understood. I am saying, however, that a child is not so dependent on her parents for learning what is good grammar. It was once supposed that children were born with minds as blank as a new blackboard. In recent years that idea has been overthrown. We shall see throughout this book that language especially is an area in which children seem to display an amazing amount of inborn interest, shrewdness, and ability. Thus, hearing children whose parents are deaf-mutes and children whose parents speak only a foreign language will learn to speak the language of their general community, even though their parents can give them no help at all.

Many readers are bound to complain that it defies common sense to say grammar can be learned without a teacher. This chapter cannot give a full portrait of the revolution which, during the past twenty years, has made such a statement possible. For the moment, let me say only that of all the many recent discoveries about children's language, the most important finding has been that the way a child uses language is more like a process of maturing than it is like ordinary learning.

Maturity comes whether or not th child or her elders expect it. Children automatically start to crawl, then walk, then run; their baby teeth come in, and years later a second set of teeth replaces the first; in adolescence they go through a series of physical changes which lead to sexual maturity. All of these events are inevitable, and each comes in the child's own good time. The onset of teething or puberty is predictable, but in any individual case such events usually begin either a bit earlier or later than the "average." Once the process has begun, however, it doesn't matter if it started late. A child whose teething was slow in coming still gets all thirty-two teeth.

Language development resembles these other maturing processes. You do not have to teach a child about grammar for her to use it. The starting time for the various stages of language development is not precise, and the speed at which a child's language matures is not a reliable measure of intelligence. In short, the basis of language is biological rather than being simply artificial.

No one should fear that these natural origins pose any threat to the obvious fact that language is something unique. I have been surprised to see how often people do seek to trivialize the remarkable fact that people, and only people, talk. I was once astonished by some letters I received after a magazine published an article of mine about baby talk. Several of my correspondents tried to insist that a word like *mama* arose because it was formed by the same lip movements a baby uses to suck. There are many faults with this sort of folk insight into the origins of language; for one thing (as we shall see), it overlooks the long history of sound-making that precedes saying *mama,* but at this point the central objection I wish to make is the way such a notion pushes language into a kind of convenient accident and the way it suppresses recognition of our fundamental need for language.

The world is full of sucking mammals, but of them all only people ever say *mama.* Talking, like walking on two feet, is built into our genes, but that fact does not make speech any the less deliberate or less remarkable.

We can get into trouble if we try to make too sharp a division between those activities which are natural and those which are cultural. Nature gives us teeth; culture tells us what to eat. Nature gives us puberty; culture defines the wedding ceremony. Nature gives us language; culture shows us how to use it.

The subtle task of parents, therefore, is to teach the value of language. We shall see that certain aspects of experience are universally recognized by even quite young children, but our attitude toward our experiences is our own. Language permits us to share these attitudes with others. Silence leaves us alienated, suspicious, and confused. A final purpose of this book, therefore, is to show parents how they can help children use language to form bonds between themselves and the people they speak with.

Indeed, from the beginning bonding is important in a child's speech, and surely much of the pleasure that comes from hearing a child's first words is that the words themselves refer to members of the family. *Mama* and *daddy* tend to head the list of any child's earliest vocabulary. Thus, one of the first things a baby's words show is that she recognizes her parents and is pleased to see them. If there are other children in the family, the baby will soon have names for them too. The priority given such words is visible proof that the family still holds first place in the life of the child.

The onset of language is thus a special opportunity. Communication has been going on between parent and child since birth. The child knows when she is being loved, and the parent knows when the child is uncomfortable or content. But with the coming of talking, communication can be much more profound and personal. No longer is the baby limited to signaling her emotions and pains. She can soon report that she sees her sister and is glad of it, or that she is sitting down, or lost her shoe. And now, for a change, the parents can begin to tell their child a few things like, "Pick up your shoe," or, "You are so cute." The possibility of the trust that comes with two-way communication has begun.

The rest of this book will pursue the three purposes outlined above. First, it will provide a detailed guide to the process by which a child uses language. Parents who understand that process will be rewarded many times with an appreciation of what their child is accomplishing and with a fuller understanding of who their child is.

Next, by observing the changes going on in your child's language, you will have a fuller picture of where your child's development stands. Any difficulties or strokes of genius can be spotted when they occur. Thus, parents using this book can help their child's speech through any problem periods.

Third and finally, along with offering practical help when questions arise, this book also offers a guide to day-to-day speech and ways for parents to promote their child's language talents. As I have said, this task is not so much concerned with the details of grammar and style. Such help has its place, but it is not the essential point. What is important is for children to realize that if they use language wisely, they can cut through doubt, mistrust, and loneliness.

Chapter 2
The Youngest Person

The heart of this book lies in the developmental chapters of Parts II and III, for they contain a detailed and practical account of children's language from birth to age five. Each of the developmental chapters has been divided into six sections.

Age: The chapters open with a brief description of the typical age range of children whose speech has reached the stage described in the chapter. Usually this section includes a chart that breaks the stage into smaller units and suggests the age and order in which the development proceeds. These age ranges have to be taken with a little caution because they report averages rather than rules. Some perfectly normal children are going to be "late," according to these charts. Fortunately, children are not trains with pressing reasons for being on time. Judge their language in the context of the whole chapter, not just on this age section.

Other Growth (found only in Part II): A brief account of other changes going on in the child. The focus of the paragraph is on how these changes relate to language development.

Playing Together (called *Talking Together* in Part III): Suggests language games that parents can play with their child. Although many of these games exercise the child's newly emerging language skills, their point is seldom to actually try and teach some aspect of language. Instead, they offer ways to speak and communicate with your child as fully as possible, given her level of development. Grammar and vocabulary come so easily to children that it seems more worthwhile to concentrate on games that enrich the social experience of language. Of course, people have not had to wait for the emergence of modern science to discover how parents can talk with children; many suggestions make use of traditional language games such as nursery rhymes. In those cases, this book indicates what these traditions are about and shows how they can be used to the fullest effect.

Problems: Any biological process can go awry. Most such difficulties are self-correcting, especially when a power as important as speech is concerned, but parents are naturally anxious about any and all problems. To help answer questions as they arise, each chapter discusses a variety of language difficulties—some likely, some extremely rare. This section should be consulted whenever a reader is troubled by the way a child uses language or whenever the developments do not seem to be as expected. It is possible that alert parents may become disturbed by one or more of the slight and passing peculiarities of a child's speech, which in a less observant family would never even be noticed. Thus, many of the momentary oddities of children's speech have been included in the problems section, not because they really are problems, but because parents may want to be reassured that the matter is entirely normal and no cause for alarm.

Some parents may have bought this book specifically because they are already troubled by some aspect of their child's speech (or lack of speech). They may be eager to turn as quickly as possible to the specific pages which can give them some idea of whether or not their child's problem is serious. I urge such readers first to read through Chapter 3, "Creating a First Language," which outlines the typical first thirty months of language development. This summary can help establish some sense of whether your child's progress really is markedly different from the ordinary.

Next, you can use this book for a fuller diagnosis. Many apparent language difficulties are really hearing problems. Chapter 14 will help you determine if your child has a hearing problem that interferes with speech. If hearing difficulties have been ruled out, use Chapter 15 to help judge whether or not you are confronted with a truly serious developmental issue.

In the case of children whose main problem seems to be poor pronunciation, the problems section in Chapter 13 will help diagnose the seriousness of that matter. If none of these areas seems precisely what you are concerned about, check the index. Your worry should be treated in one of the book's many problems sections.

Your Child's ＿＿ (in each chapter this blank is filled in with a different word): This section gives a full description of the developmental details which parents can observe. Each of these sections includes at least one chart summarizing these visible changes in speech. Most of the discussion in the section is devoted to explaining the items in the chart. For example, in Chapter 4 this section is called, "Your Child's Awareness," and its major chart indicates the emotions which children express from birth to one year; e.g., delight (age six months) or determination (ten months). The text of the section goes through the chart and discusses the expression of each emotion, one by one. These explanations can be read straight through or taken item by item, as the child progresses through the chart. The idea behind this section has been to give parents a specific understanding of their child's increasing capacities and broadening range of things to express. By consulting its charts and then observing their own child's speech, parents should have a clear indication of how their child's development stands.

What Is Happening: The final section of each chapter describes what happens during this stage of development. It is the only section of the chapter that is not oriented toward practical actions and observation on the part of the parent. Instead, it simply tries to make sense of what takes place. It is, if you wish, the purely scientific part of the chapter, providing knowledge just because it is nice to understand our children. These descriptions are limited to an account of what is taking place. The question of how a child is able to do all of these astonishing things is ignored. We still don't know how a child does it. The scientific study of children's language is still only at a stage comparable to the one which astronomy reached back in the time of Kepler (the early 1600s). By then astronomers knew what happened (the planets were in elliptical orbit around the sun), but why it happened (the action of gravity) was still a mystery. Perhaps another Isaac Newton will arise to explain how children are able to speak as they do, but none is yet in sight.

Box 1
FUNCTIONAL TABLE OF CONTENTS
(Nondevelopmental Chapters)

Subject	See	Contains
Age	Language Diary	Space to record your child's individual development
Playing Together	Chapters 11, 12	Discusses in detail the role of parents in their child's language development
Problems	Chapter 13 Chapter 14 Chapter 15	Pronunciation Hearing Unsatisfactory development
Your Child's Development	Chapters 3, 7	Introductory chapters to each developmental section
What Is Happening	Appendix	Information for those who want to know more about the scientific material

---

All other material in this book revolves around the developmental chapters. Box 1 outlines this other material and suggests how its content shares the concerns of the sections in the developmental chapters. These extra matters consist of:

Language Diary: At the back of the book are pages for keeping a personal record of your child's language development. They focus specifically on the sorts of changes described in the developmental chapters. Space for two types of entries has been provided. One group tracks the accomplishment of universal milestones in speech development, while the other notes a child's individuality and interests. I strongly recommend maintaining such a diary in the case of parents who are at all anxious about their child's language. Speech sounds so natural to our ears that we can easily overlook the many real accomplishments a child makes. Then, too, children's speech changes so rapidly and completely that it is easy to forget what a child's speech was like even a month or two before. The diary provides a way of recording and remembering developments.

The Parents' Role: Two chapters discuss the importance of parents to a child's use of language. The first addresses itself specifically to what the parents have to teach, while the second focuses on the environment which parents provide a child. The roles of books, television, and nursery school are all considered. There is no best time to read these chapters, since they concern raising children throughout the years covered by this book. Perhaps the simplest approach is to read the chapters quickly when you first begin to use the book and then refer back to them as questions arise.

Problems: The three major difficulties of children's language concern pronunciation, hearing, and unsatisfactory development. Each of these matters is considered in a chapter of its own and can be studied if and when the need arises.

Development: The introductory chapters to Parts II and III survey the period covered by the developmental chapters which follow. They should be read as a child enters the developmental period described in that part of the book.

In talking with parents of growing children I have repeatedly encountered a double-edged response to the study of children's language. On the one hand, there is pleasure and interest at the fact that so much is being learned and that so many new insights now exist, should any problems arise. At the same time, I have seen a persistent fear. Are babies and their speech now to be treated like butterfly specimens, pinned and labeled in neat rows? None of us is eager to see either ourselves or our children reduced to the sort of simple generalizations which are used to explain the issues of physics and chemistry.

Understandable as this nervousness is, it is quite misplaced.

I believe that instead of classifying and simplifying a parent's view of children, this new knowledge will greatly add to the dignity which even the youngest children can claim. If this book has a moral, it is that children are people too. Despite their size, their dependence, and their frailty, the development of infants can be understood only if their humanity and individuality are taken into account.

"Dignity" is not a word usually associated with children. "Cute," "lovable," "promising"—these are the words people generally turn to when they speak in praise of children; but to speak of dignity—that is, to focus on *inherent* worth rather than potential worth—still sounds peculiar to many ears. I am confident, however, that the growing study of infant development, in speech and other areas of social activity as well, will eventually make a phrase like *infant's dignity* seem ordinary rather than odd.

The ancient prejudice against children's viewpoints is so widespread that even boastful parents can slip into it. I was once conversing with a mother of two children who was telling me about her eighteen-month-old boy when suddenly, in the midst of her very alert and sensitive account, she made a passing reference to "the year when he made only animal cries." She was talking about the sounds that precede the appearance of English words and was implying that her son had been, in some way, prehuman. Of course, her child had gone through nothing like a year of making animal cries. The many emotional vocalizations made by babies have no counterpart in the animal world. We all know that birdcalls, lion roars, wolf howls, and so on are much more restricted and more predictable than human language. It turns out that those sounds are also quite unrelated to the coos and babble of babies. Rather than reinforcing old prejudices against the minds of children, the new science argues for a fuller recognition of an infant's humanity.

Adults need a tool as flexible and creative as language because they have such a variety of things to say that a more fixed communications system would not serve. Children too are so unpredictable in their points of view, feelings, and interests that only language will do. Of course, children do not yet need a language as rich and complicated as that of adults, but the many differences between the speech of individual children are still great enough to make it impossible to always predict what a child will say in a particular situation. The kind of precise predictions which biologists can make about animal-world communications cannot be made in the human world, not even in the language of a child.

When children's language is seen from this new angle, it looks quite different from the traditional view. Instead of arguing that children's first language is simple because they have not yet learned the full language, it says the language is simple because they still have simple things to say. The older view wasn't wrong, just beside the point, like saying that I am writing in English because my French is so atrocious. The truth of the statement provides no insights into what has actually been said.

This new approach has paid a great dividend by making sense of the transitions from one stage of development to another. The stages themselves (single word, two words, etc.) have long been recognized, but the change from one to another always seemed perfectly arbitrary. Now, however, we can see that the transitions come as a result of the child's increasing number of things to say. Her older verbal forms no longer serve.

Personally, I have found this discovery most exciting. It has made me look at children with even more wonder. Recently, for example, I was holding a fifteen-month-old boy who was a real chatterbox, although most of the sounds he made were part of no established language. The old way of responding to this child was to think how cute he was, but to ignore what he was saying or to dismiss the sounds as animal gibberish. This baby suddenly looked me straight in the eyes, made a very emphatic *ehh* sort of sound, and pointed with one outstretched finger toward a vase. I had heard him make the same sound before while pointing and realized that *ehh* was what is called, aptly enough, a "pointing sound." It is, in the child's private vocal system, the equivalent of saying *look* or *I see*. This baby had not been making random noises as he chattered; he was expressing (in a tongue of his own devising) his interest and awareness of the world around him. The recognition that so much consciousness is present in young children can only increase our admiration for them.

Because of these findings, any and all parents using this book should keep in mind the simple fact that their child is a person, not a scientific stereotype. If the book says that a child of such and such an age typically uses language in such and such a way, and your child does something else, there is no need to get upset. Chances are she is revealing her individuality rather than developing some important problem. Children with serious and long-lasting difficulties in learning the technical side of language (words, phrases, grammar) are profoundly rare.

Box 2
MAJOR TRANSITIONS BETWEEN STAGES

Typical Age (in months)	*Formal Transition*	*Personal Expansion*
12	From babbling to using words	From expressing emotions to translating situations into sounds
18	From speaking single words to combining words	From seeing a situation as whole to analyzing its parts
30	From using primitive sentences to speaking English grammar	From awareness of parts of situation to awareness of parts of language
42	From speaking sentences to conversing	From awareness of language to awareness of audience

An area of especially notable variety is in the age of transition from one stage of development to another. Box 2 notes the typical ages at which the transitions occur; however, probably very few children make all these changes at the "typical" age. The box illustrates why these transitions cannot be expected to occur like clockwork. Two changes take place. One is the switch in the form of speech which we can all hear. This is the change which has provided the standard way of sorting out the stages of language usage; however, these changes are really symptoms of a private enlargement of the child's subject matter and perhaps a growth in the very consciousness of the child. These expansions add new powers of thought which are retained throughout life. These are not passing phases the way the various formal stages are, so these powers are what really matter.

Even when the formal transition has not yet been clearly accomplished, the personal expansion may be well behind the child. I recall once talking with a man about a fifteen-month-old girl. He told me, "She's a bit behind in linguistic development," but as the conversation proceeded it became apparent that the child was "behind" only in terms of the formal transition to using English words instead of babble sounds. She was, however, jabbering away, using many recurring sounds of her own devising, drawing attention to herself, her ambitions, and her situation. Intellectually and personally, she was right where she should be, but (at fifteen months!) she was already being labeled as *behind.*

One final word about this book and how to use it—those boxes I keep referring to. They provide a handy way of summarizing and displaying a lot of information, and they should make it easy for readers to check the main facts in a chapter; however, they do tend to simplify and reduce complex matters to an over-tidy little relationship. Usually, I have tried to elaborate on the contents of the boxes in the prose paragraphs that surround them, but such clarification is not always possible. The "personal expansion" column of Box 2, for example, reduced a great deal of the next two parts of the book to four pithy phrases. Obviously, the developmental process is more complex than the outline. Even so, the point the box makes is still valid: From birth your child is a person, a young person, a needy person, but still a person. Her development is not so much a process of humanization (she is fully human from the start) as it is one of expanding awareness.

PART TWO
THE FIRST LANGUAGE

Many are poets that do not think it.
—JOHN KEATS, *Letters*

Chapter 3
Creating a First Language

AGE: BIRTH TO THIRTY MONTHS

It is tempting to label the period described in Part II as "the time of natural language." Tempting, but not quite convincing. Children do follow many of their own instincts and inclinations while creating the language they speak during the first two or two-and-a-half years, but the final product is not quite their own. The words a child uses and her intonation are part of her cultural heritage. So I have followed the lead of the psychologist and linguist Roger Brown and call this period's speech the "first language." Yet we should not be overly impressed by the fact that American children start out speaking English words, while Parisian babies use French ones. This self-evident fact can easily blind us to the deeper truth that natural drives and personal creations are what dominate early language development.

During this period the purposes of speech are much narrower than for three-year-olds, and, although the vocabulary and intonation are supplied by a particular culture, the way children use the first language is much the same, so matter what the tongue, technology, or culture of the parents. Even more striking is that the developmental stages of the first language are identical around the globe and are not altered by any idiosyncracies of the parents' grammar.

Thus, the following chapters are less about learning English than they are about beginning to talk, no matter what the child's future language will be. They describe a process that is fundamentally the same for American children in a Denver suburb, for Italian children in the bustle of Rome, and Korean children on a farm near Seoul. It is a very old process; my own estimate is that it is several millions of years old and was found among at least some of the proto-humans who hunted beside the shores of the ancient soda lakes in East Africa's Rift Valley.

When people step back to think about it, the development during these first thirty months seems astonishing. Starting out with little more than an alert eye and a tendency to doze off, a child quickly builds up a set of interests and attitudes, plus a vocabulary for expressing them. Yet, as you watch these changes on a day-to-day basis, they all seem quite natural and in keeping with the state of things. Viewed from up close, the transitions in stages of development are hard to identify. Changes like the first word and first sentence look very precise on a chart but are less neat in reality. Children do not seem to wake up radically different from the way they were when they went to sleep. Instead, there is a slow gathering of small modifications, so that from time to time it strikes an observer that, although the child is not so very different from the way she was yesterday, she is quite changed from the way she was a week ago. A child who walks with strides, who looks you brazenly in the eye, obeys her mother's verbal commands, and says *bye-bye* as she is carried off to bed seems well removed from the child of a month before who was taking her first cautious steps, did not catch your eye so confidently, and who seemed more fascinated than comprehending when her mother spoke.

The changes do build up, and somewhere a hazy line is

crossed. One day you think it might be stretching the point to say she has left the first stages, but soon thereafter it seems absurd to even wonder if she has entered the single-word stage. Sometimes, trying to observe the development feels like trying to watch the Grand Canyon grow. The forces are unseen, the changes are minute, but the end product is layer upon layer of natural beauty.

Box 3
WATCHING A WORD GROW

Tim began to wave good-bye around his eleventh month. It was an amusing sort of wave, limp-wristed and not aimed in any special direction, but it was most definitely a wave. Naturally, all who saw it felt compelled to wave back and say *bye-bye.*

Just before his first birthday Tim was busy mastering walking, so he wasn't talking yet, but his comprehension was progressing. When I was about to leave after one visit, I went to the door to get my coat. Tim's back was to me as he sat playing with his toys, which were piled up before him. *Bye-bye,* his mother said to me. At once Tim turned to look, not at his mother, but toward the door and me. So, I noted, he knows *bye-bye* means I'm about to leave.

I was back at Tim's on the evening he turned thirteen months old. When it was time for him to be taken to bed, his mother picked him up and stepped toward his bedroom. Tim gave that wave of his and this time said loudly and clearly, *bye-bye.*

I had managed to see each of the steps toward the production of a word. First, the situation (in this case, departure) is recognized. Then the word appropriate to the situation is understood. Finally, the word itself is quoted when the situation recurs. The growth is as natural as the color of a dandelion.

The absence of artificiality is the persistent theme during the growth of the first language. Certainly, a newborn baby's crying seems natural, a little too natural, in fact, and it is more with relief than wonder that parents greet the arrival of a few more pleasing sounds. By age six months, quite a large repertoire of these sounds has developed, and already it seems old hat to notice that the tone of the baby's voice expresses her general emotional state. Unremarkable as this fact appears, it constitutes the emergence of a major part of language for it goes without saying that throughout the baby's life, tone of voice will be important. When she begins to use written language, she will find she needs greater precision in vocabulary and grammar because her tone cannot be heard.

Equally in the nature of things is your child's interest in the speech of others. In fact, children are responsive to the human voice almost from the moment of birth. A soothing voice is far more calming to a baby than the sound of a rattle or some other artificial noisemaker. In my own experience I find four-month-olds particularly pleasant to talk with. They listen with wide-eyed attention while I ramble on about whatever I choose. It seems so different from talking with a one-year-old who so clearly has a mind and interests of her own and will not long endure such chatter. By one year that rapt gaze of attention has been replaced with greater understanding. At best, a child of this age will speak only a few words, but she understands and reacts to many.

It might seem that we could draw an absolute line between the time when a child has not yet spoken a word and when she has. If we ignore all questions of understanding and tone of voice, surely then we could say, "At this point the first word was used," right?

Maybe. There is certainly a first time the child uses an English word. It may be *cat* said while pointing, or *mama* while looking, or *bye-bye* while waving. Yet even this dramatic turning point is preceded by so much development that when it comes, the onlooking parents are not taken by surprise.

The baby has been gaining the ability to speak correctly in a few concrete situations. The notion of what is "correct" and which aspects of a "situation" merit attention will grow more complicated as the child grows older. In the beginning these situations are simply emotional. The baby expresses contentment or surprise or some such primal feeling. Her tone of voice is expressive, but the sounds she forms do not matter.

Goo could just as easily be replaced by *tah*. The only kind of error even theoretically possible at this point would be an inappropriate tone of voice, such as expressing surprise when all that was felt was contentment. Personally, I have never seen or read of such an error, so natural are these sounds to people.

Eventually, however, children do settle upon a few syllables for particular situations. It may be that *dah* accompanies stamping feet, or *ap-ap* is said while reaching, or that *kloo-kloo* is used only in the presence of a bottle. From our point of view, any other sound would serve just as well, but the child has settled on these sounds. To her they are as correct as English words.

Meanwhile, of course, parents have their own set of such arbitrary sounds. *Bye-bye* is the sound English speakers make while waving; *bottle* is a sound we say when in the presence of drink; *hi, there* is the sound we make while picking up the baby and kissing her. So one day the baby reaches and quotes her mother, *"bottle,"* at the same time. It is a great social advance—the first official word—and yet it is right in keeping with all that has come before.

None of this naturalistic description is intended in any way to put down or trivialize the child's achievement. On the contrary, it is to me so remarkable and wonderful a thing that I have astounded my friends and family by spending years learning and thinking about it. The point is that the achievement is the child's own doing. The word has not been learned because the parents have been sufficiently diligent, nor has it been imposed by society through some means which we must be careful to preserve lest our children not learn any words and all power of speech be lost to future generations. Thanks to you, your child will learn English; but thanks to her own inborn capacity, she will create her own language first. If she had to, she could create and use just her own language. Doubtless, the original languages grew up in just this instinctive way of translating a few specific situations into personally chosen sounds.

For quite a while a child speaks both English words and meaningful sounds of her own devising. The balance, however, slips from the private vocabulary to the more social one. Slowly the number of English words increases. It is common for fifteen-month-olds to have spoken about ten different words from the parents' language, and after that point the growth accelerates. The words spoken at this stage generally name something in the environment (e.g., *doggie*) or something the speaker is doing (e.g., *sit*).

One puzzle each child has to resolve is just how similar two situations must be in order for a particular word to be appropriate. Since no two experiences are identical, a certain flexibility is required if a word is ever to be repeated. Waving good-bye from your mother's arms is different from waving good-bye while standing on the sofa. Are both situations similar enough to merit the sound *bye-bye?* Yes? Well, then, are dogs and cows enough alike to both be called *doggie?* No? Then how about a toy dog and a neighbor's pet? These questions have to be resolved on a word-by-word basis.

In the midst of confronting this philosopher's quagmire of word suitability, children suddenly begin to use two words to define a single situation. This switch from speaking words to using primitive sentences has impressed many thinkers as a remarkable and unexpected step. For a while during the 1960s, it looked as though the first sentence was going to replace the first word as the milestone that marks the beginning of "true language," but this view is no longer so popular. It turns out that for all its dramatic promise and its seeming unexpectedness, two-word combinations emerge very naturally from the single-word stage.

Three things are happening during the single-word phase: the size of the vocabulary increases; the use of particular words is brought into closer agreement with general practice; and the number of situations that provoke speech increases. It is this last development that justifies the combining of words.

If you and I vowed never again to speak a whole sentence when one word would serve, we would still not settle for many single-word statements. There are too many ambiguities in single words; too many important details go overlooked. The listener could imagine too many reasons why that particular word might have been used. It would be foolish to expect a baby not yet two years old to appreciate all of these matters, but she is not so blind that she cannot appreciate any of them. By the late part of the single-word stage, a child's awareness of a situation has grown so rich that any of several words might be said. For example, she begins to name things associated with particular objects, so if she sees her father's hat, either of two words could be used: *hat* or *dada*. If either is appropriate, neither is sufficient, and the child begins to speak both words together, *dada hat*. All by herself the child has created a sentence. It is a great milestone, and yet it is also a perfectly natural modification of all that has come before.

The ease of growth of a baby's first language has surprised many people. Babies are so natural, while language seems quite artificial. There appeared to be no easy way for the two to come together, even though common experience shows us that babies and speech do link up without much effort. The ease of this linkage was considered a puzzle and much research grew out of a desire to explain that "puzzle." The answer has been found in a baby's instinct to express herself. Folk wisdom had always assumed that when a baby spoke, she was doing no more than learning English. It supposed that children begin making only single-word statements because so far this simple skill was all they had learned. That idea has now crumbled under the weight of twenty years of close observation and careful description. Every child begins by creating her own language. She turns to using the language of adults because it is handy and powerful, not because she would be forced to silence without it. She speaks in single words and primitive sentences because they are sufficient to express what she has to say. When those forms cease to be adequate, children abandon them in favor of more powerful ones.

Because the creation of the first language is so firmly rooted in the nature of your child, you can confidently expect that during the first two or two-and-a-half years after her birth, she will go through the development process I have outlined. It is as sure as any other process of natural maturation and growth. The problems and concerns that may appear during the rise of the first language are listed in Box 4. Most of the items covered by that list are not terribly serious. The most common difficulty is slow development.

Box 4 **PROBLEMS AND CONCERNS**		
Stage		*See page*
Baby Sounds	• Cry is screechy and distorted	34
	• Vocalization is rare	34
Single Word	• Words are nearly unintelligible	49
	• By age 15½ months child still does not	49
	• respond to any English words	
	• speak any words	
	• Many English words are used incorrectly	50
	• Child never uses gesture to express herself	50
	• After a promising beginning, speech has largely disappeared	50
	• Child is lazy about language	50
	• Child is now 18 months old but still is not speaking English words	50
Primitive Sentences	• By age 24 months child still does not:	68
	• combine words	
	• reply to parent's speech	
	• Words are combined into nonsense	69
	• Child speaks only in clichés	70
	• Child says one thing, means another	70
	• Child almost never initiates speech	69
	• Primitive sentences still absent at age 30 months	68
	• Child frequently gets tangled in her speech	70

Many readers of this book will know some other baby of about the same age as their own child whose language development seems more advanced. This point is doubly true if your child is a boy, since boys' speech often develops more slowly than girls'; however, in the longer run these developmental rates don't usually forecast much about verbal power. At the same time, no one should be complacent; the rare but real problems of the first language ought to be detected as early as possible. I urge readers to consult the pages listed in Box 4 whenever questions arise.

Throughout the first-language period, speech can be considered as a kind of toy. It is something to enjoy, to get to know as well as possible, to get a sense of its pleasures, but it is not something for a parent to be frightened about or something to be turned into fearful seriousness. The watchwords for this period are *enjoy, talk,* and (why not?) *brag.*

Chapter 4
Cries, Coos, and Syllables

AGE: BIRTH TO ONE YEAR

The sound developments of a baby during her first year are so numerous, so extensive, and change so rapidly that, for clarity's sake, they have been summarized in a chart.

Box 5
FIRST-YEAR SOUND DEVELOPMENT

Birth	CRYING begins
	Able to make bursts of rhythmic movement with lips
2 wks	Human voice can halt crying
3 wks	Fake cry appears
1 mth	Schwa sound appears
1½–2 mths	COOING emerges
2 mths	Duration, pitch, and form of sound can be changed
2–3 mths	Familiar faces produce cooing
6 mths	BABBLING emerges
6–7 mths	Intonation patterns appear
7 mths	Adult intonation is imitated
	Request intonation appears
7½ mths	Responds to adult speech with babbling
9 mths	Calling sound appears
	Can imitate *ah* sound
10 mths	TOY WORDS created
	Gesture and eye contact accompany vocalization
	Insistent intonation appears
12 mths	Vowel sounds begin to have adult form
	Questioning intonation appears

OTHER GROWTH

Among the many astonishing physical changes during the first year is the development of the human vocal tract. The human head and breathing system is marvelously shaped to promote speech. At birth the vocal tract is, in essence, a simple tube, unadapted to speaking, but by the first birthday it has developed many of the features necessary for controlled speech. Since these changes are internal, they are largely invisible; however, a symptom of the change is the eventual appearance of a chin. At birth babies are quite chinless, but as the head rearranges itself for speech a chin does appear.

PLAYING TOGETHER

The object of the games in this chapter is to suggest ways to encourage your baby to vocalize in social situations. As the year goes on, the richness of these situations increases.

Box 6
AGES FOR GAMES IN CHAPTER 4

Age (in months)	Game
2	Coo to you, too
2	Say "clean"
6	Play chitchat (first game)
7	Play chitchat (second game)
7½	Play chitchat (third game)
10	Pat-a-cake

Coo to you, too. In this game the purpose is simply to encourage your baby to make sounds. Starting from the second month, you can often induce the baby to make cooing sounds by looking at her, smiling, and speaking a few words.

The surest ways to inspire your baby to vocalize are: first, speak yourself; second, smile, laugh, or click your tongue; third, touch the baby.[1]

By about the third month your baby can distinguish between

familiar and strange faces and usually will not coo in response to the smile of a stranger,[2] so guests may find they cannot persuade the baby to play this game.

Say "clean." Babies are particularly likely to vocalize when they are naked.[3] Thus, in the bath or after changing a diaper is an especially good time to encourage your baby to speak. When the baby is cleaned up, but before she has been wrapped up again, try stroking the baby and saying, "Say 'clean.'"

Play chitchat. At around six months it becomes possible to have pretend conversations with your baby.[4] In these games parent and child speak back and forth. This conversational ability develops in several stages:

First game: at this stage the baby can repeat her own babble sounds. Thus, before the game can begin, your baby must say something. You then repeat what she said. With a little luck your baby will then repeat the same sound. You can continue the game by imitating the sound the baby made. For this stage of the game it is best to let the baby be the one who changes to a new sound. A sample of this pretend conversation:

BABY: nuh
PARENT: nuh
BABY: nah
PARENT: nah

Second game: around age seven or seven-and-a-half months the parents can start these pretend conversations themselves by looking at the baby and speaking a babble sound which the baby responds to. This game is best if the sounds the parent makes start out easy and become more difficult. Box 7 gives a series of initial consonants in order of increasing difficulty. In the table all the consonants are followed by *oo,* but, of course, any vowel can be used in your games. When playing this second version of the game, begin with one of the consonants to the left of the dots (h, y, d), and only gradually advance to consonants further to the right. Sample game:

Box 7
INCREASINGLY DIFFICULT BABBLE SOUNDS

---

hoo—yoo—doo ⋮ *too—goo—whoo*

PARENT: yaw
BABY: hoo
PARENT: yoo
BABY: yah
PARENT: dah

Third game: some children become quite good at imitating intonations. For example, parent says, "Who that?" with a questioning intonation, and the baby replies, *guh,* with the same rising sound at the end. Other sorts of intonations possible at this age are requests (e.g., smile!) and calls (e.g., yoo-hoo).

Note: at eight or nine months children may suddenly abandon all interest in such imitation and this game becomes impossible.

Pat-a-cake. This classic game has many virtues, including the fact that it is extremely simple. Hold your baby's hands and clap them together to the rhythm of the song's first couplet:

Pat-a-cake. Pat-a-cake. Baker's man.
Bake me a cake as fast as you can.

Another important quality of this game is that since it is chanted, the sounds and intonations are easily recognized by the baby. Also, it calls for touching and vocal contact, both strong needs in the child. (By age eleven months, touching is more likely to evoke sounds from the baby than are smiles and laughter.)[5]

Because of the increasing importance of touching, Box 6 lists this game for age ten months. Many parents will have been playing this game long before then. Nothing is wrong with this earlier introduction of the game.

It is unlikely that the baby will join in vocally during this game, but by the end of the first year she may be observed clapping her hands by herself and making some rhythmic sound.[6]

PROBLEMS

At this stage serious problems are rare. The one which parents should be most alert to is the question of deafness. Box 43 in Chapter 14 lists "hearing milestones" that should be observable in your child during the first year. Check to see that they are passed. One symptom of deafness is a typical change in the baby's cry.[7] It sounds more screechy and distorted than a hearing child's cry. The fact that your child makes a lot of sounds is not sufficient evidence that she hears. Vocalizing is so powerful a human instinct that even profoundly deaf children go through cooing and babbling stages.

Children who vocalize only to cry are extremely rare. If in reading this chapter it seems to you that your child is seriously behind in development, you can make a special effort to encourage coos and babbles. First, determine when the baby seems most likely to vocalize at all. Typically, these times will be during a bath, after the diaper is changed, or while lying nearly naked and waiting to be dressed. The least likely time to vocalize is usually when she is all bundled up or is quite warm. Place your baby in a situation where vocalizing is most likely and play the "Say 'clean'" and "Coo to you, too" games described in this chapter.

If you find that your child really does not vocalize or that she once vocalized but has now almost completely stopped, you should bring the matter to a doctor's attention.

YOUR CHILD'S AWARENESS

Children are alert to the world from the moment of birth.

The baby's eyes catch hold of things and follow them. She turns her head when noises are made. As the first year passes, the baby's awareness of the world continues to grow. This steady development is expressed in sounds, and as a baby's awareness grows more complex, her vocalizations too become more elaborate.

At this stage it seems impossible to speak of the child's sounds as a language. The vocalizations are natural and worldwide, rather than cultural and learned. On the other hand, with the exception of crying, the vocalizations have no counterpart in the rest of the natural world. The many sounds used by animals—bird songs, coyote howls, elephant trumpets—are used to control and organize situations. They proclaim territory, attract a mate, frighten intruders, and so on. By two months, however, babies are already beginning to make sounds that have no such immediately practical use. Their vocalizations express moods and awareness, a task that seems more artistic than functional. So, although these sounds cannot be called language, they are purely human. The child's use of the sounds to give voice to her feelings is so like the task of language that it seems arbitrary to call these vocalizations "prelinguistic," as they were formerly termed. The child is in a mysterious territory where her urges and her awareness are specifically human, but not yet part of any culture.

Box 8 **BABY SOUNDS**		
Age at appearance (in months)	*Expresses*	*Sound*
Birth	DISCOMFORT	Crying (cry—inhale—rest pattern)
	PAIN	Cry portion of pattern is prolonged
	IMPATIENCE	Loudness of cry increases

Age at appearance (in months)	Expresses	Sound
2	CONTENTMENT	Coos (at 6th month becomes babbling)
6	DELIGHT	Exclamatory intonation
	EFFORT	Struggling intonation
7	WANT	Requesting intonation. May have a preferred sound
	AWARENESS OF LANGUAGE	Babble imitation
10	DETERMINATION	Insistent intonation
	DETAIL	Toy words

Box 8 lists the precultural sounds of babies and what they express. These days it is common for parents to have one or two acquaintances who openly doubt the cleverness of children. "It's hard to know what a baby really thinks," is their polite way of wondering if your child really does feel what she expresses. This attitude is a holdover from nineteenth-century science, which often tried to deny the reality of anything that could not be seen at firsthand. Since speech is the tool nature has given us for letting the world know what would otherwise be private and secret, it is hard to directly refute such doubting acquaintances; however, if precultural speech is meaningless, there should be a stage when the child discovers meaning and begins to change from empty sounds to significant ones. No such stage has been found. On the contrary, the history of a child's speech shows progressive growth and maturation in which new abilities emerge from old ones. So, although it is maddening to hear people doubt the obvious alertness of your child, you can confidently pooh-pooh their skepticism.

Precultural vocalizations can express:

Discomfort. Crying is a necessary instinct if the baby is to be rescued from troubling situations. It appears immediately after birth. In fact, a nephew of mine was crying even before he had fully emerged from his mother. (Such during-birth crying is common in childbirths which use no drugs.) Not only is the cry natural to the baby, but parents need no explanation on how to interpret what they hear. For the sake of completeness, Box 8 lists the distinctions between the ordinary basic cry, the cry of pain, and the angry cry that indicates the infant's impatience. Parents will have no trouble recognizing these distinctions.

Contentment. Crying is welcomed at birth as a sign of vitality, but it soon becomes a bit wearing, and parents are relieved when, at one-and-a-half to two months of age, coos of contentment begin to be voiced. Surely the baby has known many times of contentment before this age, but only now does she begin to express it vocally. Once cooing begins, parents quickly discover that their baby has preferred situations for vocalizing.

The expressive feature of cooing is in the tone of voice, not the details of the particular sound that is formed. As time passes, the sounds themselves become more varied and more intricate. Around the sixth month these sounds blossom into an enormous variety, and sometimes a particular sound can take on a more precise meaning.

By coincidence, one of my godchildren has entered the babbling stage while I have been working on this chapter. He has developed the habit of rolling a long series of *r-r-r-r* sounds after nursing. His father, who long ago became able to sleep through these late-night feedings, reports waking up in the middle of the night to hear a soft voice saying *r-r-r-r*. The tone expresses contentment; the *r* sound narrows the contentment down to the particular sort felt after a satisfying meal.

Delight. The phrase "squeals of delight" pretty accurately sums up this expression of surprise and pleasure. It is a refinement of the contentment expression, permitting parents to distinguish between two of the forms of happiness known to their baby.

Effort. During their steady and active exploration of the world around them, babies often engage in physically difficult struggles, trying to pull things, etc. These struggles are frequently accompanied by an intonation indicating hard work.

Want. A calling or requesting intonation appears in the baby's voice.[8] Sometimes a particular sound may be favored. One mother reported to me that her six-and-a-half-month-old child called *ay* whenever he sat in his walker and saw his parents seated at a table, drinking from glasses. The call was accompanied by a reaching for the glass. So already the baby's vocalizations can refer to specific features of the setting.

Awareness of language. Childish conversation becomes possible at or just before age seven months. The "play chitchat" games described earlier in this chapter take advantage of this development. The expressive tone used in this stage is usually one of contentment, but already the linguistic waters are getting a little muddied, because by seven months many children can imitate the intonation of the adults around them.[9] The range of replies to adult speech at this point varies considerably. Some babies tend to respond with babble sounds of their own; others prefer to smile or laugh. Furthermore, the reactions change rapidly with time.

Toward the end of the year, rather complicated replies to adult speech can appear. One child, for example, replied *mamam* whenever she heard either the word *mama* or *papa*. The sound was not yet used as a call or a name. It was simply a reply made to two particular sounds, but it is strong evidence of a well-developed awareness of language. A month later, the *mamam* reply turned into the word *mama* and was used spontaneously, rather than simply as a reply.[10] This sort of process foreshadows a child's power to use the language of her parents. As we shall see, the ability to speak the language of a group depends on the ability to quote what others are already saying.

Determination. An insistent intonation appears at about ten months.[11] Like the angry form of crying, this intonation is loud and clear. It is a further development of the wanting expression, and, as in wanting, a baby can settle on a particular sound to indicate a particular demand. For example, one child studied used the sound *daeh-daeh* to mean "come."[12]

At this same age, babies start to use eye contact and gesture to express requests and to direct adult attention.[13] The intent to communicate for practical effect is evident in both vocalization and deed.

Detail. At about ten months, precultural sounds take a radical turn, for the baby begins to use specific sounds to report her awareness of some environmental detail. These sounds are not quite words since they are still precultural, but because their use is so like actual speech I call the sounds toy words. This appearance of wordlike sounds is most important, and its discovery destroyed forever the old theory that babies at this age are merely imitating, and expressing nothing.

Toy words can be names for definite things, or they can define situations. One child, for example, used to say *ah-ah-ah* when she was pretending to read aloud from a newspaper. When a wagon came by, she would say *mmmmmm*.[14] During the early stages of my own interest in child language, a nephew of mine (age thirteen months) surprised me by his toy word *ay-day,* which meant "pick me up." The incident brought home to me how creative and open to language children at this stage have already become.

The creation of toy words constitutes a great stride toward language. First of all, they translate awareness of detail into sounds, even though the immediate need for such translation may not be apparent. Language does the same thing. Thus, even before the first word appears, a baby begins to show some of the most profound and mysterious uses of language.

A further astonishing aspect of toy words is that they are symbolic, but invented by the child herself. Normally we think of symbols as tools which a person learns to use. Here, however, the symbol has been created by the baby. We shall see this pattern time and again throughout this book. Language development consistently begins with evidence of some new consciousness of the world. Then the child tries to express this awareness as best she can. Finally she turns to the accepted cultural way of expressing what she has discovered.

This creative process sits at the heart of language and human development. It shows itself before the baby's first birthday. In less than a year parents have seen their child's mind grow to a level of creativity worthy of a poet itching to express herself.

WHAT IS HAPPENING

It is tempting to think of the whole first year as a time of speech practice, which climaxes with the first word. That idea, old as it is, has proven false. During this stage the baby is maturing rapidly. Both her awareness and her ability to make sounds are growing, and by the first birthday vocalization has become extensive and varied. The great progress visible on the first birthday is only natural in a person who has become physically able to make so many sounds and who is now aware of so much which ought to be expressed. The first year is not a time of verbal practice. Instead, it is a period marked by the rapid rise of things to express.

The minimal need for practice was one of the surprising early discoveries of the revolution in the study of language. Eric Lenneberg recounted the unhappy story of a baby who had had to undergo surgery and for six months, from ages eight to fourteen months, had breathed through a tube. In this condition it was impossible for the child to make any sounds at all. Yet even when verbal practice was impossible, only one day after the tube was removed the child could make the advanced babble sounds typical of children her age. The tube had not hindered the development of vocalization at all.[15] Practice at making the sounds is the least important part of this stage of language development—indeed, it is physically impossible for a baby to make the same sounds adults make—and there is quite a range in the amount of sounds normal children produce.

Box 5 at the start of this chapter summarizes the sound development of the first year. The first sign of advance is the "fake cry," or softer sound, that begins to precede the basic cry.[16] At around the first month, the *uh,* or "schwa" sound, appears. This is the same neutral sound as the *a* in *about* and is the most bland sound of language (although to my ear there is very little blandness to the sound when it is spoken by a baby). The schwa turns into cooing. From the age of about two to six months, babies go through a period of cooing.

Box 9 COOING SOUNDS[17]	
Age (in months)	*Sound*
1½	schwa (uh) *nk-, k-,* and *g-*like sounds
2–6	schwa varies (becomes more like *ah, aw,* and *oh*) *h, t, d, y,* and *s* sounds

Box 9 shows the cooing sounds a baby can make. The spellings given are, of course, only the roughest approximations and are for ears accustomed to listening to English. Americans spell the first such sound as *goo.* Germans, on the other hand, hear the same sound as *arra,* while Arabs say it sounds like *nikvh,* quite a mouthful, indeed.[18] Different as these forms strike us, they are all produced at the back of the throat, and babies at this point do make their sounds there. By the end of the cooing stage, the baby's vocal control has extended to her whole mouth, and when she vocalizes you can see her entire jaw moving.[19]

At six months, the range of possible sounds expands dramatically. It is often said that during this babbling stage a child produces all the sounds of all the world's languages. The claim is now recognized to be an exaggeration, but it is true that a babbling baby can produce an astonishing variety of sounds; many of them appear familiar, but others seem as remote as the click sounds of the Bushman languages of Africa. Careful observation, however, has found that the most common babble sounds are much like the sounds which are most widespread in a child's early speech.[20]

Box 10
BABBLING STAGES[21]

1. Interest in vowels
2. Interest in consonants
3. Speaks in syllables (consonant + vowel)
4. Word patterns (2 syllables together)

More important than the variety is the developing form of the sounds. Box 10 lists the progressive stages which babbling goes through. With babbling comes an audible distinction between vowel sounds (which are formed by opening the mouth) and consonants (formed by closing the mouth).[22] Children begin by playing with vowel sounds. I remember once being at a dinner party where off to one side, in a crib, was a baby. All of a sudden I heard him go through a series of five sounds ranging from *ah* to *aw,* and I realized that he had definitely entered the babbling phase. A week later he had moved on to consonants, spending one full afternoon going *f, f, f, f, f.*

As we saw in the preceding section, these rather technical developments in the nature of the child's sounds are accompanied by a steady increase in the range of emotions that are expressed. These expressions depend simply on tone of voice; the details of a particular segment of sound (whether the child says *f* or *aw)* don't matter. Thus, there is no reason to suppose that the sounds made will be consistent.

Of course, at the same time the child's awareness expands, her body is growing physically. This growth includes a strong maturation of her vocal equipment and the muscle coordination necessary to operate it. A notable result of all this simultaneous development is that babbling progresses toward an adult structure and intonation.[23] After a period of concentration on simple sounds, combinations appear as syllables. This stage immediately gives the baby's vocalizations a more languagelike quality, since, to the ear at least, syllables are the basic sounds of language.

The stages of sound growth—from crying to toy words—are universal. No matter what race the child belongs to, no matter what language is spoken around her, this pattern is followed. Indeed, even deaf children go through these first stages of vocalization. But as the child's awareness has been enlarging, the influence of her cultural setting has grown more powerful. The first signs of differences between the speech of children in different cultures come at the end of this period of vocalization.

Analysis of the sound waves made by American and Japanese children when they babble found that by the toy-word phase, children destined to enter different societies have measurably different intonations.[24] Already, then, their sounds have gone beyond the natural and the personal. The first hints of culture are voiced.

Chapter 5
The First Words

AGE: FIRST TO SECOND BIRTHDAY

The stage when children express themselves with single words is commonly said to begin when the child is one year old. In some cases, particularly for girls, this stage begins a month or two early, while for boys it can come a little later. Typically, by the fifteenth month a child of either sex has spoken ten different words or names.[1] This single-word stage ends when the child begins joining two words together with some regularity. That more advanced speech may come as early as eighteen months or may be delayed until the second birthday.

OTHER GROWTH

The most dramatic nonverbal development in the child's behavior is the onset of walking. Usually, walking precedes the use of English words, but this pattern is not universal. Once the child begins to concentrate on mastering walking, her language development, wherever it has reached, seems to stay on a plateau.[2] No further progress is likely until after walking is under control.

Attending to two separate and demanding tasks is quite difficult for adults and is probably no easier in children. Thus, children who are making good progress in their various physical skills may be continually putting language development on hold while they tackle some new bit of muscular control. As a result of this start-stop process, any judgments about your child's language development have to be made in the context of her overall development.

44

PLAYING TOGETHER

Box 11 WORD GAMES FOR ONE-YEAR-OLDS		
Game	*Purpose*	*Best age for playing*
Give Me the Toy	Promotes comprehension	First part of single-word stage
Silly Things		
Question Time		
Introductions	Teaches important words	Once single-word stage is under way
Do and Say		
Thingamajig		
Grouping Things	Promotes sense of richness of experience	Latter part of single-word stage
Sorting Things		

Box 11 indicates the purposes of the games listed in this chapter and suggests a general order for playing them. Children are going to begin using single-word speech instinctively, so these games are designed to enrich a child's sense of how and when to use words.

Give me the toy. Your child's toys should have names. These names can be either specific—e.g., Kermit, clothespin, cat—or they can be general—e.g., doll, block—but the more specific the names the better, especially at first. Use these names for the toys in front of the child so she can have some opportunity to learn them. Look at her and say, "Please, give me the clothespin." No reaction? Reach over, take the toy clothespin, and say, "Clothespin." Play with it a moment and then ask for something else, using the same formula, "Please, give me ——."

Children can learn this game pretty quickly. If your child seems to understand that you are asking for something but still hesitates, point and repeat the one-word request, "Clothespin." Because this game teaches social interaction as well as vocabulary, I recommend that anytime the child does hand you something (right or wrong), you reply, "Thank you."

Silly things. Pointing and asking for things makes it easy to practice nouns. Verbs are harder. Fortunately, children are eager to follow silly suggestions, so ideas like, "Why don't you eat Snoopy?" or, "Put shoes on your ears," or, "Drink the clothespin," inspire laughs and action.[3] If your child seems reluctant to act, do them yourself as encouragement.

Question time. Ask your child a lot of questions, and if the child does not respond, answer them yourself. "Who's that?" "Where is ——?" "What's this?" are questions that ought to be asked once or twice a day during play. There is a strong relationship between the number of questions asked at thirteen months and a child's comprehension at twenty months.[4]

Introductions. By now every person who comes into the room should be announced to the child. "It's Carolyn." Announce yourself when you return. Very quickly the child should be able to make some of these announcements herself. Answering *who's that?* comes early,[5] and since the swiftest road to people's hearts is by speaking their name correctly, this social skill should be encouraged. Ask *who's that?* when somebody familiar comes in, if the child does not spontaneously say *hi* or call out the name.

This social activity can be turned into a game by using snapshots. Show the child photos of familiar faces, and ask whom she sees. This game can take a little practice since the child may need to get used to the relationship between people in photos and people in the flesh.

Do and say. Many words grow out of actions, and if you teach the action, the word follows. Three actions that lead to words are:

• *waving:* whenever a person leaves the home, wave and say *bye-bye.* Encourage the child to do both, but first emphasize the waving, since the action is learned before the word.

• *sitting:* by thirteen or fourteen months children are old enough to start saying *down* when they play Ring-Around-the-Rosy.[6] Dancing in a circle is still rare at this age, so it is better if the child is held up and the parent does the turning in a circle. At this age the whole verse may be too long for the child, so reduce it to:

> Ring around the rosy
> We all fall *down.*

On "down," set the child down. The routine can be quickly repeated just by lifting the child and putting her down again while saying "down."

• *taking:* children at this stage like to take hold of interesting things, even if someone else is already holding onto the item. By this age the child should be under enough control to pull back if you say no; however, in cases where you don't mind if the child takes what she reaches for, try saying *please* as she grabs for something. After a little while she should be saying *please* as she reaches for things. This action plus word is the first step on the road to saying "please" before reaching.

Thingamajig. The world of the one-year-old is full of things with unknown names. If your child points at something and says *here, that,* or if she makes some general pointing sound, assume she is interested in the thing but doesn't know its name. At the very least you should reply, "Yes, it's a——," and then repeat the one-word name. Children at this stage catch onto words quickly, so there is no need to go overboard repeating the name. If it is spoken once or twice during play, that is a good beginning.

Grouping things. Children in the late single-word stage are quite interested in how things are similar and the ways they are different. This imaginative skill ought to be encouraged. Go through a picture book playing a game of calling out some word and pointing every time you see a picture which could be classed with the word. For example, if you use a book full of animal pictures, you can look for animals with long tails, crying *tail* and pointing whenever you see an appropriate picture. Your child might surprise you, classifying a rabbit's ears as "tail." That's OK. Use the correct word, but praise the imagination. "Yes, its ears are so long they are like a tail." The idea of this game is to find imaginative links between things, not merely to learn the stereotyped rules of English classification.

Sorting things. In selecting toys for your child you will naturally want some that are unique and distinctive, but you should also include several that are used in the same general way. Language is a good tool for distinguishing between things that might otherwise seem similar. For example, each stuffed doll should have a separate name. A child may favor playing with her unique toys but speak the names of the similar ones more often.[7]

Picture books are also good for this sorting. If, for example, an animal book shows three lions (perhaps a mother and two cubs), give each lion in the picture a name, as a way of individualizing them. You have to be a little careful here because you may forget the names you selected, while the child remembers. It is easiest to stick with famous sets of names: Huey, Louie, Dewey; Humpty and Dumpty; Napoleon and Josephine; Tinker, Evers, Chance; etc.

The classic nursery rhyme for sorting out things that would otherwise seem indistinguishable is played by counting off the child's toes:

> This little pig went to market;
> This little pig stayed home;
> This little pig had roast beef;
> This little pig had none;
> This little pig cried, "Wee, wee, wee!"
> All the way home.

PROBLEMS

Pronunciation is so poor that words are nearly unintelligible.
This is the most common difficulty, and ordinarily it is not
fully resolved for several years. Because the question of
pronunciation continues over such a long period, the matter
has been given a chapter of its own (Chapter 13). The single-
word stage is a little early to expect much in the way of
consistent or accurate pronunciation. It is standard for strangers to find a child at this stage completely unintelligible.

**Child is fifteen-and-a-half months old and still has not said
her first word.** By this age, most children are speaking at least
occasionally. Also by this stage, users of this book should have
been alerted to any deafness, but ask yourself if the child does
react to noises made outside of her line of vision and if her cry
sounds normal, without a screechy and distorted quality.
Chapter 14 considers a number of signs of hearing loss. If
hearing problems can be eliminated as the source of the delay,
the only other important consideration is comprehension.

Does the child respond to any specific word or names? Can
she play the first game described in this chapter? If the answer
to *both* questions is no, the situation needs correcting. I
recommend a thorough doctor's examination, including hearing, eyesight, and development (physical, mental, emotional).

If the child understands some words, is generally alert, and
is physically curious, there is probably no cause for concern. It
may be that she is so active, experiencing so much, that
language (which is in part a symbolic substitute for action) is
not yet particularly important to her. If your child is both
active and interested, chances are strong that there is no
language problem to be concerned about. Follow the game
suggestions for converting action into speech (**Introductions,
Do and Say**) listed in this chapter. Keep such play lighthearted,
since in some cases slow development is likely to be caused by
parents pressing too hard. Leave the child alone with a group
of her toys (toys which you refer to by different names) and
see if perhaps when she is playing by herself, she doesn't speak
a name or two.

Child never uses gesture to express herself. By itself this fact is surprising, but not important if language development is as expected. If this lack of gesture is part of an overall absence of communication, you should read Chapter 15 to determine whether or not a serious problem is appearing.

After a promising beginning, speech has largely disappeared. If this situation persists, it is a disturbing development. You should check Chapters 14 and 15 to consider the matter more fully.

Child is lazy about language. Many parents can see that their child is bright and alert, so they conclude that a general absence of language comes out of sheer laziness. This explanation is almost never correct. I suggest you reread the list of headings in this problems section and determine if any apply to your child.

Child uses English words but uses them incorrectly. Over-generalization of words is the most visible error of this stage. For example, the word *dog* may be applied to any four-legged animal. The phenomenon is discussed in the last part of the chapter; it is entirely normal and no cause for alarm.

When your child uses the wrong word, you should supply the correct one; however, teaching a child the correct word calls for a little bit of care, because a child can easily misunderstand and think you are agreeing with her. Do not repeat the word she misused. For example, do not correct her by saying, "That's not a dog," and don't ask, "Is that a dog?" Instead, make a point of using the correct word. If your child sees a cow and says *doggie,* reply, "Yes, I see the cow," stressing the word *cow.* Later, point to another cow, or a picture of one, and say the one word, "Cow." Simple as this direct system is, it works.[8]

Child is now eighteen months old but still is not speaking English words. The matter could still be a question of simple delay, but it is now time to determine whether the child is developing normally or if there is a problem. Look at Chapter 14 for a consideration of the hearing matter and Chapter 15 to determine if, indeed, language is merely delayed.

YOUR CHILD'S POINT OF VIEW

It is an exciting moment for admiring elders when a baby says her first recognizable word. By happy example, only this morning, shortly before sitting down to resume work on this chapter, I received some pleasing news about a ten-and-a-half-month-old girl; she has said her first word, *cat.* Clearly she understood "cat," for her parents have three cats in their apartment, and, as she spoke, the girl looked and pointed at one of the cats. It is a great milestone for her speech.

Yet dramatic as the moment is, the precultural sounds described in the preceding chapter show how very natural is the eventual appearance of the first word. The baby's awareness of herself and the world has been growing since birth and has been expressed vocally. Now her sense of things is beginning to take on a deeper social character, and she changes from private words to English ones. At first, the central element of her awareness was how she felt about a particular situation, and, of course, that emotional aspect of the matter never disappears. Tone of voice continues to be important in speech, but now the details of the experience matter as well. Out of the totality of the sounds, movements, and colors of any particular experience she has found a part to focus on and to name. It is a first step along the road toward the conscious criticism of experience which is part of every adult's life.

At this point, of course, that criticism is pretty simple. We can translate a baby's one word, *cat,* into the simple claim, "I am aware of a cat." In fact, during the whole of the single-word stage, the adult version can usually be rendered as a simple statement of awareness. The reasons for such awareness, however, expand quite impressively. By the end of this stage, your child will have talked about things because they were immediately at hand, or because she remembered them, or (slightly different) she was reminded of them, or she experienced them, or she wanted them, or she didn't want them, or she was greeting them.

After surveying these many reasons children have for

talking, one nineteenth-century scholar remarked, "How exceedingly misleading it is to say a child's vocabulary consists of only ten or fifteen words, or the like. Those ten or fifteen sounds may do duty as a hundred or more words."[9] This sense of the richness of their child's speech, not its limitations, is the main idea parents should gain from hearing their child's first use of language. Naturally, parents are interested in their child's vocabulary and want to see it grow, but more exciting and important is the growth of the way children use the words they know.

Box 12
TYPICAL FIRST FIFTY WORDS

NAMES

Things	*People*	*Food*	*Clothes*	*Animals*
airplane	baby	banana	button	baa-baa
ball	dada	bottle	hat	bird
book	mama	cake	mitten	bowwow
car	SanClaus	cookie	shoe	horsie
clock		juice	sock	kitty
dolly		milk		meow
flower		orange		quack
hair				
light				
there				
this				
toys				
tree				
two				

ACTIONS

away	hug	thanks
bye-bye	jump	uh-oh
down	more	up
eat	no	yum
hello	open	

By the time of her first English word, a child's sense of the world permits her to talk either subjectively about herself or objectively about other things. During this stage, children will naturally talk about both sorts of things, but some children are more interested in one general subject and some the other. Several recent studies have observed that one-word speech falls naturally into two sorts: the objective naming of things or the subjective expression of actions.[10] Katherine Nelson, the investigator who has explored this subject most thoroughly, reports that children who concentrate on naming tend to be firstborn children. They develop a larger vocabulary before they begin combining words into sentences. Later-born children obtain a more diverse vocabulary and are in the one-word stage for a comparatively short period of time.

It is interesting to see how a child's point of view grows and unifies during this period. At the start, the child's subjective statements tend to be about herself, and any investigation of these sorts of remarks is likely to conclude that when children begin to use words, they are completely egocentric. A child who says *down,* for example, means she has sat down; not Daddy across the room sat down. But as time passes, a child's one-word remarks do refer to events outside herself. It appears she has become less self-centered.

An investigation of objective naming, however, would lead to precisely the opposite conclusion. It is consistently reported that although children at this stage do respond to their own name, they seldom speak it until the very last phase of one-word speech.[11] They begin by naming other people and things. So a study of children's naming would conclude that a sense of oneself comes rather late.

The contradictions between the development of objective and subjective expression are most easily avoided by not trying to be too profound. The Freudian jargon of psycho-analysis is natural to many parents these days, but I recommend avoiding such an approach to children unless you really are trained in the field.

The difference between the development of the two classes of words seems quite normal if we consider a child's words from her own point of view. Surely, when children notice or think of something outside themselves, the main interest is the thing itself, not some detail of its activity. So out comes a name. In the same manner, the central feature of oneself is hardly one's own presence, a fact which never changes. Therefore, when talking about themselves, children naturally refer to what they are doing or have just done.

Without language this dual point of view might continue indefinitely, but with language a child soon notices that words which had been reserved for herself can apply to others. So after a while, when Mother sits down, the baby does say *down*. This development brings a new wrinkle, for although *down* does seem like a good translation of this situation, the old favorite, *mama,* is also appropriate. The solution that will soon be discovered by the child is to speak two words together; however, for most of their second year children are content to focus on just one detail of their consciousness. Box 13 lists the reasons children have for objectively naming something.

Box 13
THE REASONS FOR NAMING

Reason	*Example*	
Pointing	"cat"	Points and looks at cat
	"mama"	Hears mother's footsteps
Remember	"moon"	Saw moon earlier in the day
Wants	"dolly"	Wants doll
Association	"dada"	Sees father's briefcase

Pointing. The first reason for naming is simply a thing's visible presence. It is the most primitive form of talking and will eventually fade as the child grows old enough to have ideas about her experience, but for the present the awareness of some specific environmental detail is quite enough, and children's most frequent use of single-word speech is to name things in their presence.[12]

Naturally, children at this stage are aware of many things they cannot name. Rather than be silent, they often develop a pointing sound; that is, they make some habitual sound while pointing or reaching for something. Eventually, this sound is replaced by an English word, such as *there* or *that*. Be it English or a made-up sound, this pointing speech can be taken as saying, "I am aware of something, but I don't know what it is called." The thingamajig game described earlier in the chapter has been designed to make use of this situation.

Another way to point out something with an unknown name is for the child to invent a name of her own. This solution is especially noticeable when the invented name is based on the sound a thing makes. For example, a dog might be called a *wuff*.

Animals, by the way, are favorite subjects for children's speech. I already mentioned the child whose first word was *cat*, and apparently animal references are part of almost every child's early speech. Animals have all the qualities necessary to encourage speech. They move; they are common enough to be seen often, but not so common that they are part of nearly every situation; and, perhaps most important, they are not for touching. For the good of both parties concerned, babies and pets are usually kept separate. Combining this don't-touch rule with an intrinsic interest in the animal's activity seems to encourage speech. Using names is, at least in part, a substitute for other forms of activity. Children with the fastest-growing vocabularies talk more and handle things less than other children of the same age.[13]

Remember. Very soon after the first word a child reaches the stage of being able to name things that are out of sight. For instance, a child sitting at the dinner table suddenly said *playground*. Of course, no playground was at hand, but she had been there earlier in the day. Such a remark might be translated as, "I remember the playground."[14] It offers firm evidence that the child's awareness has expanded beyond the immediate moment.

Want. The purely symbolic use of a child's first naming has surprised armchair theoreticians who once assumed that a child's first use of speech would be for giving orders and shouting desires. We saw in Box 8 (Chapter 4) that desire is not the first precultural expression, and now we see that it is not the first use of English words either. The facts of development continually illustrate that language is first of all the simple translation of situations into words. Practical application of this activity comes later, but eventually it does come. Expressions of want are readily distinguished from pointing by intonation and gesture. Often the name is repeated until the child is satisfied.[15] After pointing, wanting is the most common type of naming.

Association. Late in the single-word stage the child begins naming things because she has been reminded of them. The most common reasons for such reminders are possession (somebody often holds or wears the reminder) and location (somebody or something is usually at the place of the reminder). A typical example of association comes when a child sees her father's hat and says *dada*. Usually, a nearby adult replies with something like, "Yes, that's Daddy's hat," and eventually expressions of property will indeed develop from expressions of association. Naming on the basis of association is a sign that the child's awareness is growing increasingly complicated.

Box 14
THE KEYSTONES OF ACTION

Action	Word	Example
Doing	"down"	Sits down
Greeting	"hi"	Father enters room
Object	"dolly"	Gives doll to parent
	"mouth"	Puts food in mouth

Throughout the single-word stage there is a steady growth in the number of ways an action is identified. In Chapter 4 we saw that the toy words of a child often translate as, "This is the sound I make when I do this." Eventually, real English words are used to accompany actions.

Just like names, the action words identify the central aspect of a situation. As time passes, the reasons a child can be interested in an action increase. Box 14 lists the different aspects of action that children can focus on.

Doing. These expressions grow out of toy words, and at the beginning they refer to the child's own actions. The words chosen focus on the change that comes with an action, rather than on the name of the action.[16] For example, when a child sits down she is more likely to say *down* (focusing on the change) than to say *sit* (naming what she does). Later in this stage a child may utter a series of such doing words, identifying the successive steps of an action.[17]

Greeting. Saying "hi" begins as an action word. It is said while a child waves hello. Typically, a child first learns to wave; then the words *hi* or *bye-bye* are said while waving; and finally, the action disappears and the words suffice.[18]

One interesting feature of saying *hi* is that there is another equally good way of greeting people. Children at this age also react to someone's arrival by calling out the newcomer's name, but saying *hi* grows out of a personal action, while calling a name grows out of the child's awareness of her environment. The two forms express subtle but different ways of perceiving the situation. The child's choice of the form of greeting is the first time we can definitely say that the rules of her speech would have permitted her to express the same general situation in another way. Along with voicing her awareness, she is unconsciously expressing a point of view. Since one major distinction between language and the communicative signals of the animal world is that language expresses viewpoint, people have naturally wondered how soon this capacity can be recognized in children. The answer is that it is present almost as soon as the first few words are spoken.

Object. In this case, the child seems to be simply naming something, but the name refers to an object being handled. It is a relatively rare usage, and typically it begins by the child handing something to a parent and speaking the name of the gift.[19] At the late part of the one-word stage, children also name an object they are handling; holding up a toy train, for example, and saying *train*.[20]

In our discussion of animal names, we saw that it is not common for children to name the things they are handling; so this appearance of naming the object of an action indicates that some sort of mental development has taken place. Whereas in the past a child eating a cookie might have said *eat*, now she is as likely to say *cookie*. The inadequacy of either lone word to sum up the situation is becoming apparent to the child, and the single-word stage is coming to an end.

Box 15 **KEYSTONES THAT MUST BE NAMED**		
Example	*Word*	*Action*
Disappearance	"all gone"	Food is finished
Rejection	"no"	Pushes food away

For the sake of neatness and simplicity it would be nice if all children's one-word statements could be categorized as focusing either on objects or events, but reality is never so tidy, and even in the single-word stage there are some situations that combine both categories.

Disappearance. This subject appears fairly early in the single-word stage and is the opposite of naming. It reports that something is finished or out of sight. Common words used to express this situation are *away* and *all gone*. *Stop* is also used to indicate that some action is over.[21] It is most unusual for the child to name the thing that has disappeared. At this stage a child's attention focuses on the fact of disappearance, rather than the item which has vanished.

Rejection. Since the purpose of rejection is the exact opposite of expressing desire, the two things might be expected to have a common origin, but they don't. The most common word for rejection is *no*. (Paradoxically, *yes* is also frequent.) *No* is first used by children as a doing word. They say it when they are doing something forbidden. For example, a child might say *no* while opening a drawer she is not allowed to open. Later she says *no* when she is only tempted to do something forbidden. (She might look at the drawer and say *no*.) At that point the word has become a substitute for action and might be classed with other action terms. But finally the word *no* does jump over to the other classes of words and is given practical application. The child begins saying *no* in order to forbid others or to reject things.[22]

So by the end of this stage parents can see that even though their child is still limited almost exclusively to single-word speech, she is expressing a much greater awareness of the world and of herself. This growing consciousness means that single-word speech is no longer adequate to the task of translating a child's sense of the situation. Single-word speech cannot name both another person and that person's actions, although by now the child is conscious of both the actor and the action. Single-word speech cannot identify both what a child is doing and what she is holding, although by now a child is conscious of both things. The child reacts to this enormous limitation on expression the way any poet would; she grows unhappy with established forms of speech and seeks new ones. The single-word stage comes to a halt.

WHAT IS HAPPENING

During the single-word stage, many separate features of language develop simultaneously. Some matters are carry-overs from the previous stage of development. Intonation and tone of voice were the primary features of precultural sounds and they continue to develop. Babbling does continue even after children speak a few words. At this stage it is common for children to speak long babble sounds that seem to imitate adult sentence intonation patterns.[23] This development is a logical and natural extension of the progress we saw in the preceding chapter, when intonation began to take on cultural features. A questioning intonation indicating that a reply is expected comes rather late in the stage.[24] A typical early question is *what* or *what that,* and it indicates that a name is wanted. By the end of this stage many elements of intonation appear to have been settled.[25] A comparison of the intonation patterns used by a boy at the end of the single-word stage and his intonation eight months later showed that there had been no further change in the established patterns, even though sentences of several words had become the rule.

Inevitably, the developmental feature which draws the largest attention and excitement at this stage is using new words. This turning away from personal toy words to the common words of English is a momentous point in any child's social development. It is a change that comes slowly, but insistently. Children entering this stage speak English words only occasionally; their pronunciation is garbled; and the context of the word is obscure.[26] Their understanding of words spoken by their parents, however, is much better. At the time of the first birthday, a child's spoken vocabulary is, at best, only a couple of words, yet she may be able to respond to nearly fifty words.[27] Of course, months earlier she was already responding to tone of voice.

Just why children understand so many words but speak so few is something of a mystery, although the explanation may be as simple as the reason why I personally never use the terms of nuclear physics. I know, more or less, what electrons, strong forces, and energy quanta are, but I have nothing to say about such things and, consequently, do not talk about them. By the same token, a child may know what "highchair" refers to but have no interest in talking about the thing.

Children certainly have favorite words. The words used most frequently and persistently by one child at this stage were *more, there, gone, away, stop, up,* and *uh-oh.*[28] These are typical of the most common first words. At any given moment other words may be used more frequently, but their popularity is short-lived, while these ordinary little words continue. The short-term popularity of new words is part of a standard pattern in language development. When a word is first spoken it is repeated often, but its use declines markedly once the word has been thoroughly practiced.[29] Unless the word is of real importance, its use will not continue the way the words just listed persist month after month. Some words disappear from use for many months before recurring.[30]

A major shift in language development is now taking place. Language is changing from a personal means of expression to a social one. That is to say, the child is beginning to be more interested in the names other people have for things; the purely personal expression possible in toy words is no longer satisfactory. Children at this stage do not yet show much interest in how well their communication gets through, but they become keenly alert to using English.

The change from speaking private words to using those of an established language involves more than a simple change in the vocabulary. A word's definition is shared generally by its users, and this social definition must be understood. At first a child may not appreciate exactly what is included in a particular word, and she might either limit its use or extend it too much. One of the hardest and most important of these problem words is one of the first, *mama.* This word tends to take on mythic proportions in the understanding of the child.[31] It can name mother, but it may also be used to catch the attention of someone other than the mother. It can be a generalized plea for help. The single-word stage may be almost finished before *mama* is usually limited to being a word for the mother.

Some examples where children's definitions have been reported to be more idiosyncratic than social include:

• a French boy who used the word for "breast" to indicate that he wanted to nurse, that he wanted a biscuit, that he saw a red button on a piece of clothing, that he saw the point of a bare elbow, that he saw an eye in a picture, and that he saw his mother's face in a photograph.[32]

• A child used the word "bird" to indicate any moving

animal, but on hearing the word would look around for a bird and would not be satisfied by finding some other moving creature such as a cat.[33]

• At the age of nine months a precocious little girl used the word "car," but only to indicate a car moving on the street below her apartment window. The word never referred to a parked car, a car she was riding in, or a picture of a car. At age ten-and-a-half months she stopped using the word altogether, and it did not reappear in her vocabulary until she was sixteen months old, at which time it had a broader definition.[34]

• Stephen called his hat "hat." Then he began calling anything a hat which he put on his head, including paper, keys, a small bucket, and play hats. Next, he narrowed the definition to indicate things which can enclose the head. Keys and paper were no longer called hats, but boxes were. Finally, the definition was narrowed even further to indicate only items of clothing which enclose the head.[35]

Box 16
NAMING FOUR-LEGGED ANIMALS[36]

English	Starting at 21 months	By 24 months
cat	tee	pushie
small dog	tee . . . goggie	goggie
toy dog	goggie	goggie
cow	tee	moo-ka
horse	tee . . . hosh	hosh
large dog	hosh	biggie-goggie

• Almost everybody writing on the subject reports instances when children used the wrong name for an animal. (Typically, a horse will be called a *doggie*.) Box 16 presents one child's experience in trying to sort out the names of four-legged animals. We can see that in a three-month period there was quite an evolution. Beginning with *tee* (as in "kit*ty*") for "cat," the word was generalized for several types of animals. Then *hosh* was substituted for *tee* in referring to a horse. Finally, the child had a full set of terms.

These anecdotes illustrate a pattern which is not terribly astonishing but whose details show how hard children must work if they are to use language socially. At first the uses of a word are as personal as for toy words. Definitions can be tightly restricted, as in the case of *car,* or enormous and powerful, as in *mama.* Definitions can also be right on the mark, and most studies these days conclude that the majority of names of things are used correctly right from the start.[37]

Many names, however, have to be worked out. There is no obvious reason, for example, why a collie and a dachshund should both be dogs, while a cat is something else. Even stranger is why living cats and dogs are different, but stuffed and living dogs are called by the same name. Every language has its own way of sorting out the things of the world, and no child is born with any special reason for preferring one language's system over some other. In cases like this, a child is not merely learning the English names of things, she is beginning to think according to the English custom.

Chapter 6
Beyond Words

AGE: BETWEEN SIXTEEN AND THIRTY MONTHS

Typically, by the end of the twenty-third month children begin to combine words into longer sentences, mostly two words long. They now begin speaking in primitive sentences. The length of this stage varies. Some children pass through it in less than two months, while others remain in it for as long as nine months.

PLAYING TOGETHER

Grammatically speaking, a child at this stage has to discover the rules of English word order, so she can say *big ball* instead of *ball big*. Socially, however, the task it utterly different. In the last chapter we saw that a questioning intonation appears late in the single-word stage. Now the child begins to explore some of the implications to her recognition that speech can provoke still more speech. The games in this chapter are all designed to promote the child's growing appreciation of the possibilities of dialogue—of conversation and questioning. A few of the games can also help draw a child's attention to proper word order.

Social expansion. One type of simple conversational device available to both parents and child is repetition. Parental repetitions are usually called "expansions," since they appear as enlargements on the sentence of a child. If a child says *mommy sock,* a parent might reply, "Yes, that is Mommy's sock." Or if a child says *throw daddy,* a parent might expand the sentence by saying, "Throw it to Daddy." It is not a good idea to try to speak to your child in primitive sentences. Children at this stage respond better to adult English.[1]

When expansions were first noticed, they caused a lot of excitement among investigators of child language. They seemed a perfect teaching tool, but experiments to demonstrate their usefulness have repeatedly found that they do not help a child improve her grammar very much. Recently, expansions have been shown to offer some subtle help in using the forms which are peculiar to a particular language,[2] but chiefly what they seem to teach is that repetition is an acceptable form of dialogue. The likelihood of a child quoting her parent's speech is much greater if the parents also repeat the child's speech.[3] Normally, we do not consider repetition to be good practice between adults, but partial quotation in speech is necessary if language is to create bonds between people. If two people are talking together and do not use the same names for the same things, you can bet there is tension between them.

Parents need not worry that their encouragement of repetition is going to stunt their child's originality or turn her into a parrot. Development is more complicated than that, and in Part III we shall see that quotations provide children with the key to English grammatical practices.

For the present, parents will find that expansions let them feel they are more firmly in contact with their child's mind. Expansions serve as a kind of "I'm listening" sentence. They inform a child that the parent is paying attention, without offering any real comment on the conversation.

Instructional expansion. There is a way to use expansions to help your child's grammar. At this stage the only grammar that must be observed is English word order. Is it correct to say *wet diaper* or *diaper wet*? There is no natural solution to this question. Some languages use one form, some the other, while a third group does not care. Word order is important in English, and the more quickly the cultural rules are mastered, the sooner a child can get on to other things.

There are suggestions that children prefer to repeat those

forms they have not yet mastered,[4] and one of the first things researchers noticed about children's quotations was that they preserve word order. For example, if a parent says, "You have a wet diaper," the child might repeat the remark as *wet diaper.* Therefore, a parent who notices that a child seems to be unsure about the order of a particular word may be of help by speaking the proper word order to the child.

It is a particularly good idea to expand a child's sentences when the word order is incorrect, to let the child hear the correct usage. But here the parent must be careful. When a child says *diaper wet,* the natural expansion is, "Yes, your diaper is wet." While the grammar of the expansion is perfectly correct, it does not help the child discover that the adjective *wet* goes before the *diaper* it describes.

A better expansion would be to say, "Yes, you have a wet diaper." This approach takes a bit more care, but it corrects the word order and provides the child with a good model to listen to.

Nursery rhymes. Nursery rhymes can be used as a kind of pretend conversation.[5] Once again, the idea behind the game is to encourage the idea that language leads to a sense of communing or sharing. The game itself is quite simple. A parent recites the first part of a line from a nursery rhyme, and the child completes it, as in:

Ring around the . . .

　　　　　　　　. . . rosy

A pocket full of . . .

　　　　　　　　. . . posy

Ashes, ashes, we all fall . . .

　　　　　　　　. . . down.

Recitations like these are easy and fun, although children often need initial encouragement by watching both parents play the game. If a child hears her mother say, "Little Jack Horner sat in a . . ." and then the father chimes in with, ". . . corner," the child quickly catches on to the rules of the game and spontaneously joins the fun.

Question time. Questions continue to be a good way to draw speech out of the child. At this stage, children are better at providing information than at saying *yes* or *no* correctly. The best questions, therefore, are general ones which call on the child to say something specific. All you need are picture books or the toys and things familiar to your child. Questions should be varied so the child gets practice at talking about a range of topics.

Children during this stage often talk about locations, ownership, and naming—the easiest things to ask about. *What's that?* a parent asks, and the child gets to name something. *Where is——?* uses the child's ability to locate things, and *Whose——is this?* gives her a chance to talk about ownership. All of these questions let a child use her first grammar. It is a good idea for parents to follow up on the reply with an expansion (as described above). In particular, a parent should be alert to the problems of word order and, if necessary, reply to the child's answer with an instructional expansion.

Yes-or-no questions are more difficult for the child to answer correctly, but there are several reasons for including a few of them in questioning games. First, because sharing and practice at dialogue, not accuracy, is the point of the game. Second, because yes-or-no questions help prepare a child for the next period of language development. Once a child gets beyond speaking primitive sentences, she must master the peculiarities of verbs, and asking yes-or-no questions speeds up the rate at which a child uses auxiliary verbs.[6] These words—like *can, have, do,* and *will*—help form tenses in English, and a child can use them only after first hearing them. Yes-or-no questions like *Can you see me? Have you got a thumb? Do you want a kiss?* and *Are you a cute little girl?* put auxiliary verbs right up at the front of a question. Children pay more attention to the first words of a sentence than to those that follow.[7] Thus, parents who include yes-or-no questions among the verbal games they play will be helping their child's future language growth.

PROBLEMS

Child is two years old and still limited to single words. If the child's second birthday passes and her speech is still taking the form of one-word comments, parents are likely to be troubled. Where are the sentences? Usually the delay is of no importance, but parents understandably want some sign that sentences are coming. One important clue that the child is on the verge of spontaneously combining words is that she has begun to wrestle with the inadequacy of single words.

In the single-word chapter we saw an increase in the situations in which a child uses single words. This increase leads to ambiguities in the child's own understanding of her words. The idea children soon hit upon is lumping words together. Thus, if you are troubled because your child continues to use only single words, keep track of the kinds of situations in which she speaks. The language diary at the back of this book has space devoted to this matter. If you find that the situational use of single words is developing as expected, even if it is not as fast as you would prefer, then relax. The sentences will appear.

A second clue that sentences are on the way is the appearance of meaningless sounds before single words. These sounds can be short vowels, or they can take longer forms. When these extra sounds are combined with a real word, they form part of a single pattern of pronunciation, just as in true sentences.[8] The distinction between the rhythmic sound of sentences and the uttering of single words is so clear that it is perfectly noticeable to parents with no linguistic training. The addition of sounds to single words is a promising sign that word combinations are close at hand.

If by age thirty months primitive sentences still have not appeared, you should read Chapter 15 to help determine whether the matter involves a simple delay or something more serious.

Dialogue not appearing. By the time two-word sentences begin to appear, children should ask occasional questions. The rise of questions which seek information marks important social progress, as the child is discovering that language gives her access to the wisdom of others. *What's that?* a child asks and is told, "That's butter." The child replies *butter.* On the surface, the child is learning a bit of vocabulary; more importantly, the value of asking becomes clear.

If a child speaks sentences and does not use this social role of language, parents should play the question game (given above) as a form of encouragement. If this play still does not lead to questioning, the child's pediatrician should be informed.

Child almost never initiates speech. "She's a quiet child, keeps to herself." "She's a shy child." "She's so serious." These are the things some parents say if they see their child doesn't talk much. Of course, there is a huge range of talkativeness and not everyone talks all the time, but a child who almost never initiates speech is quite unusual. This silence is more than shyness, for most children's speech at this stage is really addressed to themselves. It is especially rare for a child to be silent both in company and when alone. By itself this behavior may not signify much, but if it is only one thing in a series of concerns about language development, you should consider the whole situation quite carefully by going over Chapter 15.

Child speaks nonsense. Parents may be alarmed occasionally to hear their child say something that is apparently meaningless. Generally, this development is no cause for alarm; the world is full of things children wish to express and yet which cannot be handled by the precedents of their language. Instead of being cowed into silence, however, they use language freely, as a tool which, if it is bent a little, can serve well enough.

Such inventiveness constitutes the most profound solution to the problem of speaking beyond the formal capacity of one's language. At this stage children are already creative enough to invent a little grammar (a spur-of-the-moment word order) or create words. Sometimes these children's inventions become so free—saying things like *car mosquito* and *pencil doggie*—that they simply cannot be interpreted by listeners, but parents needn't fear that their child has given herself over to meaningless jabber.

Parents should only become concerned if these kinds of sentences predominate or if there is a tendency to create obscure two-word combinations in which neither word is a noun. In such cases see Chapter 15 for a fuller consideration of your child's speech.

Child speaks only in clichés. Occasionally children speak long sentences or phrases which they have heard others speak. If these kinds of sentences come to dominate a speech and are always used in the same rote way, it may be a symptom of serious trouble. You should turn to Chapter 15.

Child says one thing, means another. At this stage the child still has not mastered enough of the social complexities of language to realize how useful lies can be. I do not believe that a child at this stage can deliberately lie, but she can be misunderstood. Compared with the other communications systems in the natural world, language is unusually confusing. Misunderstanding is a continuous part of language. During the primitive-sentence stage, this confusion is likely to be particularly apparent in the case of yes-or-no questions. What, for example, are we to make of this exchange:

A child is reaching toward the top of the TV, and his mother asks, "What do you want?"

"Bottle." A bottle is on top of the television.

"You want the bottle?" asks Mother.

"No," says the child, who then takes the mother by the hand, reaches toward the television, and adds, "Want bottle."[9]

The child's desire is evident, but why did he say *no,* he doesn't want the bottle?

The basic problem is that children in this stage have not yet gotten a firm grip on the general concepts *yes* and *no.* This discovery will surprise many parents who can see that their children already use and respond to both words. The children have also learned to nod their head (yes) and shake it (no).[10]

So surely they know the difference between *yes* and *no*. Unfortunately, this conclusion is illusory. Children at this stage use *no* to indicate absence, nonexistence, or rejection. A denial is still too abstract a concept for them.

Since yes-or-no questions call for denial or affirmation, they are beyond the capacity of children at this stage to answer correctly; however, even before they start combining words, children do understand that when they are asked a question, they are expected to make a reply. Thus, when asked a yes-or-no question, children do know they are supposed to say something, even if they don't know what to say.

Children develop their own solutions to this challenge. The most common is to simply say *no* to everything. The words can be accompanied by head shaking or nodding, but the meaning of these gestures is no more precise than the words. So a child can be asked, "Do you want this puppet?" and answer *no,* while at the same time reaching for it.

If a parent is truly stumped by a child's desire, it is best to ask a more general question calling for information rather than seeking confirmation. A child can answer the question, "What do you want?" if she knows the name for what she wants. She cannot, however, confirm the question.

Child frequently gets tangled in her speech. Box 17 lists a number of frailties that afflict every speaker throughout life. In some cases, however, one or more of these problems is more the rule than the exception. If it seems to you that your child is unduly troubled by one or more of these tangles, you should read Chapter 15 and judge whether it seems serious.

Box 17
TANGLED-TONGUE SPEECH

- Knows names of things but cannot speak them when asked
- Cannot associate name with thing
- Frequently confuses words that sound alike or which share similar meanings
- Unable to imitate words or sounds

YOUR CHILD'S INTERESTS

Because children differ so much among themselves, the similarity between their early sentences is chiefly a formal one. Their sentences consist of two, or occasionally three, words arranged in a regular order, but there is a great divergence among the things they talk about. The topics available to children at this stage are so few that it might seem as though the content of their speech ought to be as similar as the form, yet collections of early sentences present an astonishing range of expression. One child's sentences are filled with invention; another's are primarily concerned with herself; while a third's are full of talk about friends and family. Even in these primitive sentences, the individuality of the child is apparent.

Often a child will be confronted by something she wishes to talk about, but she does not yet have the verbal tools to speak correctly. Instead of keeping silent, the child speaks anyway. Sometimes, in fact, children face problems which grammar can never encompass. The study of one boy's speech caught him in the midst of trying to make sense of death. Calico, the family cat, died, and the boy tried to speak of the event in a number of ways: *Calico all gone; Calico all done; bye-bye Calico; Calico bye-bye.*[11] Later, a psychologist pointed out that these sentences and others showed that the boy was unsure about where to place the words *all gone* and *bye-bye*. But when the world is so fraught with importance, a lack of grammar is not an obstacle. Children speak because they have something to say, and this need to translate reality into words pushes them to grope for and discover the rules of grammar.

The topics children at this stage can speak about and examples showing the most common primitive sentences are outlined in Box 18. The topics themselves come from the children's hearts and are not learned; however, it is notable that all of these topics were found during the single-word stage. The primitive-sentence stage does not contain any qualitative leaps in the kinds of situations that provoke speech. The development we see suggests a deepening appreciation of the nature of these situations, rather than the discovery of previously unrecognized topics.

Box 18
THE VERY FIRST GRAMMAR

Expresses	Examples	Comment
NAMING:	this ball see tree there cookie hi bird allgone light } bye-bye milk }	Names what is absent
DESIRE:	more juice gimme cake no sock } no clock }	Names what is not desired
ACTION:	car away baby hug eat cookie open toy daddy ball daddy ball jump chair jump chair no jump } no eat }	 (Daddy *caught* ball) (Daddy *threw* ball) (Jump *on* chair) (Jump *off* chair) Similar to expressions of desire
DESCRIBE:	big SanClaus little mitten hot milk happy bird	
ASSOCIATION:	dadda shoe } bird tree } cookie there	Possession Location
NOTE:	Other types of speech, particularly questions *(who that; what this),* are commonly formed as clichés rather than being produced after using grammatical rules.	

There is no known order in which the listed topics appear in a child's two-word speech. Furthermore, it is unlikely that any one child in this stage expresses all of the rules shown in Box 18. Thus, two children just starting to combine words are likely to say very different sorts of things. Each time a new topic is raised, however, the appropriate rules for word order must then be mastered. As time passes and children's two-word speech extends to more topics, their language begins to resemble each other's more closely; but different interests and experiences prevent children's sentences from becoming identical. The topics their sentences express are:

Naming. The interesting thing about two-word naming is the way it combines an action word with a name and, thus, makes the speech seem far more energetic than single-word naming. Even in the case of redundant speech which unites a pointing word *(this, that, see, here, there)* with a name, the effect is quite vigorous. *There chair* seems a more potent remark than the equally precise *chair* coupled with pointing.

This combination also resolves a distinction noted during the single-word stage. Greeting people with *hi* plus their name overcomes the need to choose between the words. This ability to unite formerly distinct ways of expressing a situation is one of the great powers of language.

Desire. The emotion children at this stage seem to be most aware of, or at least most likely to put into words, is that of wanting. In the case of one boy 24 of his 61 earliest recorded sentences (that's 39 percent) announced his wants: *want fix it* (i.e., I want it fixed), *want car, want cookie, want ball*,[12] and so on. Of course, the boy might have been just showing off his knowledge of where to position the word *want;* however, a month later 44 of 149 recorded sentences (30 percent) were still beginning with want.[13] Some children, however, use this form only rarely.

Essentially, this topic is a form of naming. It is made the same way naming sentences are created. A name is combined with some other word. Once again the union makes two-word speech seem a more vigorous way of speaking.

Action. Because two words are not enough to describe an action, this topic is still the most difficult one facing young children. If John hit a ball, we need at least three words to describe the event, *John hit ball.* Children try to get by with *John hit, hit ball,* or even *John ball.* Children do eventually master the proper order for these different abbreviations of the full action, but they do not express the whole thing until they get beyond combining words and begin to combine primitive sentences, an accomplishment which is too advanced at this stage of speech. At this point they can only express parts of the relationship.

When children use two words to report their own actions, their remarks often sound a bit odd, for they usually refer to themselves by their own name. One child, named Kendall, said things like *Kendall bite* and *Kendall break.*[14] A Swedish girl, Embla, also showed the same tendency, saying things which translate as *Embla go* and *Embla try.*[15] The appearance of making objective statements about some third person probably comes from the difficulty of the word "I." These sentences mean *I bite* or *I go,* but *I* is a hard word to latch onto.

Description. This topic seems to be the biggest present advance in the use of a child's speech. The addition of a second word to a name permits naming to become a descriptive activity. Usually children are content to describe a thing in terms of some quality it possesses: *big ball, hot milk, wet diaper,* and so on. Less common, but sometimes encountered, is a description that places things into larger categorics. One child said things like *mommy lady, Kendall monkey, Kimmy monkey, Scott monkey too.*[16]

Description also commonly involves numbers. *More* is the general word for plural or recurring things, although sometimes children use specific numbers.

Association. As in the case of single-word speech, the reasons for associating two objects with one another are usually possession and location. Some children do use the word *my,* but more often at this stage they use their own name when claiming something. As we saw in the single-word stage, not all statements of ownership are selfish, and many of these sentences report that someone else owns something.

As for location, although children may know both *here* and *there,* they do not yet grasp the distinction between the two words, and parents should not assume that *here* means nearby or *there* means further away. At this stage children do not use prepositions to indicate location, and when a child says something like *ball chair,* the most literal interpretation is probably a general one ("the ball is at the chair"), rather than a more specific one meaning *in, on,* or *under.*

Questions. Some children ask a lot of questions. Most of them ask for names: *what that?* and *who that?* are the most common. A bit later *where——?* appears.[17] Questions about ownership, requests for a description, or inquiries about somebody else's wants are not found at this time. The grammar behind the questions children do ask is fairly complicated, and the questions are known by rote, rather than being created in accordance with rules.

Negatives. At this stage a child's use of *no* in combination with another word indicates either absence or nonexistence. It is not used to deny statements. The development is more evident in some other languages. In Hebrew, *en* means nonexistence and *lo* indicates a denial, so we should expect that Israeli children will first use the negative for nonexistence. When the primitive sentences of an Israeli girl were studied, she was found, as predicted, to use *en* first.[18]

WHAT IS HAPPENING

Once a child's vocabulary grows, she begins to notice some ambiguities in her speech—to use the jargon of our age, her "consciousness expands"—and the child's use of language changes to express this new understanding. The result is a fuller expression of the situation. By the time she is five, this sort of circular process will have gone on so many times it will be hard to say who is in charge, the child or the language.

At the start, word combinations are neither elegant nor long. Usually they consist of only two words, and the child is still content to make many one-word sentences. Their brevity gives the sentences a pithy directness and an abrupt sort of charm. Children say things like *mommy oops* when their mother has just said "oops," or *eat sweater* while chewing on their sweater. Remarks like these are so original and to the point that parents love to cite them (quite accurately) as proof of their child's combined cuteness and cleverness.

In the past, these primitive sentences were often called "telegraphic" because, superficially at least, they seemed to resemble the way sentences were shortened to cut down on the cost of a telegram. The term is no longer so popular because it misdirects the reader's attention, putting too great an emphasis on what is lacking. Instead of worrying about why children omit tense or prepositions, it has been more profitable to discover how they go about including what they do say. Clearly, the child herself is trying to organize her own speech. She is not seeking to determine which of her parents' rules she can most safely ignore.

Sentences express ideas by tone of voice and by grammar. Changes in tone of voice are, by now, an ancient way for the child to express different attitudes. Unlike the words of a telegram, which lie lifelessly on paper, a child's words have a sound and rhythm to them. Children's early sentences are primitive, but they are not simple.

The grammar of primitive sentences takes a while to be established. It has been firmly demonstrated that the only grammar rules which control primitive sentences are word-order rules. This fact holds true for a rigid word-order language like English and also for a language like Hungarian in which word order is much less strict.

Of course, children say plenty of things that would be wrong in adult English. *See cold, all gone lettuce, more high, bye-bye dirty,* and *no down* are good examples of primitive sentences which no English-speaking parent is likely to say. Yet sentences like these turn up routinely in children's speech, and they do show the two critical features of language. They express something, and they are original. A child held in the air by a joyful parent may protest *no down* when the parent moves to put her back down on the floor. The grammar is inelegant, but it is sufficient. The parent understands because the words do say something.

Yet all the inventiveness in the world is not going to lead children to proper English. No evidence has ever been found that children have any inborn preference for one word order over another. The orders they settle on are learned. Since learning involves a certain amount of trial, error, and change, alert parents can sometimes see their child groping to learn an order and then finally mastering it.

Once a child has learned how to use a rule, she may go through a period of extensive use with the form. We saw this same pattern of use in the single-word stage, when children go through phases of favoring particular words. The same sort of thing now turns up in primitive sentences. For example, if the child has learned how to use the word *big,* she may go through a phase when talking about big things is a dominant verbal interest: *big car, big cow, big hot, big man, big san'wich, big doggie, big hand, big shoe.* It is as though the child thinks sentences which use *big* correctly are a kind of new toy to be played with as much as possible. Of course, this kind of self-imposed drill is invaluable in turning the use of a particular word order into a habit that is so strong it seems natural. How surprised a child would be to discover that in Africa infants learning Swahili put their word for *big* at the end of the sentence.

Even the best toys wear thin, and eventually the enthusiasm for a particular combination passes. If the child is not really excited by bigness for its own sake, the repeated announcement that something is big disappears. The rule is not forgotten. There is no return to a groping pattern with that particular word, but the percentage of times the rule is used is much reduced.

The rules that children learn are quite specific. They state that a particular word always goes in the same place. For example, one rule says that the word *little* goes first. Another says that the word *hot* goes first. Adults combine such rules and say that adjectives precede nouns. We have no evidence that children have any abstract insights into their own grammar. What they do know is how to organize individual words. The primitive sentences of one boy, for example, showed that he had learned the rules for many adjectives—saying correctly *big lion, little hat, old cookie,* and *hot fire*—but he still struggled with the problem of where to put the word *wet.* He tried: *shirt wet, wet nose, shoe wet,* and *wet diaper.*

At this stage most of the social possibilities and limitations of language are unrecognized. Children speaking primitive sentences show no notion that language can communicate an experience to someone who has not already shared the experience. They also act as though they expect to be automatically understood, and, for all their eagerness to master word order, they do not show much interest in trying to make themselves more clear. This behavior is again comparable to that of a poet, but a special kind of poet—one who is not interested in being published. As long as the child is satisfied with the quality of her sentences, she is content and does not seem to fret over what others say or whether they understand.

When a child has something to say which is too complex for her simple word-order system and which has overpowered the limits of her inventiveness, she often turns to clichés. A cliché is the reverse of an invention. Inventiveness permits a child to speak before she has fully mastered the rules, while clichés follow rules but are not fully understood. In Chapter 9 we shall see that children eventually use the structure of these clichés as the entry point to English grammar. A typical primitive-sentence cliché is *drink of water.* This phrase is treated as a single word, and a child has no notion of how its individual parts work. She cannot alter the cliché to *drink of Coke* or *drink of ice water.* Some children at this stage are quite skilled at picking up clichés. In the case of one boy studied, many of his earliest sentences began with *can I have.* This construction is remarkably advanced; however, there was no evidence in the boy's speech that he really understood the rules. By now, researchers have collected and analyzed enough primitive sentences for it to be stated as a general rule that the use of any grammatical construction other than those based on word order are clichés.

After about half a year, children begin to reach the end of the primitive-sentence stage. They speak one sentence and then add on another: *Block 'way . . . 'way away,* or *this sock . . . dirty.* Three-word sentences begin to be heard with regularity. As these sentences begin to grow, rules which were previously used by themselves are combined. For example, a child can now say sentences like *want mommy sock.* At last a child can express the full facts of an action, as in *John hit ball.*

At this point the language of a child resembles the pidgin languages used by people who do not share a common language but whose business forces them to communicate. Pidgin languages also depend on word order to express relations; gesture, pointing, and intonation do a lot of the work in filling out meaning; nouns are used without an article, and number must be inferred from the context; time is also inferred from the context, since the form of the few verbs used is unchanging; certain complicated ideas which must often be expressed are stated as clichés; questions are indicated by intonation, rather than by changing word order.

The formal similarity between pidgin languages and primitive sentences suggests that once your child has passed through this stage, she has created language in its most elementary form. The suggestion is strengthened by the fact that the relationships expressed in the first grammar are found in all of the world's known languages. Primitive sentences can be translated literally into the primitive sentences of other languages, but having now created the universal features of speech, it is time for the child to switch over to the individualities of English.

English treats many things which strike all of us as being as basic as issues of possession or description, but details of time, space, condition, and plurality are all ignored by primitive sentences and are treated differently by different languages. It is time for the child to move beyond what she knows naturally and to learn what culture has to reveal.

PART THREE
LEARNING ENGLISH

Language is fossil poetry.
—R. W. EMERSON,
      Essays, "The Poet"

Chapter 7
The Discovery of Tradition

AGE: TWO AND A HALF TO FIVE

The chapters in Part III describe a great change in the way a child speaks. During the first two-and-a-half years of life, a child's language is personal; the form and purpose of that speech is largely her own, even though she does take most of her vocabulary from the general society. Presumably, this creative process could continue indefinitely. In fact, it does sometimes happen that a pair of small children are left largely to themselves and they develop a language of their own;[1] however, it is obviously better for a child to use the established language spoken by everyone around her. The chapters in this part describe the abandonment of the first language in favor of speaking English.

This transition comes at a time of a great many visible changes in the child. Socially, intellectually, and imaginatively, she shines with many new glories. From a linguistic point of view, the development is marked by the rise of many new things to say. The language to express all these new things seems to rush forth. The systematic step-by-step approach to language is replaced by a wholesale blossoming of thought, insight, and imaginative play.

The child's world has ceased to be merely a totality of facts.

Now things that are not facts—ideas like "Look at me; I'm a fireman"—become important. A child of this age can be in a room when suddenly she imagines making a paper doll, and begins to hunt for a piece of paper and some scissors. If you see her searching, the only way to find out why is to ask her straight out, "What are you looking for?" There is no sure way to deduce from the environment what her imagination is up to.

Now more than ever the comparison of a child with a poet seems apt. The creativity of a child's words has the same sort of creativity we see in many poems and song lyrics. Its originality comes from the speaker's way of seeing, rather than from the actual invention of a new language. A child who says, "I love Mommy more than peanut butter," is speaking creatively because she recognizes an ancient emotion in an original way. The vocabulary and grammar are ordinary, but the vision they express is moving.

It would be absurd to expect a child's linguistic creativity to keep pace with this imaginative explosion. Each of the world's established languages has untold centuries of thought and experience behind it, and each has evolved a great capacity for subtle and precise statements. No single person in one short lifetime could be expected to invent all the expressive powers of English grammar, anymore than one genius could discover the whole of modern mathematics.

The growth of the child's awareness and imagination has given her more to say, but probably nothing so remarkable that English grammar is not already able to handle it. The easiest response, therefore, is to start quoting English sentences and phrases more extensively. This rise in quotation is exactly what happens.

Starting with her first official word, the child has been treating the English language like an attic trunk stuffed with random goodies. As her imagination grows, more and more of the trunk's contents are put to use. At first only a few words are taken out, but by the time she turns three, phrases and even whole sentences have been snatched as well. Inflectional endings, proverbs, songs, and cultural formulas for greetings, farewells, and so on are also there for the grabbing. Faced with this great wealth of hand-me-down speech, a child needn't spend much time inventing more vocabulary and grammar of her own. Fact is, the trunk is so full there cannot be many people who ever avail themselves of everything it has to offer.

Biology does not regulate vocabulary or grammar, but it can help with the general power of abundant quotation. Apparently children's capacities for longer quotation do improve at this age. Nature seems to have helped the child to develop the tools needed for looting the attic trunk. No doubt we could imagine people being born with a set of preprogrammed concepts or grammatical rules of some sort which would direct us in our use of language. That kind of ordered approach seems very modern and rational, but nature is more practical than rational. Instead of giving us a program worthy of a finely crafted computer chip, we have been provided with a plagiarist's ability to help ourselves to what we hear.

This unsystematic transition from the first language to English has forced Part III's organization to differ from Part II's. The natural progress of that first language was comparable to a river's course; it meandered a bit, but it reached its stages in an orderly manner, one after the other. It allowed me to describe the first language in a reasonably straightforward, stage-by-stage way, but now that river has suddenly reached a lake bed. Instead of just going forward, it has begun to spread out and to cover many different places at once. Because of this change it is no longer helpful to talk about "stages of development." Naturally, as time passes, the child's language becomes more elaborate and intricate, but focusing attention on some arbitrary stage would blind a reader to everything else that is happening at the same time.

The three chapters summarized in Box 19 all cover the same time period (age two and a half to five), but each traces the development of a different aspect of language. Each of these matters becomes so intricate and elaborate that we might pity the poor three-year-old who has to simultaneously confront them all, except we know from ancient experience that three-year-olds succeed famously.

Chapter	Concerns	Development
Box 19 **SUMMARY OF PART III**		
8	Conversation (purpose)	Child begins to make use of language's social power. Starting from a primarily individualistic position, the child becomes more sensitive to the cooperative role of language.
9	Grammar (organization)	Child makes increasing use of English grammar. Primitive sentences are replaced with clichés which are broken down and altered according to the changing situation.
10	Vocabulary (style)	The child's vocabulary triples. This increase not only broadens the range of subjects discussed but deepens them, so that a child can select the word most suited to the occasion.

The first concern of correct speech (shown in Box 19) is the most abstract. It is also universal, regardless of culture, although every culture has its own way of governing the matter. The purposes of speech come from the child herself. During the first-language period, a child's urge to speak was instinctive and her purpose was simple. She translated a situation into sounds. Now, however, her imagination has expanded so much that her ambitions go beyond simple translation. She might use language to try and control the situation at hand, or she may speak in order to share her own viewpoint with somebody else.

The consequences of this expansion threaten chaos and frustration; "chaos" because the new purposes make it so much harder to predict what a child is going to say, and "frustration" because accomplishment of these new purposes depends on the cooperation of others. In the days when a child's speech was often a monologue, the attention of others didn't matter so much, but now that language is becoming increasingly communicative, others have to listen. There may be some biological processes helping to organize matters, but so far we know only about the cultural factors. Every society has its own control system which permits speech to become conversation rather than chaos.

Much of this system is learned from parents who teach it explicitly. Good manners, including polite speech, are taught more directly by parents than good grammar. In its most powerful form these cultural rules suppress the child's own purposes. For example, every society has a greeting formula which must be followed. A child's heart may yearn to say to an arriving aunt, "Did you bring me some candy?" but stronger forces lead her to say first, "Hi, Aunt Selma." It is at this stage that language begins to take on some of the qualities of a mask, imposing specific speech forms on specific situations. Reality is hidden, and only in intimate surroundings or among equals can a child usually be completely free to follow the purposes of her heart. In the worst cases children are never free to speak their piece, and language becomes a wall cutting them off from everybody. More often, fortunately, a balance is struck. The child's purposes are framed in accordance with the cultural requirements but are not completely suppressed.

Of course, along with social correctness, speech must be grammatically correct, but what is grammatical correctness, anyway? A quick survey of the world's languages demonstrates there are an enormous number of contradictory ways in which the details of any situation can be put into a sentence.

This range of culturally different ways of speaking about identical situations has always been one of the great mysteries of language. How can there be so many ways of seeing? Which way is best? This last question is generally answered, "My way is best," but that prejudice is hard to prove. It is not so easy to show that English grammar is superior to the grammar of Latin in the age of Cicero. Language commonly concerns concrete situations which can be viewed in any number of ways, each just as defensible as the others.

The secret of a child's grammatical correctness is in her attic-trunk approach. She quotes others as needed. We already saw, during the primitive-sentence stage, that children have a number of clichés at their disposal. A child may ask *Can-I-have cookie* in which the phrase *can-I-have* is understood merely as a synonym of *want,* while the grammar of the phrase is completely unappreciated. This sort of partially understood quotation is at the heart of a child's switch to English. First she recognizes the general situation in which a phrase is used, and only later does she begin to break down the phrase to say things like *can he have* or *can my mommy have.* (An example of this process is described in Box 20.)

This speak-by-quoting method provides the practical ability to use English grammar long before a child gains any theoretical appreciation of the viewpoint the grammar seems to imply.

As for any abstract concepts which may lie buried deep in the grammar, I suspect most of them never are recognized by the majority of speakers. *Drink-of-water* is a common and early cliché of child language, but the concept which unites that phrase with *yard of wool* and *name of the man* is pretty subtle and hard to define.

The use of quotation leads a child quite naturally into a third concern of correct speech. As long as she quotes someone else exactly (or at least as exactly as she can), a child is free of further worry, but once she begins to break up and revise her clichés, the responsibility for what she says becomes increasingly her own. Suppose a mother says *Give it to me,* and the child replies *Give it to you,* switching the *me* to *you.* Could she make any other changes? Of course, *it* could be made more specific, as in *Give the doll to you.* Perhaps there is another word that could be used instead of *give: Throw the doll to you* (said with a rebellious giggle). Or perhaps the child says nothing at the time but later says to her father, *Please, give it to me.* Here she is quoting her mother exactly but has added the word *please* because, after all, she is speaking with her father.

Box 20
THE CREATION OF A NEW PHRASE

Three-and-a-half-year-old Arthur was a child of the modern age. A TV newsman stopped him for an interview, and, with no signs of intimidation, he answered the reporter's questions. "Do you know what day is today?" Arthur nodded. "What day is it?"

"Halloween." Arthur's voice was pleased.

"Are you going trick-or-treating?" Arthur's mother looked alarmed at that question. Undaunted, the reporter repeated, "Are you going trick-or-treating?"

"Yes."

"Will your mother let you go alone?"

"Yes."

Since the point of the news story was that children should not go out alone, it was the reporter's turn to look alarmed. He turned to the mother and asked, "Is he going alone?" The mother shook her head, no, and the reporter leaned down toward Arthur. "Your mother says, no way."

"Yes way," Arthur cried exuberantly.

Watching the news that evening, I smiled at this example of childish creativity. Several years after speaking their first words, children are still quoting their elders, only now they are modifying what they quote. Arthur understood the *no*, and he changed it; he didn't understand *way*, but he did keep it. By quoting the speech of others, changing what they think needs changing and keeping the rest, children are able to use sentences long before they have any abstract theories of grammar.

All of these possible changes fill language with a variety that makes it continuously fresh and interesting, but they add to the problems of any child trying to speak correctly. Which of the many possible words should she use? The answer depends on her personal understanding of the situation, on the size of her vocabulary, and on how much she believes the listener can be expected to understand. In short, it depends on her own sophistication. The child is on her own. She must speak in a style that is correctly suited to the occasion, but she must determine for herself what is or is not "correct." Since this variable way of speaking depends on the personal characteristics and insights of the speaker, it is the most distinctive and individual part of any child's speech.

Box 21
CHILDREN'S WORD PLAY[2]

A particularly intensive study of children's word play traced the development of a girl named Valerie over a three-year period.

2 years, 7 months	Because . . . because . . . Becky (giggles)
2 years, 10 months	Caca-cola (for Coca-cola)
3 years, 1 month	(Looking at a picture book about animals) I like this, this . . . fis, fis, fish!
3 years, 3 months	A dishrag, a dishrag, a dishrag. A ragdish. Radish! A radish; I like radishes.
3 years, 4 months	Pop, you're my popsicle.
3 years, 6 months	Adult: They're playing Monopoly. Valerie: Like Polly?
3 years, 7 months	Valerie (describing a TV show about birds): They had eagles, bad birds. Do you know what they're called? Finches. Adult: Finches? Valerie: It's something that pinches.
3 years, 11 months	(Singing) I want you to listen, to lis, to lis, to lis, lis, lis, lis, list of names.
4 years	Just a moment, Mommy. Hey, it's almost the same, moment, Mommy.
5 years, 3 months	She's the villain . . . maybe her name is Lynne! That's a good one.

By the time she turns five, a child's speech is usually appropriate to the whole context. The purposes governing her conversations are the culturally correct ones. She organizes the details of her speech in the grammatically correct way. The words she uses are precise and clear enough to be stylistically correct.

These new powers emerge most vividly as a part of play. Some of the most important studies of children's language during this period have reported what children say in fun. For example, it is now well established that children like to play on words. This breaking up of words into sounds that can be used for fun is the lighthearted side of the insights which transform clichés into new sentences. Box 21 contains a number of examples of youthful puns. Unfortunately, French scholars have taken childish punning more seriously than either the Americans or British, so the plays on words cited in the box have been translated from the French. Puns are notoriously difficult to translate. For proof that children can do better than the box indicates, I suggest you observe your own child's verbal play. (A page in the diary at the back of this book is reserved for examples.)

The games described in Part III were designed with this lighthearted use of language in mind. Even when the point behind the game is very serious, the speech should be fun. Correct speech is a by-product of childhood, not a goal.

Box 22 **PROBLEMS AND CONCERNS**	
	See page
Matters of *grammar*	
• Previously learned grammar is being forgotten	124
• Grammar is not progressing as expected	125
• Child starts to talk and then doesn't know how to proceed	124
• Word order is seriously jumbled	125

	See page
Matters of *context*	
• Grammar is fast improving, but language still seems socially lacking	97
• Child is using her new skills to tell lies	96
• Child has no friends her own age to talk with	97
• Child's skill at conversational tasks is good, but her style of speaking is unacceptable	98
• Child's meaning is often obscure	146
• Speech is extraordinarily literal	99
• Child's behavior is beginning to interfere with speech	125

Box 22 summarizes the most common problems of this period and tells where in Part III they are discussed. Because difficulties can be either formal, having to do with grammar, or can be large and more social, I have divided the box into two sections.

Chapter 8
The Secrets of Conversation

Once children begin to move beyond the primitive-sentence stage, their speech becomes much more sociable, and the steadily improving grammar now seems like the least of their accomplishments. At this point there is a sudden leap in the amount of talking carried out with other children. In typical situations, children younger than three address most of their remarks to adults, while by age three and one half the bulk of their speech is directed to other children.[1] Now suddenly children become impatient when communication fails or proves difficult, and they struggle to clarify themselves. Better yet, they are generally successful at finding ways of correcting a misunderstanding.[2]

Box 23
THE RISE OF CONVERSATION

Age

2½ *Beginnings of conversation*
   • Speech is increasingly relevant to other's remarks
   • Need for clarity is being recognized

3 *Breakthrough in attention to communication*
   • Seeks ways to clarify and correct misunderstanding
   • Pronunciation and grammar sharply improve
   • Speech with children own age expands dramatically
   • Use of language as instrument of control increases

4 *Fundamentals in conversation are known*
   • Able to shift speech according to listener's knowledge
   • Literal definitions are no longer a sure guide to meaning
   • Collaborative suggestions have become common
   • Disputes can be resolved with words

5 *Elements of conversation are under good control*

There is also a shift in speech subjects. Three is the age when children suddenly begin to ask many questions.[3] This age is also the time when wholesale boasting appears.[4] The rise of boasting reflects the new powers found in speech. Children's talk becomes quite unlike the literal translation of situations that dominated their previous language. It is more flexible, more varied, far less predictable.

TALKING TOGETHER

Picture books. By age three, picture books should be used to promote two-way conversations.[5] You read the picture book's story, but the child also tells stories about the pictures. Well before this age, children are able to complete sentences based on pictures. A parent, for example, looking at a page with the picture of a puppy can read, "Once there was a . . . ," pause, and point to the picture while the child says, "Puppy." By three and often well before then, the imagination of the child has grown enough for her to be able to invent brief stories about the pictures. These stories are likely to be short and may not be clearly relevant to the picture at hand, but the point is for the child to practice telling someone what is on her mind, so the brevity or irrelevance of the story does not matter. (The nature of children's stories is discussed more deeply in Chapter 11.) Once a child is used to this game and has overcome any initial shyness, you can help her flesh out her stories (which are likely to contain only twenty or thirty words) by asking questions.

Who am I hiding? Children between the ages of three-and-a-half to four can begin to play this game. Take magazine pictures of famous people (famous to the children—cartoon characters, television stars, etc.) and ask the child to guess whose picture you are hiding from her. Give clues by describing the person. After you have done this two or three times, say, "Now it's your turn," and give the pictures to the child. Now she has to describe a person so that you can guess who it is.

The purpose of this game is for the child to practice telling somebody something they do not already know. Success at the game requires that she take into account your point of view and your information. Any help you give the child should focus on that requirement. If the child gives as a clue, "He did it," spell out your problem, saying, "I don't know what *it* is. What did he do?"

Parents playing this game may be tempted to give long clues, but since your child cannot do the same and might be intimidated by her incapacity, it is best to give short clues. Another technique that can encourage the child is to begin every clue with the words *I'm hiding,* as in, "I'm hiding a friend of Elmer Fudd." That way, when it's your child's turn, she will already have some words to quote and get her started.

Puppets. The use of hand puppets is an excellent way parents can speak with their children while stepping outside the role of parent. If a parent holds a puppet and the child holds a puppet, the parent can put a wide range of speech into the puppet's mouth. In the natural course of events, much parental speech addressed to the child is the language of control. Puppets provide a way of expanding the kind of language your child hears.

There is one important rule for this game: the parent's puppet should speak only in a socially acceptable style. Punch and Judy dialogue with a lot of anger, shouting, nagging, and so on may seem like fun and it is sure to please your child, but it radically subverts the idea behind this play. Television, friends, and your child's own energy are going to promote these unwelcome speaking styles. The idea behind the puppet game is to be sure and let your child also hear more desirable forms of conversation.

Table talk. Children from age three on up are practiced enough at speech to be able to report in some detail what is on their minds. The question is whether they will learn to use their ability or learn to keep their thoughts a secret. I recommend that by age three both parents begin to really talk with their children. It is common for one or both parents of a three-year-old to have fallen out of the habit of speaking with the child except as a means of controlling her. Now is the time to return to fuller conversations. At this age formal conversation, with everybody seated properly in the living room, is a bit much to ask of a child, but if you slip in such talk while seated at a table sharing a snack, the conversation is natural.

Children at this age are unlikely to say many things which, in themselves are particularly fascinating; however, if you look behind the literal meaning of the words, they will reveal much about themselves and their attitudes. At this age there is no need to press for a particularly lengthy talk. The idea is to promote the conversational habit, not to set time records.

Parents dutifully seeking to talk with their children are notorious for developing mechanical questions (e.g., "What did you do in school today?") which interest neither the adult nor the child. A more creative approach is to begin with a statement of your own, rather than a question. Once table talk is established as a part of life, almost any sort of statement will do.

PROBLEMS

Child is using her new skills to tell lies. This is the stage when children generally begin to lie. Lies start with unjustified boasting and can then spread to many of the other purposes of speech. Their appearance in boasting is a way of maintaining a front, of reasserting one's social rank. If a child brags, "My dad flies airplanes," then your child will be tempted to make the same claim, even if it isn't true. It is a way of preventing the friend from getting a leg up the social scale.

Parents should not be shocked and should not overreact, but at the same time should not ignore this new discovery. Children have to learn that telling the truth is important and that lying is wrong. You certainly don't want them deciding that it is all right to lie to other members of the family. Of course, children will never learn not to lie if they aren't brought up in a circle of truth.

As for lying with friends, this tendency is harder to control because children decide among themselves the rules for what is or is not acceptable speech.

Child has no friends of own age to talk with. A three-year-old's horizon expands to include extensive talking with other children of about the same age. Up until this point, language development has not much depended on this kind of talking, but now it does. The social skills of conversation are developed at this age, and parents should be alert to this need. Children who are growing up in isolation from other children or whose friends consist mainly of the friends of older brothers and sisters are not gaining the conversational experience that will be important throughout their lives. Parents of three-year-olds should make an effort to insure that their children know and regularly see children of about the same age to talk with.

Child's grammar is fast improving, but language still seems socially lacking. Box 23 at the front of this chapter outlines the conversational development of children during this period. On rare occasions, children have no sense of language as a social tool.[6] The parents of such children probably have long feared that something was wrong but told themselves it was only that the language was still so underdeveloped. Now with the transition from primitive sentences, the grammar is fast growing, but the imaginative use of language remains absent and speech is still fully tied to the objective situation. This problem calls for attention, and parents should turn to Chapter 15 to consider their child's language.

More common, and a lot less serious, is for a child's social use of language to be growing but for a few of the powers listed in Box 24 (p. 100) to be unexpressed. Here the problem appears to be the absence of a skill, rather than the absence of imagination. The solution is to provide help in the specific uses that are lacking. Play the puppet game described in this chapter, and make sure your puppet uses the powers that need practice.

Another important way to help a child who lacks a particular skill is to use it yourself. Let the child hear how to say something. This help may require a bit of self-conscious effort on your part. For example, part of your own speaking style may downplay comparing yourself with others. If so, you may not be providing your child with a model for even occasionally performing this task. There is no need to revise your entire conversational style, but you should make an effort to include such speech at least sometimes in your talk with the child. Once you begin, you should find it becomes easy fairly quickly. In comparing yourself, for example, you can deliberately open a brief conversation with the point of letting your child hear how such an exchange takes place. After eating some ice cream you might ask, "Did you like that?" and when the child says *yes,* you reply, "I did too." That final and simple addition of a self-comparison line in a quite ordinary parent-child exchange is a valuable way to give the child a richer sense of how language can be used.

Child's skill at conversational tasks is good, but her style of speaking is unacceptable. Children can easily discover the social powers of language but then develop maddening ways of expressing them. Expressing desire, for example, may take the form of begging, nagging, shouting, whining, cursing, or some other obnoxious style. Do not excuse this speech as the behavior of a little child unless you want her to learn that her style is indeed acceptable. Harsh punishment would also be unfair, since the child has yet to learn what the acceptable form of expression is. Tell her in a serious tone of voice not to speak that way.

Teaching your child to speak acceptably makes a subtle demand on the parent. If you want to keep language open as a means of sharing thoughts with your child, you must speak to her in a socially acceptable manner yourself. Imagine this conversation:

CHILD: I want ice cream.
PARENT: No.
CHILD: Please, please. I want ice cream, ice cream; want ice cream. Please, please.

What do you reply?

The worst answer is to give in, "Oh, all right," and thus teach the child that whining and pleading is a good way to express desire.

A firm reply, however, has its failings too. "I said *no*. Now stop that nagging," will eventually teach a child that nagging is unacceptable, but it puts up a barrier toward ever having a richer conversation with the child. Parents who only use language to control children cannot expect that the child will ever speak to them on a more personal level, not when they are fifteen and maybe not even when they are fifty.

Even though the child is only three or four, she ought to be addressed as a person of some worth. The solution in the ice-cream example above is to give a better answer to the original question. You would never answer a friend with so abrupt a *no*. Children benefit from the same sort of respect. "No, it's too close to suppertime," is a better answer to the request for ice cream. Then the nagging can be stopped with the reply, "I said it's too close to supper. Now stop nagging."

One study found that if a request is denied without a reason being given, children do tend to nag.[7] No doubt puritan discipline methods can soon put a halt to that sort of behavior, but if you ever want more than submissive speech from your child, you are going to have to be more imaginative.

Speech is extraordinarily literal. Because of the ambiguous nature of speech, children must be able to understand what is not expressed. For example, they have to realize that when asked, "What would you do if you cut yourself?" the question calls for a description of how they would go about seeking help. An answer like, "Bleed," if given with a straight face, is simply wrong.

There are a few children who cannot get beyond the literal meaning of any speech. Usually their difficulties with language are so profound that they are discovered long before they abandon primitive sentences; however, if your child is not developing the ability to understand any of the implicit purposes of conversation, you should turn to Chapter 15 and consider whether or not there is a potentially serious problem.

YOUR CHILD'S PURPOSES

With the end of primitive sentences, children's speech takes on a great richness of purpose and possibility. More and more, speech is shaped by imagination, and the results are increasingly personal and captivating. By the time she is four years old, a child's language has powers and concerns that would never have been predicted by anyone who knew only the nature of primitive sentences.

Box 24
EARLY POWERS OF CONVERSATION[8]

General	Specific	Example*
	Emotional	Oh, well.
Translation	Factual	My mom told me. I don't care if it changes.
	Express desire	I want my voice to change.
	Claim possession	My voice . . .
Control	Assert rank	No, your mommy's wrong.
	Direct others	Pretend this is my car.
	Imaginative	We'll stay little.
	Assert links	Oh, well, we'll stay little, right?
Sharing	Compare self	I care.
	Asking	Did your mommy tell you?
	Playing	I have a grandma and grandpa . . . I know, I know, I know

*All examples, except for the "Direct others" and "Playing" categories, are taken from the Andrew-Betsy conversation about growing up.

Box 24 summarizes the social powers children's speech can have during this period. All parents have their own opinions concerning which of these uses are most important, but I do urge every reader to treat all the powers listed in Box 24 as serious. We all have our biases and priorities, but the more able a child is at expressing all of these categories, the fuller her potential will be. The ability to say, "Oh, well," may seem trivial, but it is quite necessary if emotional contact with others is to be developed and maintained. Profound communication problems arise when someone has something to say but is not skilled enough to say it. Just because a child never says *oh, well,* we cannot conclude that she never feels the defeated resignation that *oh, well* voices; however, if she does feel it, no one else will ever know.

A heartening and remarkable fact is how rapidly and extensively children do develop these skills. By the time they are five, they can speak with astonishing range and sensitivity. Consider this conversation between two children approaching their fifth birthday. They were talking about a most abstract and remote subject—what they were going to do when they grew up.

ANDREW: If I grow up, my voice will change and your voice will change. My mom told me. Did your mommy tell you?

BETSY: No, your mommy's wrong. My voice . . . I don't want it to change. Oh, well.

ANDREW: Oh, well, we'll stay little, right?

BETSY: What?

ANDREW: We'll stay little.

BETSY: I don't want to. I *want* my voice to change. I don't care if it changes.

ANDREW: I care.[9]

Of course, not every childish conversation can so richly illustrate the remarkable ways humans combine ego, abstractions, and conflicting fears, but this little drama between Andrew and Betsy sets forth the capacities of conversation with a stark directness we usually expect from only the greatest artists. In developing Box 24, I discovered that, with only two exceptions, I could take all of my examples from this seventy-word exchange. Thus, in my discussion of the different powers, I will refer repeatedly to the way they were expressed in this single conversation.

By referring back to a single bit of dialogue, I can stress the point that these separate powers are part of a larger whole. Speech is more than the sum of its parts. The purposes of a speaker can change as a conversation sets off in one direction and then shifts toward another. Social speech meanders like a river more often than it flies straight to the target. In order to give some sense of the overall direction of meandering speech, I have included three general powers in Box 24 which lie behind the narrower ones.

Translation. This general motive is the oldest in children's language. We have seen it from the beginning. Even in the days of precultural sounds, babies are translating their situations into cries. The rest of language grows out of this speech. By the time children are three years old, naming has largely given way to reporting. Translation now serves as a way of defining the situation under consideration.

The opening sentences of the Andrew-Betsy conversation quoted above is typical of translation at this stage. Andrew recalled something he had been told and reported the news, "If I grow up my voice will change, and when you grow up your voice will change. My mommy told me." The rest of the conversation arose from this initial objective report.

During the stage discussed in this chapter, children's use of speech as translation remains static. The amount of time devoted to this sort of speaking does not change much.[10] As adults, translation is especially important in white-collar work, where memos, reports, papers, and so on all require the translation of situations into words.

Emotional. Of all forms of speech, emotional translation has the lowest general prestige. Commonly, we do not even consider it language. "Ouch," "uh-oh," and "wow" are dismissed as a sort of animal grunting, but these sounds are culturally determined. In Africa, for example, cries of surprise and astonishment are quite unlike those made by American children. *Wow* is an English word and must be learned, just as the word "table" must be learned.

In the Andrew-Betsy conversation, Betsy's emotional, "Oh, well," was critical in keeping the conversation alive. This interjection revealed that despite her vehement protest over Andrew's report, Betsy was grudgingly resigned to its truth. That little, "Oh, well," gave Andrew something to reply to.

Factual. Modern philosophers and traditional theologians have commonly assumed that factual translation is the major purpose of speech because it gives us access to the truth. This position seems terribly narrow, but there is no denying that this use of speech is vital in letting others know what you are talking about. In the world of computers, factual exchange is one of the two major communication tasks.

In the human world, however, even this task is too complex to be so straightforward. Andrew began his comment with a simple report, but then he added a remark which was mistaken; Betsy's voice will not go through the extraordinary change that Andrew's will. Furthermore, Betsy's, "I don't care if [my voice] changes," is presented as a fact but is clearly false.

Express desire. This power might be listed as a subcategory of factual translation. I have placed it separately because it is such a prominent part of children's speech, although it is one of declining importance at this stage.[11] The facts reported here share the grammar and vocabulary of objective statements, but they are as subjective as the emotional *ouch*. All of Betsy's sentences about what she wants are charged with emotion. We have seen expressions of desire since the days of precultural sounds, and although there has been a lot of formal development of the way to voice these wants, the idea remains pretty much the same.

Control. The powers of this general group are necessary to all living societies. In the animal world they are expressed by body displays, chemicals, natural sounds, and ritualistic behavior. Among humans much of the work has been taken over by language. These uses are important because they maintain social order, but they are also rather crude. Betsy's first reaction to Andrew's news was purely the language of control, "No, your mommy's wrong. My voice . . ." Then she shifted to the more complicated truths of human feeling.

Claim possession. In the world of natural communications this use is one of the most common. Bird songs, wolf howls, and lion roars often proclaim the possession of a territory. While humans can use language in this proclamatory manner (e.g., put up signs saying, "No Trespassing"), these expressions commonly have an emotional aspect to them as well. Betsy's remark, "My voice," reflects a concern about herself, not just a claim to a bit of property.

Assert rank. Societies typically have dominant and submissive members and a way to remind everybody of their status. While these relations vary greatly between cultures, children usually have to express submission to their parents. Much of this dependence is expressed by body movements, but it appears in language too. If a four-year-old routinely spoke to her parents as equals whose wishes were to be considered but given no special weight, she would sound like a very strange child indeed.

When speaking with children of their own age, however, children sometimes assert dominance, and sometimes equality or submission. A symptom of this is the boasting which suddenly becomes quite widespread at this stage of development. Put-downs of the listener are also common. The issue in such exchanges is seldom the point under discussion. Rather, it is the pecking order of the arguing children.

Human complications set in to this category as well. Betsy's reply, "No, your mommy's wrong," is a typical form of childish dominance. It is right in the my-dad-can-beat-your-dad line, but the issue here is not the pecking order of Andrew and Betsy. At stake is the difference between the way Betsy would like the world to be and the way Andrew's mother says the world is. A little girl like Betsy does not feel the authority to seriously challenge a statement attributed to a grown mother, but her prompt put-down of Andrew's remark is a classic use of language to try and dominate a situation.

Direct others. This power was not used in the conversation between Andrew and Betsy. It constitutes the regulatory use of language. Statements of the *do this* sort fall here. During the age of three to five years, this type of speech increases greatly.[12] Particularly common are collaborative directions of the let's-do-such-and-such type. This sort of speech becomes important for children as they develop the ability to imagine new goals and want to enlist the help of others. "Let's see who can hold their breath longest," is the sort of ambition that depends on language.

Regulatory speech also becomes important during this stage as a means of correcting someone else's behavior. *Don't* becomes a favorite word for many children.

Since cooperative efforts are dependent on directive speech, it is too bad that once children enter school they come to associate it almost exclusively with instruction and giving orders. Many adults seem to be quite unfamiliar with the idea of giving directions between equals, and parents are well advised to encourage the cooperative form of this speech at home.

Perhaps because directing others is a sensitive matter, we often speak around the issue. Quite commonly, the point of expressing a desire is to direct the listener to help fulfill that desire, but the point is not spoken aloud. Instead of saying straight out, "Give me a cookie," a speaker is more likely to choose some other form, such as expressing a desire, *I would like a cookie,* or asking a question, *Can I have a cookie?,* or, if the other party is uncooperative, asserting rank, *If you don't give me that cookie, I'll knock your block off.* Regulatory purposes are also behind manipulative lies: *There's a monster coming and he loves to eat cookies. Better give me that one so I can hide it.*

These many ways of voicing a single purpose have driven social scientists close to despair in their attempt to systematize the way language is used. Children seem to have less trouble with this tangle, and by the time they are three and a half, children are well aware of the subtle aspects of this speech category. One study of children at this age observed that when one child said, "I need that pencil," another replied, "Here," and tossed the pencil.[13] If children reacted on a purely literal level, the response would not be so prompt and correct.

Already, at this young age, children can understand the unspoken.

Sharing. The powers in this general group are specifically and exclusively human. The animal world contains many examples of communication as a means of objective control, and computers can communicate for purposes of mechanical control or data analysis; however, only people communicate to share what is on their minds. When we speak of the need to communicate, this sharing power is the role we generally have in mind. Without such communication, trust, understanding, and sympathy would be more difficult.

Since it is characteristic of people to have different points of view about any given situation, we need language rather desperately. We should not be surprised to learn, therefore, that throughout this period a child's use of sharing speech grows.[14] It is the presence of so much of this type of language in the Andrew-Betsy conversation that makes the exchange seem so profoundly human and true.

The objective purposes of speech all have their counterparts in this subjective category. Since our attitudes are as important to social order as is our behavior, humanity would be seriously crippled if we had no means of communicating those attitudes.

Imaginative. This task is the opposite of translation. It puts airy nothings into words. "We'll stay little," Andrew proposed, imagining an impossible situation. Children use imaginative language in pretending and for announcing new ambitions. Among adults it turns up in art, philosophy, science, and in practical discussions of new goals and plans. Without such speech human adaptability might lead to chaos, rather than survival.

It is important to encourage children to speak up and state the new ambitions they have conceived, even if most of them do seem a little crazy or sad. The issue is not the quality of any particular idea, but the access such speech gives parents to their child's mind. In Andrew's case it is apparent that he is worried about growing up ("If I grow up . . . we'll stay little

. . . I care"). An alert parent overhearing such remarks ought to be willing to reassure the child.

Assert links. Just as physical dominance or submission is of great concern to the language of control, human speech must also confront the relationship between two minds. When Betsy revealed that, like Andrew, she was troubled by the thought of her voice changing, Andrew said, "Oh, well, we'll stay little, right?" This sentence is as personal as a touch.

Andrew seems quite skilled at such speech. *Oh, well* is a direct quotation of Betsy's last words. *Right?* is a clear invitation for Betsy to say *right.* Unfortunately for Andrew, Betsy was even more horrified by the idea of staying little, so she did not say *right.* Nevertheless, the power of speech to seek bonds between minds is of great importance, and people who are unable to use language in this way will find it difficult to form personal attachments.

Compare self. An inevitable result of the use of language to assert links is a growing awareness of how one's thoughts compare with others'. Without language we would still be able to recognize how others differ physically from us and we might suspect that others don't seem to share all our attitudes, but we could not turn the suspicion into understanding. With language we can find many ways in which others are like and unlike ourselves.

The Andrew-Betsy conversation ended with Andrew specifically stating one way in which he was unlike Betsy. That difference permits Andrew and the reader to get a clear sense of these two children as separate individuals.

Comparing oneself is particularly subject to many cultural and social regulations. Talking about oneself is often considered rude or too intimate for ordinary social situations. Without such speech, however, children may have a hard time getting a full sense of themselves and of the reality of other people's feelings. They ought to become skilled at such speech.

Asking. The subjective equivalent of directing another's behavior is to ask for what's in their mind—information, opinions, agreement. With the rise of conversation, children enter a stage of asking lots of information-seeking questions. "Did your mommy tell you?" Andrew asked, looking for something in Betsy's memory. Without language we could probably still discover ways to ask for a pencil, but asking for what is on another's mind would become a lot more challenging.

Playing. This is the one category of sharing language which has no counterpart in the language of control or translation. It is the verbal equivalent of physical play. In its social form, children invent monologues and songs which they say together. It is a way of having fun with language even when you have nothing to say. Susan Iwamura, a linguist who has made a most valuable study of this sort of children's speech, has insisted that the kinds of repetitive phrases common to such speech are not "simply simultaneous monologues during which the children have some vague notion of companionship. It was an activity which used language as the object to be played with in the sense that a ball or a doll is a plaything."[15]

Playing is serious business, and we should not let the fact that it is also pleasurable distract us from that seriousness. It is through playing that children explore, discover, and remember the ways of the world. One of their favorite playthings is language. They are aware of speech as a toy to be used and gotten under control.

WHAT IS HAPPENING

The focus of your child's verbal development has suddenly shifted. The inborn drives and prejudices which had been of central importance to language development have now become minor and may ultimately disappear. The long apprenticeship through babbling, single words, and primitive sentences has led your child into a world where she has the ability to speak, but where her instinctive reason for speaking is apparently much reduced. It is now largely up to her culture to determine how things can be done with words.

From now on, your child's verbal competence will depend

on her ability to say what has to be said. The nature of *what has to be said* depends on the specific individuals involved, on cultural rules, and on the speaker's intentions. Earlier in this chapter we saw a list of the powers that can appear in the social speech of children; however, it is not enough to simply want to use one or more of these powers. Along with having something to say, the child has to know how to go about saying it. At this point the child must take her own situation into account. The discovery that preschool children are able to shape their speech according to the overall context came as a surprise to observers of child language because the child psychologist Jean Piaget has denied that children of this age are capable of changing their behavior in accordance with their different roles. His idea has become so widespread among psychologists that it is expressed in a number of books parents might easily come across. The idea was long accepted by language scholars too, but during the 1970s it came under examination and did not survive systematic observation.[16] Children at this age do speak differently when they are in different roles. (See Box 25 for a summary of these roles.)

Box 25 CONVERSATIONAL ROLES		
Child speaks with	*Nature of speech*	*Child's purposes*
Adult	Grammar is more formal	Translation Sharing
Child (same general age)	Style is intimate	Translation Control Sharing
Younger child	Shorter, to the point	Translation Control

In general, when a child is speaking with parents, the two

important facts shaping her speech are the inequality of the relationship and the difference of interests. One study found, for example, that it is very unusual for a child to reply to an adult's reply. A child may speak to an adult and get a reply, but then the child does not ordinarily come back with still another remark.[17] Yet even during the single-word period, children know that they are expected to reply to adult questions. Thus, by age eighteen months we already see a child developing routine answers to questions like *what's this?* when she cares about neither the question nor the answer.[18] We don't usually like to admit that the generation gap can begin so early, but if parents have only routine things to say to their small children, they can only expect routine replies.

Not surprisingly, a similar gap appears in the speech between a young child and an even smaller child. Studies consistently report that there is a noticeable change in speaking style when a child of three and a half speaks with a two-year-old.[19] Often such speech seems like a parody of adult-child speech. The older child may speak mainly to control the younger one or may speak as a fond elder, increasing the use of terms of endearment and even offering attempts at teaching proper behavior, especially proper language.

It is when children are speaking with other children whom they see as equals that they are most free and creative in the way they develop conversation. Studies of this speech have caught sight of the main process of using conversational elements that must be mastered. Before the third birthday, conversation is quite primitive and simple, but by the time a child is five, her conversation sounds pretty sophisticated. During the age range of two and a half to five, finding and inventing rules of conversation is at least as critical as developing more grammar. In speaking with equals, in fact, conversation appears to be taken more seriously than the rules of grammar. The grammar of child-to-child speech at this stage is less complex and less developed than in child-to-parent speech.[20]

Before conversation itself is established, children must

realize they cannot behave like a Gilbert and Sullivan chorus in which everybody simultaneously says something different. A study of twins, age two years nine months, found them in the act of discovering this fundamental rule of social speaking. The two children were both talking, but one of them became insistent that the other acknowledge his remarks.

TOBY: moth . . . moth . .
DAVID: goosey goosey gander . . . where shall I wander . . .
TOBY: moth . . . moth . . . moth . . . moth . . .
DAVID: upstairs downstairs lady's chamber . . .
TOBY: moth . . . moth . . . moth . . .
DAVID: moth . . .[21]

And so at last there was success. Instead of two separate and simultaneous monologues, the two have come to a tentative and early form of verbal harmony. This increasing relevance of speech is the first part of its becoming social. By their third birthday, children's replies to parents have become more to the point than previously, and they can now stick more easily to somebody else's topic.[22]

Once children establish the possibility of conversation, they move on to larger issues. Perhaps the first element that has to be appreciated is intelligibility, or precision in one's choice of words, since no conversation will last long unless the words used are understood by the listener. Fortunately, this matter can often be easily clarified. If the word used is too ambiguous or badly pronounced, the listener can ask for help. Children are familiar with requests for clarity well before they are three. Typical is this snatch of speech with a little girl who was still in the primitive-sentence stage. She was playing by herself, not conversing:

GIA: uh-oh missing.
ADULT: uh-oh, what's missing.
GIA: missing tank car.[23]

This sort of exchange teaches the need to speak clearly, and by the age of four, children are surprisingly sensitive to what the listener does and does not know.[24]

A more serious limit to intelligibility comes from having a limited vocabulary. You cannot speak precisely when you use only a thousand words. One study observed a pair of three-year-olds going through an Abbott and Costello routine because they said *say* when they should have said *ask*:

SUZY: You say, you say what's my name?
NANI: Suzy.
SUZY: No. You say what's my name?
NANI: What's your name?
SUZY: Laur-um-Lauren.
NANI: Say what's my name?
SUZY: Your name is Lani.
NANI: No, no, what's say what's your name? What's my name?[25]

The only real solution to this sort of problem is to increase the vocabulary. Parents who observe children having these difficulties should speak up and offer the better word.

A second element of conversation is acceptability. Should the speech stray too far from this consideration, communication may come to a sudden halt. Children have to learn the rules for polite forms (e.g., say "please") and to consider when speaking is allowed (e.g., don't interrupt), what sort of words are forbidden (don't curse), and which sort of words are appropriate to the occasion (don't address your mother as "Mrs. Smith").

Parents naturally teach children that certain things are not to be said to parents, but much of what is and is not allowed in speech between children is decided by the children themselves. Below is a case of four-year-olds who express an idea about acceptability. The girls were playing doctor when one of them, Ann, got on the bed.

ANN: I want an injection.
REB: No, I have to cover you up . . . do my job . . . lie down.

(Ann lies down, and Rebecca tucks her in.)
ANN: I'm going fast asleep, and then you won't be able to kill
me. *(She pretends to be asleep.)*
REB: Don't be silly, Ann . . . Else I really won't play with
you.[26]

Ann's lesson for the day: even playful charges of attempting
murder are not acceptable conversation. The lesson is taught
by specific direction and by dominance.

Acceptable speech involves learning more than which topics
are taboo. You also have to learn how to reconcile disputes
when they do arise. A classic solution is to change the subject,
as discovered by two little girls growing up in Hawaii.

SUZY: And my grandma and grandpa in New Jersey, they going
to watch me make hula lessons.
NANI: So! My grandma's going see me watch hula lessons, too.
My grandma and grandma.
SUZY: Not.
NANI: Ye-es, ye-es, ye-es.
SUZY: Not, not, not, not, not.
NANI: I have grandma and grandma.
SUZY: I know, I know, I know.

At this point there was a pure clash of egos, and the
conversation broke apart into the kind of moth-goosey-
goosey-gander monologues of children just on the cusp of
conversation:

NANI: Is my grandma and grandma and grandma . . .
SUZY: I know, I know, I know . . .
NANI: . . . and grandma and grandma and grandma . . .
SUZY: . . . I know, I know, I know.
(Suddenly they both giggle.)
NANI: And grandma and grandma and grandma and grandma
and grandma.
(Suzy breaks into laughter.)

Since these children were well past the first tentative steps of conversation, they became increasingly aware of the strangeness of their monologues. Amusement and laughter replaced the shout of egos. They had, in fact, discovered a new way to play with words.

> NANI: Now you say your grandma and grandma.
> SUZY: I have a grandma and grandpa and grandma . . .
> NANI: I know, I know, I know, I know . . .[27]

This game kept up and grew louder until the adult present told them, for heaven's sake, to stop. The game illustrates how tensions that were raised by the language of control can be ended by sharing.

This conversation between Nani and Suzy underlines another way language changes once children get beyond primitive sentences. Previously, words tended to aim for the heart of the matter, but now that speech has taken on so many new purposes and is used in so many roles, the meaning of a sentence has become less literal. If the argument about hula lessons had been phrased literally in terms of the children's purposes (asserting rank), it would have gone:

> SUZY: I'm better than you.
> NANI: No, I'm as good as you.
> SUZY: Not.
> NANI: Ye-es, ye-es, ye-es.

Indeed, such conversations do take place, especially at the beginning level of social exchanges. The twins who were just beginning to converse did have exactly this kind of dispute.

> TOBY: you silly
> DAVID: no, you silly[28]

But this directness is distinctly childish. Suzy and Nani, who were only slightly older than the twins, have already begun to use language for purposes of control while pretending to factual speech. It is at this point that we can begin to observe the increasing ambiguity of meaning.

The tricky issue of "meaning" balances the speaker's purpose with the uses of grammar and vocabulary, as found in a particular language. As long as children stick close to the dictionary definition of words, their meaning is apparent. *Yes* means *yes* and *no* means *no,* but once children begin to use one form of speech while holding the purposes of some other form, meaning becomes more obscure. In the case of Nani above, lies even begin to appear. Lies permit a child to keep up in a dispute of egos. Otherwise, conversations would be more unsatisfactory.

> SUZY: I'm better than you because I can show off my hula dancing to my grandparents.
> NANI: Ah, well, since I cannot make the same claim, I see that you are indeed better.

But if you cannot bring yourself to give such a humble answer, lies become more attractive. Nani lied in order to insist on her rank.

Another study observed a child lying, perhaps in part to maintain her status, but also in part to maintain her links with the speaker. In this exchange, *yes* quite literally meant *no* because the girl did not want to admit she had missed a television program.

> ANN: Did you see "Peyton Place" yesterday?
> REB: Yes.
> ANN: Did you see the bit where the man said the baby was dying?
> REB: Yes.
> ANN: And she made a funny face?
> KIM: Every time someone comes she makes a funny face. That was a good part, wasn't it?[29]

Poor Rebecca. Normally she was quite articulate, but here all she could do to keep up her end was give a one-word reply.

The possibility of untruth is the price we pay for the general flexibility of language. Now that children have gotten beyond their early literal phase, they seem to believe that the purposes of conversation are more important than definitions. Thus, at this age we see children asking, "You know what?" and then having no answer when asked, "What?"[30] The child asked the original question as a way of making contact, not because she had something to report.

The formal part of meaning (that is to say, the established rules of speech) is most apparent in the cases where children have nothing to say. If playing with words or merely catching someone's attention is all a child has in mind, then any words or sounds ought to serve just as readily. But even though their purpose is so general, grammatical practices still exist, and even in their playful nonsense children continue to observe the customs. Indeed, studies have shown children sticking so closely to the forms that the play sounds like a grammar drill.

An example of such formal correctness was given by Suzy and Nani as they shouted good-bye and hopped into a car to leave nursery school.

NANI: Bye, Tsukamoto-o.
SUZY: Do you have fun, Miz Tsukamoto-o?
NANI: We have fun, Miz Tsukamoto-o.
SUZY: We have fun, Miz Tsukamoto-o.
NANI: We have fun . . .
SUZY: . . . when I go home . . .
NANI: When I go home . . .
SUZY: . . . with my mom-me-e.
NANI: with my mom-me-e.
SUZY: with a roachi-ie.
NANI: with a roachi-ie.[31]

The original intention of saying good-bye to Mrs. Tsukamoto, the nursery-school director, has gotten lost in the general pleasure of playing together with language. Since they have nothing specific to say, their word play consists of repetition and grammatical exercise. The breakdown of phrases (Do you have fun/we have fun) and combination of phrases (We have fun . . . when I go home . . . with my mommy) is characteristic of the grammatical development of this period.

The result of these conversational skills is the creation of the peculiarly human community. Once the elements of intelligibility, acceptability, and meaning are under control, a new kind of relationship becomes possible. By the time they are four, children are already skilled enough at social speech to invent new solutions to complex difficulties.

A beautiful example of such sophistication was given by the four-year-olds, Andrew and Betsy. Betsy was sitting on a large toy car when Andrew approached.

ANDREW: Pretend this was my car.
BETSY: No!
ANDREW: Pretend this was our car.
BETSY: All right.
ANDREW: Can I drive your car?
BETSY: Yes, OK.[32]

Betsy smiled and moved away from the car. Andrew climbed aboard, turned the steering wheel, and made driving noises.

It is amazing what a little progression from *my* to *our* to *your* can accomplish. Without language, this simple little conflict could be resolved only through some sort of aggressive display which would leave private grudges in its wake.

Chapter 9
Confronting Grammar

Single-word speech and primitive sentences have a communicative power which, for all its simplicity, goes right to the heart of the situation. Now, suddenly, rather puzzling remarks begin to appear. Children say things like, "I didn't see at the other pictures." What might those words mean?

During this period, children are in an awkward stage in which the units they need to organize are much more complicated than mere words, but the children do not yet know many of the organizing rules. The result is a series of remarkable sentences which are sometimes memorable ("I want the fire engine to talk"), sometimes a little puzzling ("I don't like milk because I like eggs"), and often clear but inelegant ("It isn't any more rain").[1]

Sentences like these make it difficult for parents to get a sense of how their child's language is developing. Do longer but more confusing sentences constitute progress? In order to see how your child is doing, consult Box 26. It lists some of the major grammatical forms of English and the age at which these forms are commonly mastered. The usual warnings apply to this table. Few children are likely to develop in precisely the listed order, and the influence of a person's ethnic and social environment is very strong. It should also be noted that there is a long period between the first use of a form and the time when a child can be counted on to use the form correctly.

TALKING TOGETHER

At this stage there is no need to try to give your child any theoretical insights into verb tenses, noun cases, etc., and

118

Box 26
GRAMMATICAL DEVELOPMENT[2]

Age	Part of Speech	Usage	Example
	Verb	present progressive, -ing	Daddy playing
		"can" as helping word	I can sing.
		past tense of a few special verbs	Billy went home.
2½	Other	"and" (used only to link sentences)	I ate and mommy ate.
		"not" (seldom used precisely)	I not go.
		"who," "what"	Who did that?
	Verb	past tense, -ed	I combed my hair.
		infinitive, to + verb	I want to eat.
		"is" (without infinitive)	He is here.
		"doesn't"	He doesn't want it.
		"can't," "don't"	Don't eat it.
		am + verb + -ing	I am coming.
3	Noun	plural, -s	I see two cats.
		possessive, -'s	The baby's . . .
	Pronoun	"where/what" + subject + -ing	What you doing?
		"we," "he," "they," "you"	They did it.
		"somebody," "something"	I see something.
	Other	"and" (to link objects)	I saw him and you.

Age	Part of Speech	Usage	Example
4	Verb	future tense	They going to go.
		habitual present, -s	He runs all the time.
	Pronoun	correct choice of "he" and "she"	Daddy . . . he . . .
	Other	"as" (comparative)	It's not as good.
5	Verb	habitual present, -es	He always catches it.
		passive, be + verb + -ed	Those dishes must be finished soon.
	Other	plural, -es	Look at the horses.
		to + indirect object	Daddy gave the ball to me.
		who + relative clause	You are the boy who did it.
		comparative, -est	I am the biggest.

none of the games below pay any attention to such things. Instead, the games have been designed to help provide your child with sample sentences that can lead to a practical use of grammar.

Puppet talk. One effective way to give model sentences to a child is by using hand puppets.[3] You hold one puppet, have your child hold another, and then the two puppets talk to each other. At some point in this game, suggest that the child's puppet could repeat what your puppet says.

This game can work in two ways. It can provide clichés for your child to learn, or the game can be a test to see what grammatical forms your child already knows. This second use can help you keep track of your child's development and discover any difficult spots where she may need help.

If you use the game as a test, the puppet should give the child a very long sentence to repeat, one that is too long to be remembered and quoted in full. For example, *This is Daddy's pencil* is too short, but *Daddy's pencil looks like a long, thin yellow crayon* will force the child to make up what she is quoting. Thus, if in her repetition she still says *Daddy's pencil,* we can be pretty sure she really does know to say *'s* for possession.

If you are using the game to provide model sentences, the sentences should be quite short so that they can be easily remembered and quoted. *This is Mother's book* or *I saw Mother's book* is just the right length.

Box 27 **PUPPET GAME—SAMPLE SENTENCES**		
Form	*Cliché*	*Test*
who + question	Who is that?	Who went to town yesterday afternoon?
and (to connect sentences)	He went and I went.	John ran up the hill, and Bill ran down it.
-ing (present)	I am playing.	Peter is playing with the toy cars he won.
irregular past	I went home.	Sarah went all the way to the house by the circus.
can	You can play, too.	Billy and Mary can both play in the room.
plural, -s	Two cats	He said he has two black cats with white ears.
they	They saw me.	They drove the big cars past our house today.
where + question	Where are you going?	Where were you and that other person taking my dog?
past, -ed	He walked home.	The mother and the father walked to church.

Form	Cliché	Test
possessive, -'s	I see mother's book.	Daddy's pencil looks like a long, thin yellow crayon.
infinitive	I want to eat.	I want him to stop making so much noise.
and (connects objects)	I saw him and him.	I want a peanut butter sandwich and a tall glass of water.
am + -ing	I am playing.	I am running as fast as I can to get away from a bear.
don't	Don't do that.	I don't want to go to her house next Monday.
is	She is little.	John is so little he can hide behind a toy car.
future	I am going to eat.	He is going to see the television and buy a new car.
pronoun agreement	I saw Daddy and he saw me.	
-est	He is the fastest man.	
to + indirect object	Mother read to me.	

The puppet games can be played periodically for years; however, by the time a child is five, she is too skilled a repeater for the game to be used to test her knowledge.

Box 27 gives sample sentences for the puppet game. They are listed in the order children typically master the forms. It is all right if your child can repeat only the key elements of the form and overlooks other parts of the sentence. Note, for example, that the cliché *I am playing* is listed twice; first, with the simple form *-ing* (as in *I playing),* and later, with *am + -ing.*

No test sentences have been given for the last several forms because by the time your child is ready to use them, she will probably be too good at repetitions to be easily tested.

Recasting. Now that your child has outgrown the period dominated by her own creativity, correction becomes increasingly more helpful and necessary. Studies have found that the most useful form of correction is "recasting" the sentence.[4] This approach avoids drills beginning with, "Say——" and it permits conversation to continue. Recasting means to repeat what the child has said but with a more complex verb form. For example, if the child says, "Make a ball," the parent could replay, "I can make a ball." Or if the child says, "I do this," the parent might say, "You do this, and I will do this." The point is to allow your child to hear more elaborate ways of saying what she has just said. It has been found that if sentences are conscientiously recast for some brief period during each day, the child's grammar shows marked improvement.

Group speech. Songs, rhymes, and tag lines on television commercials can all be quoted in unison. You should encourage your child to join in with this group speech. The purpose is to build up her supply of stock expressions which can be quoted as needed. The problems section of this chapter lists a number of nursery rhymes which can be recited together in a very deliberate way in order to promote the discovery of some basic English grammar.

Ritual speech. The best time to practice standard speech forms is in standard situations. Riding in the car, tying your child's shoe, washing, and eating breakfast are all examples of recurring events which make recurring language easy and natural. This standard language does not have to be word for word every time, but if you ritualize certain expressions during this period, you will do much to help familiarize your child with the facts of grammar.

In the car, for example, if before turning on the ignition you regularly ask, "Did you buckle up?" you will be introducing the very important English form: Did you——?

The problems section discusses some specific ritual sentences which can be used in the rare case of a child who is having a difficult time switching from primitive sentences to English speech.

PROBLEMS

Child is forgetting grammar she had previously learned. It is common for a child who has correctly used "went" to start saying "goed" as in, "Billy goed home." This kind of change from a correctly used irregular form to an incorrect form is both typical and, believe it or not, a sign of progress. The child has discovered a general rule and begun to apply it indiscriminately. In the case of *-ed* to indicate past, the use of this form is fine in, "He lift*ed* the box," or, "He turn*ed* on the television," but not so good in, "I runn*ed* all the way," or, "I see*ed* you do it."

The irregular forms must now be relearned individually in a process that takes several years. The best way to help teach the correct form is by recasting. For instance, a good reply to, "Billy goed home," is, "Oh, I see. Billy went home."

Child starts to talk and then doesn't seem to know how to proceed. This problem may seem like the first signs of a stutter but is rather different. A person who stammers has trouble getting the words out, but speaks them in the proper order. For children who talk and then cannot continue, the problem is a conflict between the focus of their attention and the rules of grammar.

The greatest expressive weakness of a word-order language like English is the way the grammar often blocks a speaker from mentioning the most interesting thing first. Thus, a speaker who wants to report what happened often has to be detached enough to be able to begin by talking about the less interesting parts of an event. For example, a picture book may show a boy putting a colorful fish into a bowl, but the sentence, "He puts the fish into water," sticks the most interesting thing (the fish) into the middle of the sentence. In exciting or upsetting or fascinating situations, this demand for grammatical detachment can overwhelm a young speaker. She speaks the name of what interests her but then cannot find a formula that will permit her to continue with the sentence.

If your child frequently gets excited about something but seems unable to do more than name it, calm her down and ask, "What happened to——?" The problem is with the language, not the child.

Word order is seriously jumbled. Word order in this period is commonly a strange-sounding tangle, but sometimes even the stock phrases are jumbled. Instead of saying, "Daddy gave me a big toy," the child says, "Toy gave me a big daddy." Of course, this kind of error pops up from time to time in everyone's speech, but if it is a persistent part of your child's speech, there may be a problem. On thinking about it, do any of the tangled-tongue features of Box 17 in Chapter 6 persist in your child's speech? If *yes,* read Chapter 15 to determine whether the matter deserves more attention.

Child's behavior is beginning to interfere with her speech. It is now thought that many behavioral problems are really language problems which become so severe they lead to frustration and tantrums. Thus, if speech was progressing but has now gone into a decline along with a general behavioral decline, you should consider the material discussed in Chapters 14 and 15.

Child's grammatical development is not progressing in accordance with Box 26. The one really serious problem of grammatical development is a failure to make the transition from primitive sentences, but recognizing this problem is not easy. Perhaps the best clue to diagnosis is in the development of questions. Many key helping words do not appear. Box 28 lists typical questions asked by children who are trapped in the primitive-sentence stage.

It is apparent that although these questions do develop, they don't develop at all normally. *What you do with this?* seems more advanced than *Where hang it?*, but a typical five-year-old can ask *What DO you do with this?* It appears that, instead of abandoning primitive sentences for regular grammar, the child is elaborating on her primitive sentences.

Box 28
ARRESTED DEVELOPMENT—TYPICAL QUESTIONS[5]

Age	Question	Normal development should include (at . . .)
3	Where hang it?	
3½	How . . . that wheel come round?	do
4	Why . . . you put?	did
4½	How . . . you polish yourself?	did
5	What . . . you do with this?	do
5½	Why (him) . . . take out camera?	did he
6	How . . . it turn off?	does

The child is not quoting others, and, in line with this individualism, she usually also pronounces her words poorly and indistinctly. Perhaps more significantly, on the infrequent occasions such children do repeat sentences, they omit many more words than others do.[6] Later in this chapter we shall see that the ability to quote others is absolutely necessary if English grammar is to be learned.

Box 28 stresses the absence of *do* because that helping verb is so crucial in questions. A child may know the word *do* for such sentences as *do it again,* but as a helping word it disappears. Ask yourself, however, just what *do* means in these questions. In fact, it refers to nothing. Instead, it marks the tense of the other verb in the sentence. English has many sentences with words that are grammatically required but which have no clear definition.

Children learn to use these undefinable words by quoting their parents' use of them, but if a child is not interested or not able to quote her parents, the development comes extremely slowly. The question *What you do with this?* shows a child who has figured out how to use *what* and *with* (a great intellectual achievement) but still has not learned how to ask the full sentence.

This problem can last well into the school years, perhaps for a lifetime. It is easily misdiagnosed as mental retardation and so can impose near-ruinous burdens on a child. It should be confronted as soon as possible.

Ordinarily by age three a child should pay attention to verb tense and should use words like *can't* or *don't*. If at this age your child's language does not show these signs, and if your child's previous speech development has been pretty much on schedule, you should make a serious and sustained effort to help her improve. Try to get her to start quoting you by using the group speech and ritual speech games.

The group-speech game can be expanded to provide serious practice with some of the basic patterns of English. I have listed below a number of nursery rhymes which can help acquaint your child with some basic English forms. Each set of rhymes has been grouped according to a particular grammatical pattern: forms for expressing action; and forms for saying *There was, I had,* and *don't.*

Start teaching each pattern group by reciting the first rhyme in the group, and then ask your child to say the first line with you. Do not move on to the second rhyme until you have spent several days on the first one. Encourage your child to learn and recite as much as possible with you. She should at least be able to say the first line completely before attempting the next rhyme.

Begin this project slowly, going through all the "so and so sat on a something" verses before attempting anything else.

Once this first group has been completed, you can teach the "so and so went to somewhere" and "there was a something" patterns at the same time.

When those two forms are done, go on to the last patterns: "I had a something" and "I don't something."

It is to be hoped that by the end of this exercise, some of these forms will have begun to appear spontaneously in your child's speech. If not, the problem may call for specialized personal therapy. You should study Chapter 15 to decide what to do.

Action pattern—*sat on*

A crow sat on an oak.
Sing heigh-ho the happy crow.
Heigh-ho the merry old crow.

Little Miss Muffet sat on a tuffet
Eating her curds and whey.
Along came a spider.
He sat down beside her.
And he frightened Miss Muffet away.

A little cock sparrow sat on a green tree.
He chirruped and chirruped; he sang merrily.
A little lost boy sat on a near stone.
He sighed and he sobbed, "I want to go home."

Action pattern—*went to*

Old Mother Hubbard went to the cupboard
To give her poor dog a bone.
But when she got there
The cupboard was bare
And so the poor dog had none.

Doctor Foster went to Glo'ster
In a shower of rain.
He fell in a puddle,
Right up to his buckle
And never went there again.

Little Bobby went to sea.
He'll come back and marry me
With silver buckles on his knee.

A little boy went to a barn
And lay down on some hay.
An owl came out and flew about
And the little boy ran away.

A little old man went to Reigate
And tried to jump over a high gate.
Said the owner, "Go round
With your stick and your hound.
For you shall never jump over my gate."

There was pattern

There was an old man.
He had a velvet coat.
He kissed a young maid
And gave her a groat.

There was an old woman;
She lived under a hill.
And if she didn't go,
She lives there still.

There was a little man
And he had a little gun.
His bullets were made of
Lead, lead, lead.
He went to the lake
And he saw a fancy drake.
"Fear not; I won't shoot," he
Said, said, said.

There was a little girl
Who had a little curl
Right in the middle of her forehead.
When she was good
She was very very good
And when she was bad
She was horrid.

There was a little boy
And there was a little girl
Who lived together in an alley.
The little girl said to

Her brave little boy,
"What shall we do in an alley?"
The little boy said
To his brave little girl,
"All our blessings we should tally."

I had pattern

I had a little boy
I called him Blue Bell.
I gave him some work.
He did it very well.

I had a little pony
His name was Dapple-Gray.
I lent him to a lady
To ride a mile away.

I had a little hen,
The prettiest ever seen.
She sat on her nest
And she looked like a queen.

I had a little husband,
No bigger than my thumb.
I put him in a pint pot
And there I bade him drum.

Don't pattern

I don't like you, Doctor Fell.
The reason why I cannot tell.
But this I know and know full well.
I don't like you, Doctor Fell.

I don't fly where the birds go high.
They have wings and feathers too;
While I sit here as though held by glue.

You should also use ritual speech during this period, and it should coincide with the progress in the group-speech material. During the "so and so sat" rhymes, the ritual sentence should begin, "I am sitting on a chair to——(watch television, eat dinner, look at a book, etc.). Every member of the family should join in, one at a time, with, "And I am sitting on a chair to——." The child having language difficulties should be encouraged to join in on this ritual if she does not do so spontaneously. There is no need to go overboard with this ritual. Two or three times in one day is plenty. These remarks should be treated as real rituals; that is, they should be said seriously and on recurring occasions.

Box 29
RITUAL SENTENCES

Coincide with rhyme pattern	*Sentence*
——— sat on ———	I am sitting on ———
——— went to ———	I am going to ———
There was ———	There is a ———
I had ———	I have a ———
I don't ———	I don't ———

Box 29 gives forms for ritual sentences to be used while the nursery-rhyme patterns are being practiced. When speaking the "I am going——" sentences, be careful to use *going* as an action verb, not as a future auxiliary. For example, say, "I am going to my chair," (action) not, "I am going to watch television" (future tense).

YOUR CHILD'S PRACTICALITY

There are two familiar ways to think about language. We can emphasize its novelty, the way it permits people to say brand-new things, or we can think about it in terms of its rules, the grammatical customs that determine how phrases and sentences are to be constructed. These two aspects have led many theorists into shouting matches over which is more important, but children, in their practical way, have no evident preference. For them language is a handy tool, and they focus on what they have to say. Grammar is valuable because it gives them a ready way of speaking. The ability to say something novel is also welcomed when they have something new to say. They are perfectly willing to use clichés, however, when clichés will do, and they don't blush when the novelty of their point leads them to stretch old grammatical practices.

One consequence of this approach is the paradox we see in school grammar classes. Children find it very hard to parse sentences, yet they usually speak correctly. School-age children who have been confronted with the sentence *I gave the ball to him* find it difficult to sort out the direct and indirect objects, but they have known for years where to put the word *to*. They are like fiddlers who learned to play by ear. They can play a tune well enough, perhaps even brilliantly, but they can't read music or discuss theories of harmonics.

Because of this practical approach to language, there is very little benefit to be had in trying to help a child by explaining the theory of what you are saying. The grammar of helping verbs like *have, be,* and *do* is rather intricate. Even if you, the reader, do understand that grammar, your child will not. Instead of teaching the abstract rules, your child needs to know under what circumstances something is said.

This disregard for theory permits a piecemeal and disorderly presentation of grammar. No theoretician would dream of teaching *I am playing* before teaching the present tense of *to be (I am)*. Logically, the one must come before the other, but most children do use *I playing* before they know *I am*. Logic has less to do with children than many people wish. This piecemeal learning has produced a grammar that is not at all systematic. Instead of being a neat and logical collection of rules, the grammar that develops is an accumulation of spur-of-the-moment solutions to the problems of expression. The result is a highly irregular set of practices. This haphazard nature of speech has long troubled mathematicians and philosophers who feel that a language ought to be logical. The benefit of such an approach, however, is that it does not trap a person within the limits of some particular system. Language is flexible enough (some would say chaotic enough) to be able to respond to unanticipated circumstances.

It is no simple feat for a child to learn these jumbled grammatical practices, and the learning is not done quickly. It was once commonly supposed that children are pretty well done with learning a language by age three and a half or four. Research during the past fifteen years, however, has made it clear that many of the more subtle or intricate grammatical practices are not learned until children are much older. At age ten, for example, children still do not understand the grammatical difference between *John is easy to please* and *John is eager to please.*[7]

It is true that once children get beyond speaking in primitive sentences, there is a great explosion in the number of grammatical forms used. For a while these forms seem confused and confusing, but progress comes so quickly that a child of three and a half seems light years ahead of a two-and-a-half-year-old speaker. By age five most of the major grammatical forms are known and used, so it is easy to overlook the many little aspects of English that have still not been learned.

Box 30 shows an example of how speech develops from the primitive *that milk?* to the English form, *where can I drink milk?* The box illustrates the four major developmental stages of grammatical usage: (1) creativity; (2) quotation; (3) breakdown; and (4) combination. Once a child has completed the transition from primitive sentences, she is likely to have all of these stages going on at the same time, for different aspects of English.

Creativity. The first example in Box 30 is a primitive sentence that uses only intonation to indicate the presence of a question. At this point, children have not gone beyond the stage of pure creativity. In the case of the question, *that milk?*, the child thinks she understands the meaning of both words and understands the general situation.

She does not know the standard English way of asking her question, however, and goes on to create her own question pattern.

The transition from primitive sentences to English ones begins with the second stage in Box 30. This transition is similar to the earlier change when, as a baby, the child switched from speaking toy words of her own devising to quoting the English words of her parents. Now, however, instead of quoting mere words, she quotes phrases.

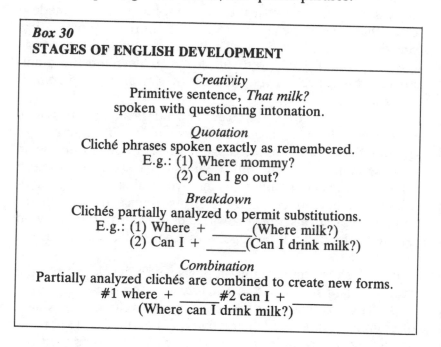

Box 30
STAGES OF ENGLISH DEVELOPMENT

Creativity
Primitive sentence, *That milk?*
spoken with questioning intonation.

Quotation
Cliché phrases spoken exactly as remembered.
E.g.: (1) Where mommy?
(2) Can I go out?

Breakdown
Clichés partially analyzed to permit substitutions.
E.g.: (1) Where + _____(Where milk?)
(2) Can I + _____(Can I drink milk?)

Combination
Partially analyzed clichés are combined to create new forms.
#1 where + _____ #2 can I + _____
(Where can I drink milk?)

Quotation. In Chapter 6 we saw that during the primitive-sentence stage, children do use some clichés as though they were single words. A child might say *want drink-of-water,* for example. She understands the general situation (drinking water) well enough but does not understand the individual parts of the phrase, and she thinks of the whole thing as being of one piece.

To us adults, the difference between words and phrases is so clear that it seems natural and inevitable. There is no evidence that the difference is at all obvious to young children. This openness to phrases was brought home to me one summer by a three-year-old nephew. The boy is French and was making his first visit to the United States. He spoke no English and during his first month here showed no sign of learning a single English word. Then suddenly he began greeting people with the phrase, *Hi, how are you?* His intonation was good, and his pronunciation (including the *h* which is nonexistent in French) was close to perfect. Instead of having a first English word, he went directly to his first sentence.

Adult grammar does not develop from primitive sentences. That form leads into a dead end. Instead, grammar comes from the clichés which are first used as a whole. Example 1 in Box 30, *where Mommy?*, is the sort of question a child can easily hear as a unit. Her father may often arrive home to find the child playing in the living room, and he asks her, "Where's Mommy?" She does not understand the details of the grammar, but she has a general understanding that Daddy is looking for Mommy. Later on, the child is able to put this understanding to good use. When she is looking for her mother, she quotes what her father asks under the circumstances (probably dropping the unstressed 's), *where Mommy?* We can see that this quotation is markedly different from parrotlike imitation. The child understands when a phrase is appropriate and her quotation is apt.

A good example of the way quotations work was provided by a three-year-old boy named Adam whose mother said, "We're all very mucky." It is impossible for so small a boy to have grasped the grammar of such a remark, but he knew the general situation his mother referred to and replied, *I all very mucky too.*[8]

All very mucky is more than a parroted imitation. The way it was used shows how good the child's practical understanding was and how poor his knowledge of grammar was. This practical orientation permits the child to talk about a situation without having any abstract notions about it at all.

Another feature of Adam's reply is that he has modified his mother's sentence. He changed the *we* to *I* and added *too,* all solid evidence that his grasp of the situation is much more firm than his understanding of the grammar of what he was quoting. No parrot could make these appropriate changes in the sentence.

Breakdown. Of course, we do not admire adults who speak entirely in clichés and quotations, no matter how apt, because these phrases suggest the speakers have not thought very deeply about what they say. We assume they have only a superficial understanding of their own words. If a child is ever to get beyond the stage of quotation, she must break the cliché apart into a general form that permits new sentences. Having learned by rote to ask *where Mommy?,* a child's next step is to discover that the location of many things can be asked about if you begin with *where* and add another word: *ball, daddy, milk, cereal,* etc.

Adam, the same boy who said *I all very mucky too,* gave an especially strong example of the start of the breakdown of a quotation into its separate elements. He developed a habit of saying *wait for it to cool* whenever a hot meal was brought to the table. After several weeks of that, Adam hung a diaper on a towel rack and said *wait for it to dry.*[9]

Grammatically, this sentence is terribly complex, but Adam was able to bypass all the rules of its construction by simply substituting one word for another in a rote phrase. On the other hand, Adam's substitution shows that his practical comprehension of the situation was remarkable. He had grasped both the idea of waiting and the further notion that some change of circumstances will have occurred at the end of the wait.

Combination. At first, of course, the only possible substitutions in a cliché are either single words, primitive sentences, or other clichés. In Box 30, the example *Can I drink milk?* illustrates this point. In this question the *drink milk* portion is a typical primitive sentence.

The final example in Box 30 shows that other general

patterns become a new source of possible substitutions in a cliché. *Where* +——is combined with *can I* +——. The result is a new rule: *where can I* +——, as in "Where can I" *drink milk, get a haircut, buy a book,* etc. Once a child's language development reaches the combination stage, the possibilities of speech begin to look infinite. To my knowledge, nobody has ever listed all the general forms of English clichés, but there must be several hundred. If you combine them, tens of thousands of sentence forms become available, and if you begin combining the combinations, you get several million possible sentence structures. Then when you begin to imagine how the different words of the enormous English vocabulary can be substituted into these general structures, you can see that a very large number of sentences have suddenly become available to your child. Starting out with simple clichés, a universe of flexibility has opened up before her.

Of course, not every mathematically possible combination is grammatically possible. For example, if rules 1 and 2 in Box 30 are combined in reverse order, you get *Can I where drink milk?* The child has to learn by rote which combinations are forbidden. In the meantime, her speech is going to sound sometimes as though it had completely dissolved into chaos.

Other sorts of errors are avoided because of context. Since practical understanding leads to rather imprecise rules, there is no formal reason why the pattern *can I* + *primitive sentence* might not lead a child to speaking nonsense like *Can I big dog?* Of course, children do not make such errors, but only because they understand the context. *Can I* is used when seeking permission, and so the temptation to ask, "Can I big dog?" never arises, but children's lack of a theoretical understanding gives them no grammatical reason for avoiding such sentences. Later on in school they may find that this purely practical orientation can make writing difficult.

Not surprisingly, this practical emphasis on understanding and intent means that the hardest parts of grammar to learn are the practices that have nothing to do with either reality or experience. For example, languages that arbitrarily sort all nouns into masculine or feminine classes pose difficulties for children (just as they do for foreigners) because the distinctions make no sense. The practices have nothing to do with understanding. One language with a particularly chaotic set of such gender distinctions and irregular practices is Serbo-Croatian. Because its rules are so confusing and arbitrary, Yugoslav children don't master the usages until they are about five years old.[10]

Modern English has (thank heaven) abolished the distinction among masculine, feminine, and neuter nouns, but we still have a few rules which express nothing about either the speaker's point of view or the objective situation. A good example of such an arbitrary rule is the expression of the possessive. In written English we have one regular possessive, *'s,* added to the end of the word. Spoken English, however, has more. In *cat's,* the *'s* is pronounced *s;* but in *man's,* the same *'s* is pronounced *z;* while in *horse's,* the correct pronunciation is *iz.* These arbitrary differences take a long time to be learned.[11]

A child does not have much trouble learning generally how to express possession.[12] She begins by quoting a possessive such as *Daddy's* and soon breaks such words down to the general form ——— + *'s.* Then she can express possession as needed; however, unless she grows up to get a Ph.D. in linguistics, she will probably never know why the possessive sound is sometimes pronounced *s, z,* or *iz.* This meaningless set of distinctions has to be learned pretty much by rote and takes years to master.

WHAT IS HAPPENING

The practical *figure-it-out-as-you-go-along* approach results in one of the most puzzling things about people and languages. They can be so profoundly different. World travelers have long known that as a person moves into more remote areas, ways of thinking become so different that even the most basic forms of common sense seem to disappear. Of course, these distant residents have been equally baffled by the absurd notions of the travelers. The problem is that common sense is not instinctive but cultural, and much of it is buried in the grammar.

The previous stages have all been dominated by the child's developing understanding. Language, of course, does have its influences. We saw that a child has to learn what is and is not called a dog, but the overwhelming development is the growing faculty of understanding. The child makes increasing sense of her experiences and uses language to express her understanding. But now a great revolution is about to take place, and by the time a child is five, language will increasingly shape the way experience is understood.

Earlier in this chapter we saw how a child's understanding can lead her to quote sentences like *wait for it to cool*. A further development of understanding can lead her to change the sentence a bit to say *wait for it to dry*. The child's comparison of one waiting experience with another is encouraged by English grammar, which permits the use of two nearly identical sentences even though the experiences they recount are rather different. Waiting hungrily in a dining room for hot soup to cool is not much like hanging up a diaper and going on to other activities. It is easy to imagine how a foreign language might encourage a speaker to see the differences rather than the similarities between the situations. Suppose a language had one word that meant to wait with a little impatience and another word meaning to wait without much caring how long it takes. Then if the child confused the two sentiments expressed above, she would be corrected. Her common sense would learn to deny there is a connection between two situations which English speakers do consider fundamentally alike.

Language promotes a sense of what is connected and what is unrelated. In the chapter about primitive sentences we saw that there are some universally expressed connections: names, desires, actions, descriptions, and associations. Apart from those universals, however, all other connections appear to depend on a person's culture.

In the worst cases it may turn out that some people become

slaves to the hidden logic of their own language. Most of us have known people so thoroughly trapped in the jargon of their work that they seemed incapable of thinking about what they were saying; however, this imprisonment is not a great danger for the majority. Once a child has become thoroughly immersed in all of the ways English offers for speaking, the critical judgment needed for selecting and combining the most apt forms should put some distance between her and the logic of clichés. She can move back in command of her own language.

At the start of learning grammar, your child has almost none of the prejudices which shape our adult common sense. Notions of time, location, and action which seem so obvious to us must all be learned by the child. Even the categories of experience have to be learned. For example, it strikes an English speaker as beyond question that we need to use a verb to distinguish between *he read the book* and *he was reading the book*. Yet for a Finnish speaker, the verb (to read) in these two sentences would be identical, and the noun (book) must be changed to express the difference between the two situations.[13] Finnish children, like Americans, learn their grammar by quoting clichés, but the clichés they use have a very different structure from English ones, and they break apart in quite different ways. The result is a radically different way of analyzing experience.

Thus, even though children around the world begin by talking about similar experiences, no two adult languages describe events in exactly the same way. Because of this variety, the language of children at age three and one half becomes increasingly difficult to translate. Whereas the primitive sentences of a child are translatable into the primitive sentences of children all over the world, a year later the same child is already speaking a language so steeped in her own culture that translation is becoming ever more difficult and less precise. With almost no apparent effort, your child has begun to think like an English speaker.

Chapter 10
The Emergence of Style

B y the time a child is four, most of the things she says could have been phrased some other way. Although her grammar has still not developed enough to allow much variety, the increased vocabulary and complexity of social relationships do permit a great many differences in speech. Thus, the great shapers of nursery-school speaking style are words and social variety.

Box 31	
CHILDREN'S VOCABULARIES[1]	
Age	*No. of words*
2½	800
3	1,000
3½	1,300
4	1,700
4½	1,900
5	2,500

Box 31 lists typical vocabulary sizes for small children. Unfortunately, the problem of counting the words children actually use has never been satisfactorily resolved; the counting process breaks down once the number gets over a couple of hundred. It grows ever more difficult to spot the new words which are sprinkled like rare gold nuggets amid the flood of older ones. Further, as variant forms of words appear and as words are given multiple definitions, it becomes harder to decide just what is and is not a new word. Thus, the estimates given in Box 31 are based on psychological tests which really check for comprehension rather than use. Children understand a lot more words than they use.

TALKING TOGETHER

Vocabulary. Vocabulary size has been traditionally considered a strong indicator of intelligence. There has been no really good basis for this belief, since vocabulary depends so much on the range and variety of a person's experiences. In the adult world, a vocabulary which emphasizes obscure rare words is commonly the sign of a smugly empty mind. Yet it goes without saying that children should be encouraged to develop their vocabularies as rapidly as possible.

From two and a half. One route to a bigger vocabulary is for your child to continually broaden her experience. A summer trip is almost bound to increase her vocabulary just because of the many new things and experiences she will encounter. Vocabulary builders of everyday life spring from the many details of existence that can be pointed out and named—things in the background of pictures, or things on television, or incidents you see when you venture out from the house.

One simple vocabulary strengthener is to ask your child to report what she saw during some ordinary excursion like a trip to the supermarket or to the zoo. Places like these pack many differently named things into a small space, so if a child visits such a spot with one parent she can recite a long list of names to the other parent. For example:

"At the grocery store we saw cookies and oranges."

"Yeah? And what else?"

". . . and potato chips . . ."

"Did you see apples?"

"Yes, apples."

"And what else?"

"Uh, boxes."

Because attention to detail is a good vocabulary promoter, you should consider the richness of illustrations when selecting books for your children. Pictures don't have to be complicated, but they should have enough detail for you to be able to say more than, "And there's Jack," when you point to an illustration.

Another vocabulary game is a rhyming one. Suggest a word like *dog* and urge the child to try and think of as many rhymes as she can *(hog, log, fog, frog)*. This is a game that can survive for years, especially during long rides in the car.

By three and a half. Once children have a vocabulary of over a thousand words, many of their new words should help deepen experience, rather than just endlessly broaden it. By age three and a half, words which distinguish between similar things or words which group different things together can promote precision in speaking and thinking. Box 32 lists word distinctions and groupings that three-and-a-half-year-old children can easily handle. You will probably find that your child already knows many of these words. Others can be taught by using pictures and giving examples. By the time they are five and have outgrown this book, children ought to be able to use all of these words without difficulty.

By four. One widely sold game that can encourage the deepening powers of vocabulary has the commercial name of *Blockhead.* Children age four have the physical skill to play it. The object of the game is simple; two players alternate placing variously colored and oddly shaped blocks of wood on top of each other. The one who knocks over the pile loses. Normally, each player picks up a block and tries to set it delicately on the stack. A simple addition to the rules permits vocabulary practice. Tell your child she can be the "carpenter" in charge of the blocks. Thus, when it is your turn to play, ask the child to give you a particular block ("Can I have the orange short one?"). The only way she can comply is by understanding the request. If she has no difficulties, try asking without giving the color clues. There are so many different ways the pieces in this simple game can be described and distinguished that many basic descriptive concepts can be introduced. Lists 21 and 22 in Box 32 suggest words for this game. After the child is practiced enough to be able to handle her "carpenter's" duties pretty well, the adult can take that role and give the child practice at using these distinctions to make clear requests.

Box 32
A FOUR-YEAR-OLD'S THESAURUS

1. mountain, hill, bump
2. run, jump, skip, hop
3. mother, father, aunt, uncle, sister, brother
4. crayon, pencil
5. house, building, garage, tent
6. television, stereo, radio
7. cookie, toast, bread
8. clock, watch, tick-tock
9. morning, night, day
10. in, on, under
11. go, start, stop
12. people, animals, bugs, fish
13. pie, cake
14. apple, orange, banana, fruit
15. zipper, button, snap
16. shoe, sneaker, sock, boot
17. wood, plastic, metal
18. street, highway, alley, driveway
19. red, black, white, blue, green, yellow
20. for, from
21. long, tall, short, thin, fat, round, flat, curved*
22. block, cylinder, plank*

---

*See vocabulary discussion for *Blockhead* game.

Telephone. Talking on the telephone is a great test of a person's speech skills. The absence of visual clues and the impossibility of pointing demands more precise language. Children age four and a half are skilled enough to talk to each other on the phone, although they tend to pause between speeches longer than adults do. Younger children can speak on the phone to adults, but when they try talking to other children it does not work well. They are not yet skilled enough at taking turns in conversation.[2]

PROBLEMS

Most of us think of "style" as something literary, an extra flourish added to language. While literary style constitutes the most conscious and complex use of language, style itself is simply the way something is said. It is as much a part of an English sentence as grammar or vocabulary. If your child says "please" when asking you for something, and never says it when asking another child for something, that variation is an aspect of her speaking style. In theory it might seem possible for a child to be absolutely predictable in what she will say in every situation; however, in practice such a mechanical use of language is unknown apart from a few serious language disorders which are certain to be discovered before this age. The problem that the child is not acquiring a style of speech, therefore, does not arise.

The greatest stylistic difficulty of this stage is speaking precisely. So much variability is suddenly available to the child, she must be sure not to omit anything crucial to being understood. This problem is discussed more fully later in the chapter. (Box 33 summarizes the chief sources of verbal confusion.) When speaking with your child, you should be alert to these difficulties and ask for a clarification whenever something seems seriously muddled.

It takes a little care for parents to actually get a clarification when they ask for one. The child's reply can really just be submission, particularly if a parent tries to clear up a point by suggesting a meaning. For example, a child might say, "I saw something outside." A parent who asks *what did you see?* is more apt to get a real answer than the parent who suggests a specific interpretation, such as *you saw Mr. Smith's new car, right?* Many children simply cannot contradict a parent's flat suggestion and will voice agreement even if they actually meant something else. Instead of clearing up matters, the confusion just spreads.

Another difficulty comes when the child thinks she is being clear and cannot understand why you are so puzzled. This frustration is especially acute when the child has used a vague pronoun. She thinks to herself, "I said *it*. Why can't Mother understand?" A good habit is to try and make your own questions fairly specific. Thus, if the child says a cryptic "she," ask *who is "she"?* instead of simply asking *who?* An unidentifiable "this" should be challenged by *"this" what?* instead of *what?*

A lot of imprecisely phrased speech is quickly understood in context, and, since you don't want to end up by discouraging speech, it is usually best to let most of those sorts of intelligible errors pass. The final example in Box 34 contains a spectacular case of jumbled yet intelligible pronouns. When matters are intelligible but seem to be getting a little too sloppy, the best approach is to recast what has been said, sharpening up the blurs. For example, if the child says, "And he and he gave it to me," you might reply, "I see. So John and Bill gave it to you."

YOUR CHILD'S CLARITY

Ambiguity is the glory and the weakness of language. It permits flexibility and the sharing of thoughts but threatens total confusion. It seems unfair to ask a three-year-old for the precision which is the mark of great artists and thinkers, but if she doesn't make some headway, the transition from her first language will lead only to bewilderment. Fortunately, children at this stage want to be understood and are usually willing to try to clarify themselves; however, if they are going to find ways to speak more clearly, they need to be alert to the source of the confusion. If all they can think to do is repeat themselves, conversation becomes frustration, like the amazing one quoted below between a pair of three-and-a-half-year-olds. Yvonne seems infinitely willing to repeat what she said, but she leaves it up to Xen to try and make sense of it:

YVONNE: Going to camp. *(Intending:* I'm going to camp.)
XEN: What?
YVONNE: Going to camp.
XEN: What?
YVONNE: Going to camp.
XEN:What?
YVONNE: Going to camp?
XEN: Can?
YVONNE: Camp.
XEN: Campin?
YVONNE: Campin.
XEN: Campin?
YVONNE: Yes.
XEN: What?
YVONNE: Go to campin.
XEN: You go campin?
YVONNE: *(Screams)* Yes!
XEN: Oh.[3]

Difficulties of this sort threaten to burst forth at any moment. The astonishing point is how rare this breakdown is. Already children have such a variety of interests and attitudes that they cannot rely on some sort of unified or childish viewpoint to promote understanding. They must find ways of keeping their meaning clear whenever problems arise, and they do. By this stage children's conversation is already peppered with attempts to bring its participants together in closer harmony. Children have begun to recognize the confusion that comes from unclear speech, and they are discovering ways to resolve it.

The fault can lie with either the speaker or the listener, so children must be sensitive enough to respond in either role. Box 33 lists the sources of subjective confusion which trouble children, and it suggests a solution. (I call these problems "subjective" in order to distinguish them from the more mechanical difficulties of poor diction or listener inattention.)

Lacking information. Leaving out information needed by the listener is a common problem. Sometimes the difficulty

Box 33 PERSONAL CONFUSIONS	
Problem	*Solution*
Speaker has not given enough information for other person to understand remarks	Elaborate on what has been said
Speaker has not thought her own words all the way through	Think harder
Listener is surprised by remark	Explain reason for the remark
Listener's expectation blocks appreciation of what has actually been said	Point out the listener's error
Listener is not sure whether or not she understood	Seek confirmation

stems from the listener's ignorance of the subject matter. Overcoming that problem demands the speaker be able to explain herself, a rather sophisticated task to require of a small child. The example of these four-year-olds shows, however, it can be done:

ANDREW: Look it. We found a parrot in our house.
BETSY: A what?
ANDREW: A parrot. A bird.
BETSY: Wow.[4]

At other times the confusion stems from the speaker's omission of some necessary detail. These problems are a little harder to resolve because the speaker has to be more self-critical in spotting the flaw to what she said, as in the case of these two children:

YVONNE: Look at the little mirror up there.
XEN: Where?

YVONNE: Up there. *(She points.)*
XEN: Where?
YVONNE: Up. Up. *(Points again)*
XEN: Where?
YVONNE: Do you see it over there in that corner? *(Points again)*
XEN: No. Oh.[5]

It is interesting to note that by this age clear distinctions are already more helpful than pointing.

Lacking deep thought. A peculiar problem associated with language is the way speakers don't always pay attention to what they are saying. It is hard to imagine a lion roaring and then thinking, "Oops. I didn't mean it just like that," but it is common among people. We are frequently unaware of the implications of our words. Even at so young an age, children respond to this confusion in an appropriate and distinctive way. The questions listeners ask are the same sort as the ones they raise when they need more information, but the speaker's reply is quite different. Instead of repeating or elaborating on what was said, the speaker is challenged to find a good answer. Here are two such conversations. In the first, the children were playing with a teddy bear.

> ANDREW: For sale, for sale, fifty-nine cents, fifty-nine cents. A big bear who's bad, who wasn't being nice. He'll be nice to you . . . fifty-nine cents. Good. Somebody just bought him.
> BETSY: Who?
> ANDREW: Oh . . . a worm.[6]

The second conversation was between a mother and a four-year-old daughter who had just built a doll-sized hut. The conversation began in earnest, but as the daughter grew more alarmed about the implications of her remark she turned to a joke, and the talk ended with everybody laughing.

> MOTHER: Who lives in it? *(Pointing toward the hut)*
> CLAUDIA: We. *(Intending: me)*
> MOTHER: And I remain outside?

CLAUDIA: No, you, we'll make it bigger.
MOTHER: What will you make it with?
CLAUDIA: *(Laughing)* With the telephone.
MOTHER: How can you do that? *(Laughs too)*[7]

Listener surprise. Listeners can sometimes be so astonished by what has been said that they ask the wrong question. Usually, they ask *what* when some other question is more appropriate, so instead of getting an answer, they get a repetition. In the example below, even the second try at asking the question was botched a little.

ANDREW: We have to go now.
BETSY: What?
ANDREW: We have to go right now?
BETSY: To who?
ANDREW: A little birthday party.[8]

Expectation too strong. A very difficult problem arises when the listener's own expectations block paying close attention to what the other person said. Often in that situation nobody has a real sense of what the problem is. The solution requires one of the people to realize just why there is confusion, but such insight can be much too difficult for a child at this age. The conversation below simply increased the confusion.

A pair of four-year-olds were talking on the telephone when one of them decided to tease the other by pretending to be about to hang up. Apparently that bit of teasing was so unexpected that the listener didn't even notice it. At the end of this snippet of conversation nothing had become more clear.

MARKO: All right, bye. Bye-y-y-ye. Hi, Sonia.
SONIA: Hi, Marko.
MARKO: I'm just kidding. *(Laughs)* Hey, hey, Sonia. Didn't you hear me say bye-bye?
SONIA: No, I didn't say bye-bye.
MARKO: I-I said bye-bye. I-I just tricking you.[9]

Few of us are immune to this sort of confusion. Earlier in the same telephone talk, it was Marko who had a hard time understanding what Sonia quite plainly said.

> SONIA: Can I ask Nelly something? *(Nelly is an adult at Marko's home.)*
> MARKO: What, Sonia?
> SONIA: I wanna ask her—something.
> MARKO: What-what do you want to tell me?
> SONIA: I want to ask Nelly something.
> MARKO: Hey, Nelly, Nelly. Sonia wants to talk to you.[10]

Listener is unsure. The worst sort of confusion is the kind that persists because people are unwilling to acknowledge its presence. When in doubt, the only solution is to speak up and see if the other party will confirm or deny what you think was meant. This approach is within the grasp of three-year-olds, and they should be encouraged not to assume they understand. Two examples show that children can seek confirmation. Sometimes their suspicion is right:

> ANDREW: Call the police, OK?
> BETSY: OK. To get the snake 'cause it's killed?
> ANDREW: Yeah.

On other occasions, the listener's assumption is denied:

> ANDREW: She's in with somebody else.
> BETSY: With Mrs. Strock?
> ANDREW: No.[11]

All of the problems listed in Box 33 arise from the individuality of the child—individuality in knowledge, intention, and expectation. Individualism is already a major characteristic of a child's mind. One study of the content of speech by nursery-school children found that while a third of their remarks were about their family and home, the other two-thirds ranged over a great variety of subjects. Most topics were discussed by only a very small percentage of children.[12] Naturally, this individualism can often block understanding. It can also promote the many wonders of humanity: personality, ingenuity, accomplishment. Maintaining a society of individuals is difficult at best. Even four-year-olds can sense the problem. Happily, they can also begin to sense ways language can be used to maintain the balance.

Box 34
LONGING FOR MOTHER

Insecure boys in a nursery school were overheard wishing that their mothers were present. They expressed themselves in the following ways:[13]

Age	Remark
2	"Mamie" (shows no interest in playing).
2½	"Want my muddah."
3	"Mama coming back pretty soon?"
3½	"My mama be up after me in two more minutes; I want to stay right here where my mama can find me."
4	"I want to look out the window and see if my mama's coming."
5	"I don't want to rest. If Mother comes, she won't know where to find me. She'll ask the lady who washes dishes, 'Have you seen a big boy?' And that'll be me; and she'll say, 'Yes, he's upstairs,' and she will come get me."

WHAT IS HAPPENING

Box 34 gives examples of how boys in a nursery school voiced their wish for their mother at different ages. The emotion seems unchanged from start to finish, but the boys grow increasingly long-winded about it. The box illustrates that, by itself, the increasing capacity of grammar does not give a child anything new to say. The content of her interests and concerns comes from her. Parents can introduce as much of their world to the child as possible, can encourage some interests and discourage others, but ultimately the child is going to decide on her own what she thinks and what she cares about. Indeed, if she did not have that private imagination, language would be much less valuable, since it would be limited to reporting either objective facts or universal opinions. The toys, books, and trips you give your child will be the raw material for her imagination; what she makes of it will both reflect and determine who she is.

The easiest way we can learn what is in the imagination of others is through language. Of course, we are not restricted to speaking only with people whose imaginations match our own, but the more unlike ourselves a person is, the more we have to use the formal tools of precision and clarity. A natural result of this fact is that people speak less formally and elaborately to those who are closest to them in experience and thought. Style, therefore, reflects not only the mind of the speaker, but the relationship between speaker and listener. We can see this fact even in children's speech.

Children as young as three can share an intimate style. Intimate speech is the opposite of a clear style; it compresses and obscures things. The conversation below quickly produced a secret new word understood only by the two children, a pair of four-year-olds who had just hopped into a car to be taken home from nursery school:

ADULT: Have a nice day, girls?
BOTH: Ye-e-es.
NANI: *(Giggles)* No-yes, no-yes, no-yes, no-yes. You say no-yes, no-yes.
SUZY: Say no-yes, no-yes.
NANI: No-yes, no-yes, no-yes, no-yes. Say no-yes, no-yes.

Soon the no-yes sound they had been shouting was reduced to a stylized minimum.

NANI: You say *nowis.*

After a little bit of work to get that form right, the children began to really play with it.

SUZY: *(Very fast and slurred)* Nowisnowisnowisnowis. Your
    turn, say *nowisnowis.*
NANI: *Nowisnowis.* Your turn say *nowisnowis* again.
SUZY: *Nowisnowis.* Your turn say *nowisnowis.*[14]

Between the two of them, they were able to keep that up for
much of the ride home.

Language development based on quotation does often
promote obscurity. Particularly troublesome is pronoun development.[15] Back in the primitive-sentence stage, names
rather than pronouns were almost always used. Later, children
go through a period when they might use either a name or a
pronoun, and finally they end up using mostly pronouns. This
last stage sounds like progress but is often a decline into
confusion. A child might use *she* three times in one sentence
and refer to a different person each time. (In context, this
practice is surprisingly comprehensible.)

Confusion over pronoun references is especially easy among
children because their speech contains so many quotations.
For example:

CHARLES: I, I getting this one. *(Points to object A)*
CYRIL: I'm getting this one. *(Points to object B)*
CHARLES: Huh?
CYRIL: I'm getting this one.
CHARLES: I'm getting this one. Give me the same, the same you
    lookin' at.[16]

As her vocabulary grows, a child also has to become more
adept at choosing the right word. Distinctions such as those
between *come* and *go* or *bring* and *take* begin to be important
to a child. The mastering of nuance is not terribly speedy.
Although the difference between *come* and *go* is understood
by age four, *bring* is only really perfected at around age six,
and *take* needs yet another year.[17] This shifting appreciation of
word use leads to occasional oddities. A common one concerns the word *big.* At age three this word is used in the
general sense of a large overall area, but at age four it is

frequently limited to the sense of *tall*.[18] This kind of change in the use of words probably continues throughout a lifetime and surely leaves each speaker with a set of words that have taken on connotations and limits not found in anybody else's speech.

There is a further wrinkle to the emergence of style. The context of our remarks grows increasingly subjective.[19] At age two actions and objects are so important to speech that the words are largely superfluous and predictable. By age three, however, a child's imagination need not depend on any objects at all, and her thoughts can be seen only through words. A pair of Italian four-year-olds gave a good example of the power of words alone to work on their imagination.

CLAUDIA: I saw the wolf outside. *(She moves from the door and feigns fear.)* Let's go and look.
FREDDY: No, no.
CLAUDIA: Why?
FREDDY: Because I scared. He's got a saw in his hand. *(He looks at Claudia.)* It's not true. *(Looks at Claudia again)* Go away! Agh! I saw him with a saw in his hand.[20]

All this excitement is literally about nothing. Claudia imagined the wolf; Freddy imagined the saw.

Now that the world of the imagination has entered so forcefully into speech, the range of possible remarks has expanded like an exploding star. Imagination frees children from having to talk about immediate experience and creates the potential for innumerable points of view. It also permits children to use a lot of metaphorical speech. (In fact, the children of this period use many more metaphors than grade-school children do.[21]) Suddenly the things that might be said are beyond counting.

Naturally, no individual is so random that any of the limitless numbers of things which could be said are said. Ways of thinking, personal interests, knowledge of the situation, and point of view all shape a child's speech. Gradually, as we get to know an individual child, we come to recognize the sorts of things she says and the way she says them. This smaller number of likely remarks is still astronomically large, but you will recognize her words as being part of your child's style. Well before her fifth birthday her speech will have revealed that in mind, just as in body, she is unique. And over the years, as you keep talking and listening, you might occasionally pause to admire the power of language which lets you and your child share what would otherwise be invisible and beyond all reckoning.

PART FOUR
QUESTIONS ABOUT COMMUNICATION

So much that is being said is correct, so little is right.
—GEORGE STEINER, *After Babel*

Chapter 11
The Parents' Role

The traditional linguistic ambition of parents has been, and presumably remains, to see that their children's language becomes as effective and acceptable as possible. In practical terms, this ambition means seeing that the child has the opportunity to make as much use as she needs of what the English language has to offer. Earlier I compared the way a child learns English to rooting through an attic trunk. To keep up the metaphor, the parents' role is to make sure the child gets a full acquaintance with the contents of that trunk, although ultimately it will be the child who decides for herself what to take from it. As with other things, the fundamental role of the parent is as a provider, in this case a provider of language.

Put this simply, the task of providing language sounds quite traditional and unextraordinary, but in practice there is a new twist to this old idea. The old theory of language development was that language is an artificial creation imposed on the child by her elders. The child herself was imagined to have been born with a mind like an empty clean slate. Implied in that simple view was the idea that the chief duty of the parent was to be careful that only the right things went on the blackboard.

In practice, this theory meant that the concerned parent was to be more censor than provider. The advice given parents said that, in order to avoid confusion, a parent should make sure the child hears only proper pronunciation and doesn't hear baby talk. Naturally, this theory urged parents to speak as grammatically correctly as they could to the child. Even more important was the need to erase any errors which appeared on the board. Thus, when a child spoke and made a grammatical error, the best response (i.e., the one most in keeping with parental duty) was to immediately correct the mistake. Of course, there were also fancy extras to the theory. For example, many people have thought it would be nice if a child were never needlessly frightened, and they concluded, therefore, parents should never use language in a frightening way, such as by telling spooky stories. The promise of traditional theory was that as the child got older and more was written on the blackboard, the less attentive parents need be toward linguistic development. The child would be increasingly able to handle herself.

This theory was an ideal. Nobody could live up to it fully—probably none wanted to completely live up to it—but the practical implications of the blackboard theory were clear, easy to understand, and, at least to some extent, have been accepted by almost everybody. The parental role was to watch over the language that the child heard and used.

The recent overthrow of folk theories about language learning has meant the overthrow of its practical applications as well. The fundamental and universal role of the parent as provider has survived. The ambition of parents to see their children's language develop as fully as possible need not be questioned; however, the specific recommendations which flowed from the old notions can no longer stand.

The injunction against baby talk, for example, is an idea that came easily to anyone who accepted the folk theory and then began to wonder about how language might be helped. It turns out that the ban was a superstition. Strict standards of parental pronunciation are irrelevant to both the age at which a child starts using words and the rate at which her powers of articulation develop. Hearing baby talk cannot hurt a child's speech. At the same time, many people find that their tone of voice is far more affectionate if they say, *Oh, whad a cude widdle baby. Ye-e-es!* than if they go for the more formal, *Oh, what a cute little baby. Yes!* So, for them, the use of baby talk leads to a greater sense of warmth and closeness. In short, the use of baby talk won't hurt language and may help the emotions. There is no reason to persist in the superstition that baby talk should be forbidden.

This new defense of baby talk shows how radically the ground has shifted in thinking about the parents' role in child-language development. The folk theory forced arguments over baby talk to concentrate on learning the technical details of language. Anyone who chose to defend baby talk was forced to suggest it might be some kind of a teaching aid. The new consideration of the parents' role comes at the question from a wholly different angle—one that focuses on the social context of the language. Parts II and III of this book continually reported that language development is a deepening response to situations, not a reflection of changes on some imaginary blackboard. As soon as the context of speech moves to the foreground of consideration, the teaching value of baby talk ceases to be an issue. If it promotes closeness in a parent who uses it, that parent should go right on and use it. The parents' role is to provide practical experience with language, not to sharpen technical insights. There is no conflict between the parents' love and their duties.

Parents who fail in their linguistic role do not risk misleading the child (that was the fear of the old blackboard theory), but her ability to speak what is in her heart might be stunted or enfeebled. This crippling can last a lifetime. The seriousness of this risk is more visibly real than the fantasy fears of the older theory. If we look around ourselves at the adult world, people who cannot express themselves are common. People who speak in baby talk are unknown.

What the old theory missed, and what parents have to be

alert to, is that the child brings a lot to this verbal relationship. The parents' role in language development cannot be considered apart from the child any more than we can contemplate the lone role of one member of a kissing couple.

We saw repeatedly in the developmental chapters that what a child brings to her speech is her own consciousness. In fact, although for simplicity's sake we speak about language development, it would be more precise to speak about subject development. The language develops only as there is an increase in things to be said. A child's speech grows so much more quickly than the parents' because she is finding new things to talk about at a rate far beyond anything an adult can match.

On the parents' side, they bring their cultural knowledge to the linguistic relationship. They already know how to express the many things the child is discovering. The parents keep providing examples of language, and the child keeps finding new uses for it.

The closest sort of relationship in the natural world is on the coral reef. A coral is a small sea animal who lives and dies in a habitat created by its ancestors. When it dies, its own body is added to the reef where it has lived. Language is found in the mind rather than in the visible world, but like coral, language is the natural residue of generations of living beings. The established languages have been created by the minds of countless people who have seen a new way to express themselves and have then been endlessly quoted by their appreciative peers and heirs. The result of this steady creation and conservation is a marvel to contemplate. Language lives only in the minds of people and yet is broader and more powerful than any of the minds that contain it.

At first, the child has no idea of how to express her discovery in the language of her parents, but she speaks anyway, inventing her own way of talking. Parents then provide examples of the established way of speaking, and the child changes over to the customs of everybody else's language. This three-step pattern—going from subjective awareness, to personal expression, to social expression—is at the heart of every child's use of language.

Parents have to consider their role in light of these steps in the pattern. Maturation is largely up to the child. The complex role of the environment in the growing awareness of the child is too large a subject for this book, but some of the aspects most directly relevant to language are discussed in the next chapter.

The second step, the intermediary one between private realization and social expression, is where the parents' role is largest. There is never a point when the cultural way of organizing language becomes so inevitable that the child can invent it on her own. There is also no automatic limit to the level of organization a language can have. During their first five years, children go from using simple sounds to organizing them into words; the words are then organized into sentences; and well before the fifth birthday, sentences are organized into paragraphs. The parents must consistently provide the examples necessary for their child's language to develop.

Success calls for openness and imagination on the parents' part. The more alert they are to the sorts of things that a child is expressing in her own individual way, the more they will be able to deliberately provide a child with the cultural ways of expressing what she means. In direct contrast to the old theory, as the child grows older, the parents' task grows harder. It is relatively easy to provide single words to a child. Providing the conversational and structural examples a three-, four-, and five-year-old needs calls for a lot greater insight on the parents' part. So much is now being accomplished by the child, it is easy to overlook the things she is still groping for.

Although conscious folk theory has been misguided about the parental role, cultural traditions have been wiser, and there are numerous social forms of language (summarized in Box 35) which take advantage of different stages of language development. These traditions are only a starting point, of course, since the content of those forms (especially as a child grows older) depends on individual needs and interests. The developmental point of all such forms is to provide society's way for organizing and stretching these emerging powers.

Box 35 **LITERARY FORMS FOR CHILDREN**		
Starting age (months)	*Form*	*Coincides with*
10	Action chants (e.g., pat-a-cake)	Objective speech
18	Nursery rhymes	Attention to clichés
30	Fairy tales	Combining sentences

The "fairy tales" listing in the box is a particularly interesting example of how the new understanding of the parental role has led to insights quite unlike those anticipated by the old theory. Age three was when the blackboard theory thought the parents' role was completed, at least so far as language development was concerned. Some proponents of the folk wisdom even argued that fairy tales, with their frightening elements, should be suppressed to keep all disturbing thoughts away from the child.

Now, however, we know that while children of this age are speaking sentences, they still need help in making their sentences part of a larger unit, such as conversational flow, explaining an event, or thinking privately. A particularly clear picture of how a traditional form like the fairy tale helps children's language continue to evolve can be found in the details of a study made by Evelyn Pitcher and Ernst Prelinger.[1] They investigated the stories told by children aged two to six and found that these stories include all the great themes of literature—pain, death, violence, sex, love, exploration, resurrection, healing. The whole kit and gory caboodle was in the tales. Naturally, many parents are going to be a little unsettled by the discovery that their three-year-old has the concerns of Shakespeare, but the exciting point is that the stories also showed a development similar to the stages that go from toy words to English sentences. In the process, the children are able to organize and overcome their anxieties.

The first stage is very much tied to the child's own experience. Two-year-olds talk about what they have known. Characters in their stories are people associated with the home; animals mentioned are domestic animals, and objects named in the stories are familiar things like cars and buses. Then, at a slightly older age, children begin to mention elements they have found in other stories. This change is comparable to the transition from toy words to English words. The viewpoint does not change much, but its terms have become the more social ones. The structure of these stories grows more complex, but as in the case of primitive sentences, the first structure comes from the child. By the age of five, however, the structure of the stories clearly owes a lot to the stories children have enjoyed. In fact, after age five it becomes harder to persuade children to make up a story, so eager are they to repeat tales they have already heard.[2]

Lest readers doubt that small children can really tell stories, let me quote a couple told by two-year-olds. The first is by a little girl aged two years ten months. Its theme, pain plus comforting, is typical of stories told by girls at this age: "Pussy cat played with the little car. He fell down, poor kitty cat. She picked her up. She taked the kitty cat down cause the kitty broke her head."[3]

A boy aged two years and eight months told a similar story. Its uncertain resolution is typical of boys' stories at this age. Their tales seem to focus more specifically on the pain: "Pussy scratched. He cried. He's a bad boy. He banged. He stopped crying. He's a good boy. He cried again."[4]

Even a minimal acquaintance with Freud is bound to make parents concerned when they hear their child dwell on such fear and anguish. Where could such ideas have come from? The child leads such a safe and comfortable existence; why do so many of her stories talk about pain? The old blackboard theory insisted that these fears and fantasies must have come from somewhere outside the child. The new look at language says, hey, of course fears and worries are going to trouble the child. They come with being human. A parent cannot protect the child from the dragons of the mind.

The old theory had no further advice. Once something was indelibly marked on the blackboard, the matter was lost. Hope for better luck with the next generation.

Newer insights argue differently. If fears and anxieties are natural to life (can anybody really believe they are not?), parents will be more helpful if, instead of trying to censor their expression, they suggest ways of facing and thinking about the fears.

Difficult as this task might sound, it can be done quite naturally. Consider this story told by a boy named Barry at age four years and nine months. A year earlier he had told a typical vaguely resolved story of "bad pirates" sinking boats. Now suddenly he tells this complete fairy tale: "Once upon a time there was a little little boy and his mother and father died and he was left all alone with nothing to eat—poor little boy. And one day he went out shopping and he looked around for a friend of his—a boy—friend who said he would be at the market and he didn't find him. So he looked all around and the more he looked the more he got lost until he came to a policeman and he said, 'Mr. Officer, would you please bring me home?' And the officer said, 'Yes, only I have to know where you live.' And then the policeman took the boy to his police car where there was another policeman. And that policeman said, 'All right, now we're ready.' And they went to his home. And then a fairy godmother came, and the fairy godmother was bad and the fairy godmother killed the policemen and made them into jars. And she cooked the boy and the boy was so strong that he pushed the fairy godmother into the oven like Hansel and Gretel. And then he slid the door and locked it. And then he ran out the door and locked her in there baking. He locked all the windows and put rocks and stones and pieces of gold and brick with gold piled up. And then that little boy lived happily ever after and that's the end."[5]

It is not hard to figure out where Barry got his story structure. He begins with *Once upon a time,* has a climax *like Hansel and Gretel,* and ends *that little boy lived happily ever after.* Grimm's fairy tales are hardly cheerful, but they have provided Barry with a way to confidently resolve thinking about his fears. The gruesome events that beset the little boy and the mood of self-pity at the beginning of the story are typical of what we saw in younger children's tales (compare Barry's *poor little boy* with the two-year-old girl's *poor kitty cat*). The new element in this story is the use of a fairy-tale structure that can reassure Barry, rather than leave him troubled.

This process confirms what parents have to offer in the development of language. They provide the materials that can move the child from her own private development to the fuller, richer experience of society at large. In thinking about their child's speech, parents should remember that a language is more than the words in a dictionary and rules in a grammar book. It is the stories, songs, clichés, and idioms too. Parents have to provide all these forms of language if they really want to help their child learn to speak clearly and effectively. In providing their children with the whole of language, parents should keep three principles in mind.

First, always treat language as a social tool. The blackboard theory assumed that parents could readily step out from their personal relationship with their child into the more neutral one of censor and corrector. It saw nothing inherently wrong in the idea that a proper response to a child's speech was to merely correct it. That theory was blind. Parents will want to correct their child, of course. It is natural and right, but they must remember that they cannot step out of the complexity of their role to do the correcting. The kinds of corrections favored by this book (e.g., expansions, recasting) maintain the social flow of language even while they correct the child.

Parents must not forget that if a child pours a bit of her heart out and instead of sympathy gets only a grammatical correction, part of the message she will receive is that the parent cares nothing about her bit of self-revelation. The price of that conclusion is a persistent communications barrier.

The second principle is for parents to recognize the stage their child's language has reached. Traditionally, there have been general cultural tools available for the different stages, as noted in Box 35. Now that so much more is known about children's language, parents can be more precise and sensitive to the needs and interests of their individual child. In this book, Parts II and III and the diary all seek to help parents follow this second principle.

Finally, never imagine that the suppression of unacceptable language is the same thing as suppressing unacceptable thoughts. It is inevitable that parents will be troubled by many of the things their children have to say, and it is tempting to simply stomp on the offending speech as it emerges. Blasphemies, racial slurs, and jests about excrement are recurring features of children's language, and parents have every right to object as the words are spoken. Even so, keep in mind the main point that language is an expression of awareness and interest, not consciousness itself. People who are content to strike only at the speech of their child are like those legendary kings who responded to bad news simply by putting the messenger to silence.

Chapter 12
Language and the Home

Children prefer language over silence for exactly the same reasons they prefer companionship to solitude. Of course, they have to learn that there are times when speech is rude, or inappropriate, or unnecessary, but they should never doubt that language can bring closeness and trust. If children conclude the home has no place for what they have to say, they will soon decide it has no place for them either.

Already by age five language plays a powerful role in maintaining the many ties that keep a family together. At birth the baby's total dependence on her parents makes words superfluous. The baby's confidence that she is loved comes from the deepest of practical experiences. As the child grows older, this physical closeness continues to be the major fact of her experience, but now certain ambiguities begin to creep into family life. Everyone's will is no longer so clearly in harmony with her own.

I recall once saying *no* to a fifteen-month-old boy who was reaching for a whiskey glass in my hand. He was so astonished by what I said that he gave the infant version of a double take and then fixed me with a very penetrating look before backing away. No? How could it be? Over the years these sorts of experiences mount up and point the child toward one conclusion: she and her family do not always see things eye-to-eye.

This recognition of differences puts limits on the authority a child now grants her parents. A study of children's social attitudes found that by age four, children understand that they do not have to obey a mother who tells them to do something morally wrong or physically harmful. The authority of friends is seen as being even more severely restricted.[1]

169

Box 36
THE ENVIRONMENT OF LANGUAGE

Family. Speak together according to the following principles:
  (a) Always treat language as a social tool;
  (b) recognize the stage the child's language has reached;
  (c) never imagine that suppression of unacceptable language is the same as suppressing unacceptable thoughts.

Books. Select books that address the child's own concerns:
  (a) Stories that are merely amusing are already plentiful on TV;
  (b) simple informative histories and descriptions are not for the preschooler;
  (c) fairy tales, folk tales, and fables often get to the heart of the matter.

Television. Work to keep the child's mind active while watching:
  (a) Encourage prompt vocal response to events on screen;
  (b) ask questions and make comments designed to encourage critical judgment;
  (c) point out ways events in a program relate to child's outside experience.

Day-care. Emphasis should be on development and play, rather than on structure and control.

Children are growing increasingly aware of themselves as individuals. Parents can hear this fact directly in the words of their children, when a child comments specifically on differences she has observed between herself and the parent. Many parents of four-year-olds have described such speech to me.

Balancing this sense of individuality is the continued and deepening closeness language can provide; however, if language is stifled, a child's awareness of individuality turns into a sense of isolation. A measurable growth in social responsibility is already detectable in five-year-olds whose parents talk to them. Children express a greater social sense when their parents give reasons for their disciplinary actions than when parents impose discipline without explanation.[2]

Families must talk or fall apart. This general rule may be even more important in modern nuclear families which force parents to take on all the duties—disciplinarian, provider, educator, friend, and exemplar—that, in larger extended families, could be divided among many different people. Language can help a child understand the family as a whole, rather than see it as something that merely grows more confusing. In the warts-and-all openness that family life imposes, language provides a reassuring source of trust.

If you will forgive me for becoming personal, it is society's intimate dependence on language which led me to write this book. I first began to wonder about the nature and mystery of language during childhood, when my family moved to France. Of course, the universal presence of the French language and the near uselessness of my hitherto trusty English made a powerful impression on me. During those years in France I saw so clearly that even my teeth understood it: without a shared language, confusion and suspicion come to dominate any social setting. During our final year in France the family lived in a Paris apartment only a short walk from the American library. While I had always liked to read, I now became a fanatic, reading scores of books well beyond my official eighth-grade level. These library books stressed the happy side of language—when it is used well, language is the great unifier. It is so powerful that a person can even feel a kinship with authors who lived centuries ago. After my three years in France I suppose it was settled that language would be my lifelong treasure.

All of these lessons were retaught a decade later when I joined the Peace Corps. This time I spent two years in Tanzania, an African country containing 120 tribes, each with its own language. There was also a single national language, Swahili, and it was immediately obvious that without that common language all hopes of turning the country into a unified nation would be lost. Even the village where I lived would have been impossible, since it was composed of people from many tribes who sold goods to one another and farmed together only because of their access to a common language.

There was also something new for me to learn; these villagers had something to say. In France the people were heirs to an ancient culture, so the presence of intelligent people was not news, but in Africa I was working with peasant farmers who were largely illiterate and often had never seen a town holding more than two or three thousand people. Yet they turned out to be as imaginative, observant, and intelligent as any people I had ever known. Furthermore, despite the many profound differences between English and Swahili expressions, I became persuaded that behind the different cultural forms there lay minds quite similar to those of English speakers. This time there was no supposing about it; when I left Tanzania I was certain that language would be a powerful interest of mine.

Imagine my surprise, then, to return to the United States of the late 1960s and early '70s. Language and literature seemed to be held in near universal contempt. The anti-war students I met showed scant belief, let alone interest, in the idea that language could be put to useful social purposes. The government seemed to think, and sometimes said, that the majority of ordinary people used language best when they were silent. In the academic world, the teachers of literature appeared to have given up, and the great writing of the past was no longer considered relevant. The one thread of promise seemed to be in the exciting new studies being conducted into the language of children. There I found scientists mining gold.

Naturally, I hurled myself among these studies with the zeal of a lost desert traveler flinging himself toward an oasis; however, I don't think it would have occurred to me to write a book for parents, if it were not for the practical implications these discoveries have for the family. The oldest social institution, and surely the one language has served the longest, is the family. If children begin talking because they have something to say, it is the rest of the family they want to speak to. If children have the same sort of minds their parents have, it is from their family that they learn how they can most clearly express themselves. It is language that keeps families from becoming clusters of isolated individuals.

Inevitably societies do build some walls between people, and then language can be used to maintain the barriers. Recently I saw a sharp example of this cycle. A little boy, aged somewhere between two and three, was calling to a policeman, "Hi, hi." I have watched children say that all over the world. Even in rural Africa I have seen infants come running out from a grass-thatched hut to call the native equivalent of "hi" to a passing stranger, but in this recent instance the scene was not quite so pleasant. The policeman looked at the boy but said nothing. After the boy had stopped, his parents told him sternly, "You must never talk to the police." I suppose that when he is sixteen, the boy will be hollering something very different at patrolmen.

The final social catastrophe comes when people decide that even in the home, maintaining walls is the primary power of language. In Chapter 6 we saw that children's conversations include three powers—translation, control, sharing—and that sharing is the most important use in the home. Any parent who wants to encourage a child's fullest language development should concentrate on developing this power. The parents' own use of language provides the most notable example for the child (see Chapter 11). Books are another important aid.

Reading stories aloud to a child is a splendid social activity. Along with the interaction between reader and child, stories are able to confront a child's many unnamed concerns. This interaction underlines the sense of being part of a group. Physically a child is present with the storyteller, and psychologically she is in the company of a good story. The great message of all literature holds her in sway: you are not alone; other people think as you think; feel as you feel. In the preceding chapter we saw another power of stories. They provide children with ways to organize their thoughts into complex wholes.

The one important cautionary note is that these benefits are limited to books whose authors know children do have serious things on their minds. In a survey of modern literature for small children, psychiatrist Bruno Bettelheim reported, "Most of these books are so shallow in substance that little of significance can be gained from them. The acquisition of skills, including the ability to read, becomes devalued when what one has learned to read adds nothing of importance to one's life."[3]

Instead of providing memorable stories, the idea behind many books is either to be lightly entertaining or informative. I recommend getting as few of these books as possible. Later on there will be plenty of time to learn about the history of the Alamo, the culture of Lapland, and the fate of the dinosaurs. Right now it is time for more meaty things. Facile entertainment should also be ignored—enough of that is available from the TV.

Fortunately, parents who pay attention to their child's reading will discover that we live in an extraordinarily rich time for stories. The literature of the world is available to us; fairy tales, fables, folk tales, and myths from all sorts of cultures have been translated into English. These tales of struggle and triumph, of marvel and splendor, can hardly fail to enchant a child.

By the time they are three years old, children are ready for some of the children's magazines being published. These offer a further way to encounter the pleasurable use of language. Much of the strength of a magazine depends on the quality of its stories and activities, but, through the presence of a few regular features, a magazine can also help establish the idea of a "voice," that is, a presence which is known and enjoyed, yet encountered only through language.

A major rival of books (and usually a victorious one) is television. The hope of television has always been that it will broaden its audience's ideas and understanding by bringing people into visual contact with many new things. Work with nursery-school children has shown that television can indeed help develop a broader imagination and understanding, *BUT* parents must work hard to achieve this result.[4] Normally, the imaginative speech and play of children is seriously crippled by regular television watching. It becomes beneficial only if, instead of being left to their own devices, children watch a program in the presence of an adult who comments on the show, who asks questions, and who gets them thinking about what they see.[5] If these things are done, children do become even more imaginative than usual. Parents who get their children playing games based on the plots and roles seen on television can find that children have new things to say.

This encouraging finding meshes with everything else we have seen about language growth. Once understanding is brought into play, a child's mind becomes ever more active and imaginative. The tragedy and puzzle is that parents have to work so hard to get a child's understanding to function in the presence of television.

Nobody has yet found a way to overcome the effect of television commercials. They are the dominant form of society's use of language to control and manipulate. During the ages covered by this book, children are not yet mistrustful and cynical about what they see advertised, but by sixth-grade age this attitude will have changed dramatically, and almost all of them are skeptical and mistrustful of what they hear. There is not much a parent can do to combat these suspicions since children are entirely reasonable to begin doubting advertising; however, this early cynicism makes it twice as important that children never worry that language itself is to be mistrusted, even among their own families. Then they really will be isolated and alone.

Compared with books and television, other items in the home are usually not so directly related to the development of language; yet they have their impact. As a general rule, anything that tends to stifle either the development of things to say or a willingness to speak up should be viewed with suspicion.

One study of children aged nine to eighteen months found

that language development is noticeably stunted in children whose mothers concentrate on controlling and physically caring for them.[6] Children whose mothers spend more time talking and playing with them do better. This discovery is in keeping with the fact that most infant speech is reportorial and has nothing to do with control; however, by being so specific, the study draws attention to some of the practical implications of this new science of children's language.

Presumably, parents who use this book will follow its advice and provide their child with a lot of play and talk, but what about children whose parents cannot be so regularly at hand? Many infants are in day-care. Nobody is suggesting there are any language problems inherent in this situation, but parents will want to be sure that their day-care center focuses more on talking and action than it does on firm organization and behavioral control. Obviously, an inattentive day-care center is unacceptable, but if, as so easily happens, attentiveness turns to physical control and manipulation instead of to promoting expression and interest, the child's language development suffers measurably.

No studies of nursery schools have been as clear-cut as that study of younger children, but if we look at the language process found after age two and a half, it is reasonable to conclude that once again schools which emphasize control are not going to aid a child's language. The great accomplishment of children during this period is the rise of their ability to take the listener into account. Vocabulary, grammar, and speaking style are increasingly focused on the fact that speech involves more than the speaker's own perceptions. Nursery schools which insist on rigidly structuring (i.e., controlling and manipulating) the child's day are not helping children get the free conversational experience they should have.

Chapter 13
Pronouncing It Correctly

Mispronunciation and the lack of understanding it leads to will be a continuing problem during the whole time covered by this book. Since difficulties are inevitable, it is not easy for parents to judge how their children's pronunciation is progressing. Friends say, "Oh, she'll grow out of it," and, of course, almost all children do learn to speak correctly. But parents want a stronger reassurance than proverbial wisdom. Box 37 lists the ages at which children are able to pronounce correctly many of the sounds of English.

Box 37		
AGE FOR CORRECT PRONUNCIATION[1]		
	Words in parentheses give example of how sound is used in English	
Age	*Type*	*Sound*
2	consonant	p (*pop*)
	vowel	ă (p*a*t), ē (prett*y*)
2½	consonant	b (*bib*), d (*deed*), h (*hat*), m (*mum*), n (*no*),w (*with*)
	vowel	ä (f*a*ther)
3	vowel	ô (p*aw*), o͞o (b*oo*t)
3½	consonant	f (*fife*)
	cluster	ks (kic*ks*)
	vowel	ŭ (c*u*t)
4	consonant	ng (thi*ng*), y (*y*es)
	cluster	ngk (thi*nk*), sm (*sm*all), sp (*sp*end), st (*st*reet), sk (*sk*ate), pl (*pl*ay), kl (c*l*ean), gl (*gl*ad), bl (*bl*ue), tw (*tw*elve), kw (*qu*ick), lp (he*lp*), lt (me*lt*), mps (la*mps*), ft (li*ft*)

Age	Type	Sound
5	consonant	wh (*wh*ich), r (*r*oar)
5+	consonant	ch (*ch*ur*ch*), j (*j*u*dg*e), sh (*sh*ip), tħ (*th*in), th (*th*is), z (*z*ebra), zh (vi*s*ion)
	vowel	ĕ (p*e*t), ĭ (p*i*t)
V*	consonant	g (*g*a*g*), k (*k*i*ck*), l (*l*id), s (*s*au*c*e), t (*t*igh*t*)
	vowel	oŏ (t*oo*k)
*V = variable		

This table has to be read cautiously since it is unlikely that any child will master every sound in precisely the predicted order and at exactly the listed age. The box summarizes the work of many different studies, and no two of them are in perfect agreement. In a few cases the research disagrees so much that I have listed the age at which the sound is mastered as "variable." Several vowels have been omitted from the chart. Vowel sounds vary so much from region to region that no firm statements about their use are yet possible. In general, vowels not on the chart are learned quite late.

The pronunciation symbols used in this table will be used throughout the chapter.

TALKING TOGETHER

Helping children improve their pronunciation is notoriously frustrating. Lise Menn, in studying her son's speech, reported five stages in a child's response to correction. If, for example, a child is trying to master the *t* in *tub*, we find these phases:

(1) Correction has no effect. The error seems beyond reform. Child says *bŭb;* parent corrects, *tŭb;* child promptly replies, *bŭb.*

(2) The child tacks the correction onto her reply but immediately returns to the mispronunciation. Child, *bŭb;* parent, *tŭb;* child, *t-bŭb.*

(3) The correction can now be repeated by the child after a struggle, but even then the correction is not preserved. Child, *bŭb;* parent, *tŭb;* child (straining) *tŭb* and later, when speaking spontaneously, *bŭb.*

(4) Sometimes the correct form is spoken spontaneously, although often it is not. Now the child can be readily corrected. Child, either *tŭb* or *bŭb;* parent, *tŭb;* child (speaking easily), *tŭb.*

(5) Correction is not necessary. Child says *tŭb* routinely.[2]

This list indicates that only when a child is between stages two and four for a particular sound can parental help actually do much in steering a child's speech.

Of course, it is self-evident that a child who never hears the correct version of a sound is never going to learn it. If you talk to your child, she will frequently hear all the sounds of English. If some sound does not appear to be coming, try teaching your child a few words that include the sound so she will have an incentive to master it. A handy tool for such teaching is nursery rhymes.

Along with their other virtues, these rhymes offer a natural way to encourage children to practice the sounds they are able to learn but are still having trouble with. The sample rhymes listed below include the ages at which they can most effectively promote proper pronunciation.

The use of such rhymes is simple. They should be spoken aloud by a parent while the child is encouraged to join in with at least the first line. (In the case of the earliest rhymes, only the first word might be used by a child.) The italicized letters indicate the sounds parents should be especially alert to and should repeat for the child if she cannot say the sound correctly.[3]

The ages given for the different rhymes are averages, and, of course, parents should be alert to the needs of their own particular child. The order given for the sets of rhymes is more stable and should be preserved.

1½–2 years

Pat-a-cake, pat-a-cake
Baker's man.
Bake me a cake
As fast as you can.

Pussy cat, pussy cat,
Where have you been?
I've been to London
To see the queen.
Pussy cat, pussy cat,
What saw you there?
I frightened a little mouse
Under the chair.

Peas porridge hot,
Peas porridge cold,
Peas porridge in the pot
Nine days old.

Peter, Peter, pumpkin-eater
Had a wife and couldn't keep her.
He put her in a pumpkin shell
And there he kept her very well.

2–2½ years

Hey, diddle, diddle!
The cat and the fiddle
The cow jumped over the moon.

Baa baa black sheep
Have you any wool?
Yes, sir, yes, sir.
Three bags full.

Hickory, dickory, dock.
The mouse ran up the clock;
The clock struck one
and down he run.
Hickory, dickory, dock.

*H*ush-a-*b*ye *b*aby, on the *t*ree *t*op.
When the wind blows the cradle will rock
When the bough breaks the cradle will fall
Down will come baby, cradle and all.

*H*umpty *D*umpty sat on a wall.
*H*umpty *D*umpty had a great fall.
All the king's horses
And all the king's men
Couldn't put Humpty together again.

2½–3 years

*G*oosey goosey gander;
Where do you wander?
Upstairs, downstairs,
And in my lady's chamber.

Old *K*ing *C*ole
Was a merry old soul
And a merry old soul was he.
He called for his pipe,
And he called for his bowl,
And he called for his fiddlers three.

Old Mother *H*ubbard
Went to the cupboard
To give her poor dog a bone
But when she got there
The cupboard was bare
And so the poor dog had none.

*T*om, *T*om, the *t*ailor's son
Stole a pig and away he run.
The pig was eat and Tom was beat
And Tom ran crying down the street.

3–3½ years

Mary's *f*ears and *T*ommy's *t*ears
Will make them old before their years.

Fee-fie-foe-fum
I smell the blood of an Englishman.
Be he alive or be he dead
I'll grind his bones to make my bread.

Four and twenty *fif*ers
Went to kill a snail.
The best one among them
Dared not touch her tail.

Ladybird, *l*adybird, fly away home.
Your house is on fire,
Your children are gone.
Ladybird, ladybird, fly away home.

3½–4 years

*Sin*g a *son*g of sixpence,
A pocket full of rye.
Four and twenty blackbirds
Baked into a pie.

Pipi*ng* hot, smoki*ng* hot.
What I've got you have not.
Hot gray peas. Hot, hot, hot.

Si*ng*, si*ng*, what shall I si*ng*?
Cat's run away with the puddi*ng* stri*ng*.

*You, y*ou, beautiful *y*ou.
You shall have an apple.
You shall have a plum.
You, you, beautiful you.

PROBLEMS

Child often whispers words. During the six months after using their first word, children sometimes whisper what they want to say, especially if they are unsure of the word.[4] Usually the tendency disappears of its own accord. Parents should encourage a child who whispers by either saying "good" and repeating the whispered word or by saying the correct word.

Words are spoken very slowly. This tendency is often a symptom of partial deafness. Other symptoms include: labored and breathy speech; prolonged vowel sounds which become distorted or which split into a new syllable; a tendency to always replace *b, d,* and *g* sounds with *p, t,* and *k* sounds (this symptom is especially important if it occurs at the beginning of words); frequent addition of *m, n,* or *ng* sounds to consonants; entire utterance is characterized by an abnormal speech rhythm.[5] Children with these symptoms should have their hearing examined promptly. Deafness is discussed in more detail in Chapter 14.

Words are simply unintelligible. Box 42 at the end of this chapter lists a number of children's rules for pronunciation. A more exact title for the listing might be "Rules of Mispronunciation," since the table describes a number of speech habits that lead to incorrect pronunciations. A study of this list should explain many of the sounds your child makes. Errors based on these rules are routine and normally disappear of their own accord. (Don't expect to be able to explain every word by consulting this list, since many words are formed by use of several rules and expert analysis is required.)

If after careful study of the list, it still seems to you that only a few or none of your child's words can be explained by these rules, there are two things to do. One is to use the nursery rhymes described earlier in the chapter with the purpose of trying to shape the child's sounds. The other is to determine if there are signs of a potentially severe disorder. Speech therapists distinguish between three sorts of pronunciation problems:

Dysarthria—The inability to speak properly because of poor muscle control.

Dyslalia—There are no physical speaking problems and language development is not seriously delayed, but speech is intelligible only to acquaintances.

Apraxia—Outward signs make it hard to distinguish from dyslalia, but the problem does not clear up spontaneously in a reasonable time period.

Parents who fear that their child's poor pronunciation is more than just the usual childish difficulty want to know if the matter might be dyslalia or something more severe. In considering your child's speech, keep these points in mind:

Dyslalia and apraxia cannot be distinguished before late in the primitive-sentence stage. If your child has fluency problems, if her tongue gets in the way of her words, or if she cannot seem to control her lip movements, she may have dysarthria, and she should be examined by a doctor. Otherwise, the single-word stage really is too early to start worrying about long-lasting problems of articulation. Wait until the primitive-sentence stage is well underway, and then see how her speech compares with Box 37.

Neither dyslalia nor apraxia is a general language disorder. If poor pronunciation is only the most prominent of a number of disturbing aspects of language, the unintelligible speech may be one symptom of a more general language disorder.[6] You should check Chapters 14 and 15 to see if a potentially severe disorder is present.

Neither dyslalia nor apraxia comes from a preference for gesture. If it seems to you that your child just naturally prefers gesture to speech, you should check Chapter 14 to see if there is a hearing problem.

Apraxia is not limited to a few sounds. Apraxia can be ruled out if a child's speech is generally intelligible, although a few specific sounds are still a problem.

Dyslalia does not last forever. If at age three and a half speech is still unintelligible, you should assume your child may suffer from apraxia and should seek professional advice.

Child's development is much slower than expected. Does the child spend a lot of time playing with one or more very small children? If the answer is yes, it is important that parents make extra efforts to talk with the child and play verbal games with her. The presence of a slightly older brother or sister, or of a twin, or of a regular playmate is socially marvelous, but, of course, children who do not speak correctly themselves can hardly be expected to provide good models of pronunciation. Unless children often talk with adults as well as with children their own age, there can be a prolonging of the beginning stage of speech.[7]

Accuracy of pronunciation has gone into a decline. It is a common paradox of child development that before something can improve, it must get worse. Typically, this decline occurs at about the point where single words are linked together into primitive sentences. The phenomenon is discussed more fully later in this chapter and is usually nothing to worry about; however, if it persists or if the decline includes the appearance of symptoms described above under the heading "words are spoken very slowly," there may have been sudden damage to the hearing. See Chapter 14.

Child is two and a half; *p*, *b*, and *d* sounds still not mastered. If at this age substitutions for all three of these basic sounds are still being made, it is sometimes a symptom of cleft palate. Such a problem should have been discovered by a pediatrician immediately after birth or as a diagnosis for the reasons the baby was having a hard time sucking. Thus, the problem of prolonged consonant substitution is more likely to be simply a sign of slow development. Nonetheless, it can happen that a child may not have seen a pediatrician very often and cleft palate has gone undetected. Symptoms are: substitution errors do not decline; more errors are made in middle consonants of a word than in the first consonants; *z* and *s* sounds do not appear.[8] Surgery is required. Usually it is performed at age eighteen months.

Child does not listen to self. It does not seem reasonable to expect a child's pronunciation to improve if she does not even notice she is speaking incorrectly. Thus, evidence that the child is not paying attention to how she speaks can be alarming. A classic example of this problem was given by the child who said *fis* instead of "fish." An adult replied by also saying *fis*, but the child grew upset and said, "Not *fis*, *fis*!" This sort of thing suggests the child doesn't notice what she pronounces. The phenomenon is a puzzle but apparently does not foreshadow any serious problem. The chief lesson seems to be that children don't like to have their errors thrown back at them. One French child grew so angry at being addressed in such talk she replied, "But, Mother. Speak to me in French."[9]

Child can but won't say word correctly. It has often been observed that children are physically able to pronounce words they routinely mispronounce. For example, if a child says *kāk* instead of *tāk* but is then shown a picture of something and told it is a "take," she may very well say *tāk*. This phenomenon is an illustration of the way speech habits can interfere with correct pronunciation. Imitation is easy, but speaking correctly in context is hard. All children make some errors of this sort, and it is not a sign of willfulness, laziness, or stubbornness.

The most astonishing example of this kind of error was provided by a boy in London. He did not appear to be able to say *puddle* because he had a habit of changing the *d* sound to *g*. A word like "pedal" came out *pĕgäl*, and "puddle" was pronounced *pŭgle*. At the same time, the boy routinely changed *z* sounds to *d*. So "zoo" became *dōō*, and "lazy" turned into *dādē*. One day he followed this $z \rightarrow d$ rule, and instead of saying "puzzle" he said *pŭdle*. When he wanted to say "puddle," he could not, but when he wanted to say something else, out came puddle.[10]

This sort of thing shows the power of the rules described in Box 42. They seem to interfere with speech rather than promote it, but these erroneous habits do permit a child to get on with speaking and with enlarging her vocabulary. Children's speech rules do not help teach proper pronunciation and show no signs of being used as though they did.

Strange as this puzzle-puddle phenomenon is, it is entirely normal and clears up in time by itself.

Words of several syllables are often mispronounced. If much of a child's speech seems to be developing on schedule but some of her words, particularly those with three or more syllables, appear to be quite bizarre, your child is probably using the rule in Box 42 called "fronting." This rule leads to a reorganization of the sounds in the sentence. Children who use it develop very peculiar ways of pronouncing many long words, including *alligator, animal, candle, candy, coffee, cream,* and *Snoopy.*[11] Use of this rule is no cause for concern.

Child seems to be developing a stutter. Many parents of three-year-olds fear that their child is starting to stutter. One study of nearly a thousand children at this age found that 4 percent of them had a noticeable difficulty in getting words out, yet only one child's hesitancy persisted as a severe stutter. Two-thirds of the problems disappeared in less than a year.[12]

In this post-Freud age it is hard to tell parents not to be anxious about a sign of potential stuttering, since all such disorders are popularly diagnosed as signs of emotional disturbance (with guess-who to blame), but I urge you to put aside the idea that anything serious is going wrong. Since 97 percent of childish hesitations clear up in, at most, a few years, it is a waste of emotional energy to start worrying. I hold the position that no child is capable of a true stutter during the period covered by this book.

Hesitation is perfectly natural during the transition from first language to English. Remember what your child is going through at this period. The abandonment of her first language calls for the extensive breaking down and combining of clichés. Of course she hesitates and repeats on occasion. Even with all emotions in perfect working order, the task is just plain hard.

One important theory of stuttering maintains that early stuttering and ordinary childish repetitions are the same thing, but some parents overreact and, in effect, teach the child to persist with her hesitations and repetitions.[13] Whether the theory is right remains to be shown. The idea, however, does reinforce the notion that the best response to a suspected stutter is to take any hesitancy or repetition in stride. There is no need to draw the child's attention to her repetitiveness, and it is wrong not to let her speak for herself. You should be especially alert to adult friends who helpfully try to finish sentences for your child. Politely but firmly tell them, "She can speak for herself."

If you find that, no matter what this book says, your child's repetition of syllables, words, or phrases sounds like stuttering to you, you should promptly bring her to a speech therapist for examination. Your anxiety may be contagious.

YOUR CHILD'S HARD WORK

Parents can easily see that their child is making a deliberate attempt to overcome difficulties of pronunciation. A child may pause before trying to speak a word or syllable with a particularly difficult sound, or she can switch to using an easier word with the same meaning, and if you ask her to try a word again she may give you a direct and challenging look.[14] In short, the child behaves much like the typical American adult who has to speak the French word *hors d'oeuvre* aloud; she becomes self-conscious and troubled.

Occasionally, however, a parent knows someone who blames various pronunciation problems on laziness. From time to time these notions even turn up in print. The puritan theory that children are not at all eager to exert themselves is belied by the active babbling nature of any healthy child. Parents should pay no attention to the suggestions of friends or relatives that any particular speech habit is the result of a lack of discipline.

The development of pronunciation follows the same process we find throughout this book. The child has something to say and does the best she can under the circumstances. In this case, the circumstances are that she cannot properly control her vocal system. Furthermore, the child is probably not aware of all the details of a particular sound and so does not fully understand just what sound she is trying to make.

There is no universal way children go about learning the sounds of English. Apparently some sounds are easier to form than others, since it is true that we can prepare lists (Box 37) predicting the general order in which sounds will be mastered; however, the sounds children find easiest to make are not the most common sounds of adult languages. Many of the common sounds of English (*f, v, th, th´*) are quite difficult for children to say correctly. The only solution to this problem is for children to be willing to speak incorrectly until they master the proper sound.

Box 38
WAYS TO SPEAK WHEN YOU DON'T KNOW HOW

Stage 1—1 to 1½ or 2 years	
Bold approach	Repeat sounds
Prudent approach	Use monosyllables
Stage 2—1½ or 2 to 4 years	
Bold approach	Use of special sounds
Prudent approach	Select sounds

Within this broad solution there are two general ways of plunging ahead.[15] One is to take a bold approach, speaking whatever one wishes to say and not worrying about accuracy of pronunciation. The second approach is more prudent and limits the child's spoken vocabulary to the sounds she can say pretty well. Obviously, neither approach can be taken to extremes, since the first would lead to eternal incomprehensibility and the second to perpetual silence. Yet these two approaches dominate every child's struggle to speak correctly.

Box 38 outlines the different ways children can forge ahead with pronunciation. Since every child's speech will combine boldness and prudence, a bit of every system is likely to be found in your own child's speech. Nevertheless, children at various stages seem to show definite tendencies in one direction or the other, and observant parents can discover for themselves which route their child is following.

One note of caution: apparently neither approach is superior to the other. A study comparing children who repeat sounds with those who don't found no important differences between their rates of language process.[16] Nor should parents worry that their child seems too bold or too prudent. No connection between a child's approach to pronunciation and her later behavior in other areas has ever been hinted at. With these thoughts in mind, we can examine the various approaches:

Repeat sounds. This system is exactly what it says. A sound is made and then repeated. The word "water," for example, may be pronounced *wäwä*. In form, this approach is a continuation of late babbling in which syllables were combined; however, since such repetition is not continued by everybody, it should be thought of as a deliberate approach rather than a biologically controlled one. A British linguist, David Ingram, suggested that repeating sounds constitutes an attempt to reproduce the many speech sounds the child hears but can't quite catch. The suggestion is a good reminder that the very strange ways of speaking probably have good and simple reasons behind them.[17]

Along with duplicating syllables, this approach leads speakers to avoid pronouncing final consonants and to avoid attempting to pronounce more than one syllable. Box 39 compares how words might be said by children using the two different approaches. You can see that even where the bold approach does not lead to repetition, the sound is different from children following the more prudent line.

This approach is adopted during the earliest stages of learning English and begins to fade when a child starts combining words into primitive sentences.

Box 39
HOW FIRST WORDS SOUND [18]

Word	Bold approach	Prudent approach
water	wäwä	wät
chicken	kĭkuh	chĭk
necklace	nĕkĕ	nĕkĭs
hungry	hŭŭn	hŭngkĭ
chip	tĭ	tĭp

Use monosyllables. This approach is the one that sounds most like adult English, and children who follow it tend to please their parents and impress their parents' friends. The quality of their pronunciation is also something of a relief, since the speech development of children who use this approach is often a little slow in starting. Because this approach tends to limit a child to what she can pronounce well, it has been noted that the first handful of words attempted helps shape the sounds that appear in later words. [19]

Box 40
DANIEL MENN'S FIRST TWENTY-NINE ENGLISH WORDS [20]

Age (in months)	Word	Sound	Age (in months)	Word	Sound
16	bye-bye	băbă	22	kiss	gēf
18	hi	häy		up	ŭf
19	no	nōo		mouth	măwf
	hello	hwōw		eye	äy
19½	squirrel	gä		bottle	bä
20	nose	nō		bread	bā
	ear	ēy		good	gōob
21	boot	bōo		eat	ēh
	nice	nyäy		horse	ärs
22	light	äy		airplane	ä-ä
	car	gär		banana	nä
	cheese	jēf	22½	gate	gāy
	Steevie	ēv		carry	gä
	egg	āgh		box	khf
	apple	ăp			

This approach includes many final consonants, and different sounds may be lumped into one word. It sounds quite different from children who repeat sounds. The most important study of this approach was made by Lise Menn, who observed her son Daniel. Box 40 gives some sense of what a child using this monosyllabic approach sounds like. It lists Daniel's first twenty-nine words and their pronunciation. It is interesting to note that the accuracy of the pronunciation begins to decline a bit as the vocabulary size increases. Such decline appears inevitable if many words are ever to be spoken.

Special sounds. This approach calls for using arbitrary sounds rather than approximations of a word's actual sound. As in repeated sounds, these special sounds appear to take the place of sounds the speaker could not quite catch; however, instead of repeating part of the word, a standard sort of sound is commonly added to many words. For example, -*rs* might be stuck onto the ends of words whose adult equivalents contain several syllables.[21]

Another common aspect of this approach is the use of one sound for many different sounds. Typically, for example, *d* might be substituted for *t, g, l,* and *th.*

Select sounds. This approach is not so easy to hear and has been discovered only as a result of analyzing recorded speech. In this case, the speaker simply avoids using words that begin with difficult sounds, while favoring words with sounds that can be readily pronounced. Children using this approach will also substitute easy sounds for difficult ones, but the substitutions are far less automatic. Instead of always using, say, *d* for a particular sound, the substitution rules are much more complex.

By age four these various approaches have all paid off and most of the basic sounds of English are spoken correctly. What remain to be mastered are many of the consonant clusters like the *scr* in "scribe," the hardest English sounds (those which are the least common in other languages), and the most subtle rhythms of English sentences. For the most part, however, at this age family and strangers alike can understand what the child says and the problem of incomprehensibility is forgotten.

WHAT IS HAPPENING

One boy's language development from the age of two and a half to four showed him struggling to pronounce *chocolate* (chô´ kuh-lĭt). He progressed: gôgî; gôkdĭt; gôkĭt; glôklôt; gôklĭt; kôklĭt; tôkĭt; trôklĭt; tsôklĭt; sôklĭt; chôklĭt.[22]

This sort of progress appears to lead to increasing complexity and accuracy. Chocolate is a hard word to pronounce. It contains three syllables; the last syllable begins with a difficult sound *(l);* the second syllable is pronounced so weakly it is hard to hear; and the first syllable begins with a sound *(ch)* that is even harder to pronounce than *l.* Each one of these aspects of the word makes speaking difficult, and when all four reasons are lumped together in one word (even in so important a word), the problem increases ferociously.

Box 41
EARLY STAGES OF PRONUNCIATION[23]

Age	Stage
Birth to 1 year	*Earliest vocalizations.* No attention is paid to how sound should be pronounced. This stage is described in Chapter 4.
1 to 1½ or 2	*First 50 words.* Some words are pronounced better than others. No systematic method of pronouncing has yet been discovered.
1½ or 2 to about 4	*Mastery of simple sounds.* Begins about same time words start to be combined. During stage, child has a number of systematic ways for pronouncing words, but often this system leads to mispronunciation. By end of stage, however, a substantial number of sounds have been mastered and child is generally understood by strangers.
4 to 7	*Full mastery of English sounds.* The English sounds which are least common in other languages of the world are brought under control.

Children speak in response to the urge to express themselves. Because they have little experience in controlling the forms of sounds, they speak incorrectly. Pronunciation is a stunningly complicated process, and articulation of the syllables in words is only one part of it. There are also intonation, stress, and a large section of speech rules which are so poorly understood we don't even have a name for what they regulate. All of these rules are being learned more or less simultaneously and all affect the speech of adults around the child, so making sense of these many sounds is no simple task. Furthermore, most of these rules are learned on an entirely unconscious level.

Speech sounds reach children as bundles of many sounds piled on top of one another.[24] Progress in pronunciation requires a child to become aware of different parts of these sounds and then to discover how these separate parts are made. Anyone who has ever tried to learn a foreign language knows how hard it is to break the huge flow of sounds into their separate elements. Tourists with a small knowledge of the local language often complain, "The people here speak so fast." By that remark they admit the sounds are washing over them so freely that it is almost impossible to catch them individually. Children have exactly the same problem. Most parents slow down their speech when talking with young children, but it is impossible to speak so slowly that only one sound is heard at a time, and if parents did succeed in speaking that slowly, they would be teaching their child a very distorted system of pronunciation.

Thus, when children begin to speak, there is much variation between the sounds and in the correctness of individual words. During this initial stage, generally called the "first fifty words" period, most of the pronunciation processes do not yet apply. The sounds a child makes tend to be quite unstable. A vowel in one word, for example, may range from ă to ō during different pronunciations.[25] Even such classic words as *mama* and *papa* can vary. One girl had two months of trouble before stabilizing the sound. In the case of *papa,* one child began saying it correctly, then the sound began to vary, and finally it became fixed at *baba*.[26]

An interesting side development during this stage is the way some children begin to use pronunciation rules that are rare in English but found in other languages. They provide good illustrations of the fact that children are ready to speak any sort of language in the world. If they were Chinese or ancient Romans, these systems would continue to grow, but for English speakers they lead nowhere and fade as primitive sentences arise.

One such system uses tone changes. Chinese and many African languages distinguish wors on the basis of the pitch given a particular syllable. Adult English speakers find this approach almost impossible to master without long and hard training. A number of children, however, have been observed using toncs.

At about the time a child begins to combine words into her first primitive sentences, she finds that if she generalizes certain linguistic habits, she can quickly use many more words and speak about many more things.[27] So at this point there is a broadening of subject matter and a rapid growth of vocabulary. The price, however, is a sudden decline in the quality of pronunciation. The classic example of this decline is the case of a girl who had been pronouncing *pretty* accurately for about a year and who suddenly switched to say *pity*. It was to be a long time before she was able to restore the *r* to the word.

Fortunately, once the primitive-sentence stage is passed, children begin to show a serious interest in being understood, and they work steadily at getting the sounds right. Many of the habits of mispronunciation listed in Box 42 are overcome by age three. The result of this effort is a sudden blossoming, and at age three many children whose speech development had seemed slow speak clearly with a dramatic suddenness.[28]

It may seem odd that since so much of language development, particularly the physical structure of the vocal system, is biologically controlled, so little of the development of pronunciation is automatic. The rules children follow in the matter are very much the result of their own style and approach. Wouldn't it be simpler and quicker if biology regulated the practice?

The lack of such regulation, however, is consistent with everything we have seen about the development of language. The foundation of speech is biological; that is, nature provides us with the physical and intellectual tools necessary for language. It also gives us an instinct to express ourselves to others, but the content of language is almost entirely free of such regulation. The thoughts we express come from our hearts, not our genes, and since so much expression is bound up in sounds, the sounds we use are selected by us rather than by heredity.

Box 42
RULES OF CHILDREN'S PRONUNCIATION [29]

Name	Rule	Age Range
To Express Incomprehensible Sounds		
Beginning filler	A vowel like *uh* or *u* or sometimes a whole syllable beginning with a consonant is attached to the beginning of a word. Works rather like the sounds of hesitant adults who start off with *well* or *er*. May be associated with the prudent approach.	Can last from 1 to 3 years of age.
Repeat syllables	Two-syllable word formed. The second syllable is almost identical to first. Discussed earlier in chapter as part of bold approach.	Disappears about time words are combined.
Special sounds	A routine sound such as *-rs* or *-i* is added to the end of word. Discussed earlier in chapter as part of bold approach.	Disappears at about age 3.

Name	Rule	Age Range
	To Change Sounds	
Vocal strength	When the speaker begins a word with the consonants *b*, *d*, *g*, *p*, *t*, or *k*, she automatically vibrates her vocal cords, making pronunciation of *p*, *t*, and *k* impossible at the start of words since they all are said without use of vocal cords. When speaker ends a word, her vocal cords do not vibrate, making *b*, *d*, and *g* unpronounceable. This rule appears to be universal and is identified with both approaches.	Most control is achieved by age 2½, but problems with *g*, *k*, and *t* sometimes last longer.
Consonant shortening	When several consonants are lumped together, the tendency is to pronounce only one of them. Found in both approaches.	By age 4 many clusters can be pronounced, but some are not mastered until age 7.
Consonant repeating	Tendency to give two consonants in a word a similar sound. The consonant pronounced is one the speaker can usually pronounce correctly. Appears to be part of prudent approach.	Considered an early process. Usually does not last past 3rd birthday.
Assimilation	Adjustment of sound in accordance with neighboring sounds. Typically, anticipation of a sound about to be made leads speaker to put tongue in wrong part of mouth. Part of both approaches.	Lasts a long time. Indeed, some forms of assimilation are part of adult speech.

Name	Rule	Age Range
To Change Sounds		
Substitution	The consistent replacement of one sound with another. Which sounds are chosen in place of the correct one depends on the individual child. Some substitution is found in every child, but it may be most common in the bold approach.	Can last until 5 or 6, when the final difficult sounds of English are mastered.
To Omit Sounds		
Final consonants	No effort is made to pronounce final consonants of a word. A common rule of bold approach.	Very early. Disappears when primitive sentences begin.
Initial syllable	In words of 3 syllables, the first syllable is simply dropped. A familiar example is the use of *nana* for *banana.*	Largely gone by age 3 (merges into next rule on chart), but some holdover words last longer.
Unstressed syllable	In words of 3 syllables the syllable with no stress is omitted. *Elephant* becomes *elphant.*	Largely gone by age 5, but parts last so long they are heard in adults.
To Reorganize Sounds		
Rely on consonants	At first most syllables are formed by using a consonant plus a vowel. The early vocabulary of children favors words that begin with consonants. Later on consonants may be added to multisyllabic words to make the transition from one syllable to another easier.	Not widespread, but aspects can last a long time and become part of adult speech.

Name	Rule	Age Range
	To Reorganize Sounds	
Fronting	A tendency to pronounce the second vowels and consonants of a word further back in the mouth (or at least no closer to the front) than the first vowel and consonants. This rule often leads the sounds in words to be reversed. For example: *animal* becomes *manoo* because *m* is formed closer to the front of the mouth than *n*.	Begins at 1½ or 2. Reversal of vowels (e.g., putting ē before o͞o) can last a long time.

Chapter 14
Hearing Difficulty

Partial or total deafness is the most common cause of serious speech difficulties and should be considered whenever a language disorder is suspected. During the first year, parents should note all the hearing milestones listed in Box 43. Space to record their passage is provided in the diary. If any one of them is more than three months late in appearing, you should have a doctor examine your child's hearing; however, successful passage of the milestones is not a guarantee that there is no partial deafness, and, of course, a hearing loss can be acquired at any time. Do not allow common sense to rule out deafness, particularly partial deafness. A hearing loss that affects speech need only concern low-frequency sounds, since the human voice operates in the relatively low range.[1] Thus, a child may be deaf to language and yet still be able to hear high-frequency sounds well enough to enjoy listening to records and to react to loud noises. This kind of partial loss can be diagnosed only by a specialist. Amateurs sometimes see that the child is not fully deaf and conclude that the language problem must be mental.[2]

Box 43 HEARING MILESTONES[3]	
Age (in months)	Condition
3	Startled by loud sounds, soothed by mother's voice; turns in general direction of sound source.
6	Responds to mother's voice; turns head and eyes toward sound but may not find source on first attempt.

200

Age (in months)	Condition
10	Looks directly, promptly, and predictably to the sound source.
12	Begins to show voluntary control over response to sounds; may or may not pay any attention to a sound. Thus, a hearing loss becomes harder to distinguish from concentration.

Whenever you suspect a language disorder, you should reconsider the matter of your child's hearing. Note particularly:

- *any regression in speech development.* This sign does not automatically imply the onset of a hearing loss or any other language disorder, since there is plentiful evidence that talking children can briefly revert to babbling, especially if there is a younger brother or sister in the family.[4] It is also common for children who have gone through speech therapy to show a decline in speech development just prior to a general stabilization of proper articulation.[5] Nevertheless, a real and lasting decline in the level of speech may well be a sign of an acquired hearing loss.[6] If the decline persists, the hearing should be examined.
- *peculiarities of pronunciation.* The problems section of Chapter 13 covers a range of odd ways of speaking. If your child's speech sounds distorted, breathy, or out of rhythm, you should consider that list of problems to see if these sounds are ordinary childish peculiarities or are typical of hearing impairment.
- *an especially attentive child.* Children typically cannot be counted on to look at the speaker until they are fairly well along—age four or five. If your child isn't even three and she always looks, particularly if she looks at your mouth, this behavior can be a sign of partial deafness. Children

are astonishingly clever about language. Your child may be reading your lips,[7] and very few parents are ever going to suspect their baby of so remarkable a skill. If your child always watches you speak, make a point of determining if her comprehension declines when she can't see the speaker. While her back is turned, ask her to fetch something and see if she can do it. (Don't just ask her to come. She might do that anyway, just to try to find out what you said.)

- *a particularly troublesome child.* Some profoundly deaf children are first brought to a doctor's notice as behavior problems.[8] The frustration of not being able to communicate or to understand can lead to violent and frequent temper tantrums.

- *a child who is a brilliant mime.* If your child does not talk much but has developed a series of marvelously expressive gestures, she may be compensating for deafness.

If none of these conditions seems to describe your child, a hearing loss is probably not the major reason behind any trouble with language, and you should consider what Chapter 15 has to say about language disorders. While none of the conditions given above are unambiguous, parents who are concerned about their child's language, and who recognize one of the warning conditions mentioned, should see a doctor about a hearing examination.

If the doctor does report a hearing loss, parents will naturally wonder what this diagnosis means for their child's future and ask whether she is to be forever denied language. Not at all. Keep in mind the fact that deafness is a physical problem, not a mental one, and a diagnosis of some form of hearing loss is in no way a diagnosis of lost intellectual or linguistic potential. While the mental powers which create language (perception, imagination, voluntary decision) are complete mysteries, the mechanics of hearing are well understood and present no fundamental challenges to scientific assumptions. The ear is a major organ, but it is not part of the mind.

Since the problem is physical, it can often benefit from a physical solution like a hearing aid. I have known a hearing-aid user all my life and can report what the devices are like from close-range experience. They are more of a nuisance than glasses because they require batteries, the volume has to be adjusted, and sometimes they give off feedback, but there is no question about their ability to permit hearing when otherwise there would be only blurred noise. Their nuisance factor is nowhere close to being strong enough to tempt a user to abandon one. They keep getting lighter, louder, less conspicuous, and more hi-fi. Since hearing technology benefits so much from the modern techniques of miniaturization, sound recording, and information processing, it seems reasonable to assume that many children of the 1980s and 1990s who are diagnosed as deaf will eventually benefit from this work, even if they cannot do so today.

Unfortunately, deafness is not always treated as a purely physical disorder, so the diagnosis has taken on social implications as well. The prejudice of many hearing people toward deafness was concisely endorsed by Aristotle. "Those who are born deaf," he wrote, "become senseless and incapable of reason." For many hearing people confronted with deafness, simple smug prejudice takes over.

Prejudice is never so innocent that it results only in misunderstanding. It leads, instead, to all sorts of strange contempts. In this case, the sign languages of the deaf are assumed to be inferior to speech simply because the users are deaf. The physical problem of deafness is treated as comic or as a moral or mental weakness. Worst of all is the pervasiveness of the prejudice. Its smugness and contempt can turn up anywhere. Few people have completely escaped the poison in at least some of its forms. Hearing parents whose children are diagnosed as deaf are likely to find that no matter how open-minded they thought they were, some of the prejudices of the hearing world have sunk into their being. If they are going to appreciate the full humanity of their own child, they must now recognize and shed those hearing-based prejudices.

None of these prejudices are more profoundly built into our

culture than the link between language and thought. We commonly assume there can be no true thought without speech. One psychologist who worked with deaf children reported the recognition of his own hearing-based prejudices and how they were pervasive in psychology itself. "Linguistically determined notions such as the dependence of thought on language, 'inner speech' and its relationship to the regulation of behavior, and the verbal basis of concept formation in children . . . came to appear facile precisely because of their linguistic determination. They failed to survive the prolonged study of the speechless deaf."[9] If parents are to recognize fully the humanity of their deaf child, they too must grasp this notion that language and thought are different.

Language is the intermediary between a person's subjective thoughts and the rest of the world. It makes public what would otherwise be eternally private. It is a translation of awareness, not awareness itself.

The practical implication of this distinction between language and awareness is not that deaf children are going to have a hard time thinking but that they will find problems in making their thoughts known. Frustration, not mental retardation or a lack of imagination, is threatened. The growth of understanding is the first phase of every step in language development. It will continue, but now that growing understanding is threatened with imprisonment behind bars of silence.

The obvious solution is to use some alternate form of language. Hand signs and writing seem the most accessible, but this theoretically simple solution is loaded with practical difficulties, especially in the case of deaf children born to hearing parents. If the parents are deaf and use sign language, the children will use signs too. Children who use sign language can express themselves as early as hearing children; however, 90 percent of deaf children are born to hearing parents,[10] and if these children use sign language, the parents are going to have to learn it too. Understandably, most parents are doubtful about their ability to learn to sign. As hearing parents of deaf children turn to the question of education, therefore, they will have a natural bias toward schools which concentrate on language forms already known to the parents—speech and writing. Tragically, the record of achievement in this area of education is pitifully weak. Most graduates of the special schools for the deaf cannot speak well and, even more disappointing, cannot read on even a junior-high level.

If your child is diagnosed as having a hearing problem profound enough to impair speech, you will soon discover that disagreements over how to help these children have produced a ferociously bitter battle. The dispute is far more intense than the lofty philosophical terms of the argument would seem to justify. The combatants ask, what is the purpose of education anyway; is it to help a child enter society, or is it to develop her individuality to its fullest potential? Of course, the ferocity of the battle comes from the practical implications of that lofty question: what kind of future is *my* child to have?

Those who incline toward the notion that education is training for entrance into society believe that any education for the deaf should stress speech and speaking. The argument is: a person who cannot speak at all is going to be left out of a great deal of modern society; a person who can speak a little and read lips a little will still be on the margin of a lot of social activity, but not quite as completely as the totally speechless. Thus, people who stress the social role of education insist the deaf should be given special training to promote speech. For them, the great enemy is any tendency to downplay speech. The opposite approach, one focusing on the strengths and potential of the individual child, leads to the decision that education for deaf children should include teaching them a sign language.

For the past century most American education of the deaf has stressed speech and scorned sign language. Previously, sign language had been the primary focus of education for the deaf. The abandonment of sign-language teaching came largely because it suddenly seemed possible to teach the deaf to speak. Even before his invention of the telephone, Alexander Graham Bell had created a splash by demonstrating his system of "visible speech," which could teach deaf children to articulate sounds. After Bell became the great inventor, his prestige added even more weight to his ideas about teaching the deaf.

Yet the prestige of Bell alone cannot account for the long survival of speech-oriented education, especially in light of its unimpressive results. There have been notable and inspiring exceptions, but on the whole the education based on Bell's principles has failed to provide more than a quite minimal entrée into general society. Years of boarding school with drills in articulation and lip reading still do not provide the emotional expressions which are so fundamental to speech. Particularly disheartening has been the low level of reading skills this intense education has yielded. Less than 12 percent of deaf students aged fifteen and a half to sixteen and a half can read above the third-grade level.[11] The persistence of speech-oriented education in the face of these failures has come partly out of the desperate hope of parents that their child will be the exception and partly out of the philosophic inability of educators to grant the distinctions among thought, speech, and language.

For a long time the agreement of educational philosophy and parental desire kept the speech-sign controversy below the boiling point, but now our knowledge of language has overthrown the old harmony. A new interest in the nature of symbols and information has given the lie to Aristotle's antideaf prejudices. Thus, the argument over how best to educate deaf children has again reached explosive proportions. Because values and purposes are at issue, the matter cannot be argued to a simple logical conclusion. At bottom there are conflicting ambitions—education for society vs. education for self-development—and no amount of reason or data is going to defeat a point of view.

Recently a compromise approach has been developed and been given a public-relations-sounding slogan, "total communication." It combines speech with signing. Proponents of the other sides of the dispute dislike this compromise. The speech advocates see it as guaranteeing that speech will never be mastered to any important degree, while the sign-language advocates consider the sign system used in total communication to be a very crude replacement for the power and beauty of the American sign language, Ameslan. Perhaps its major attraction is that the sign system used in this approach is easier for the hearing parents to learn.

In trying to reach a conclusion concerning their child's future (in effect, her whole life), parents will find that the old antideafness prejudices of a hearing society are not dispelled so easily. What is reasonable to hope for in a deaf child? Again and again the question asked at the start of this consideration will return: does a diagnosis of hearing loss mean that a child must be forever denied full language? If not, then why have the practical results of language training been so poor?

Wherever there is a social prejudice, there is a temptation to blame the victims for any social failure. Thus, it is inevitable that many will wonder if the poor record of deaf education is the fault of the deaf themselves, rather than of the educational system. Some will argue bluntly that since, after years of training in special schools, most deaf teenagers still cannot read anything but the simplest sentences, it must be that deafness profoundly degrades the ability to use language in any complex form. Is there any reason to reject this argument?

Cases like Helen Keller don't have much impact against this kind of thinking. Prejudice can always dismiss them as "the exception that proves the rule" (whatever that phrase means). Fortunately, we don't have to rely on drawing up a list of famous deaf people. Generations of the speechless deaf have left a legacy as remarkable as the spoken tongues of the majority. Just as English is the product of centuries of individual consciousnesses, so too are the sign languages of the deaf. Elsewhere in this book I have argued that English is comparable to an attic trunk or a coral reef. It is a living testament to past thought, experience, and linguistic sensitivity. Sign languages are exactly the same sort of testament, only this time they testify to the thought and linguistic expression of the deaf. They are a visible refutation of Aristotle's smugness.

It is only the prejudice of the hearing that denigrates sign language. Although hand signs have certain technical limitations (e.g., can't be used in the dark; require conversants to look at one another; etc.), there is no reason to imagine that a spoken sentence is inherently superior to a signed one. Indeed, there are times when the technical limitations of speech become apparent and even hearing people turn to a sign language.[12]

The evidence is strong that we are biologically prepared to speak, but it is also apparent that if speech is blocked for some reason, sign language will appear. A particularly dramatic illustration of this tendency was recently discovered on the remote Polynesian island of Rennell. The place is so isolated it didn't even have missionaries until the late 1930s, and they quickly left when World War II began. The people there had never heard of congenital deafness until 1915, when a child named Kangobai was born. He grew into manhood without ever speaking. Today, in old age, he seems to be completely deaf and probably was so all his life. Because of the island's remoteness, there was no way the outside world could either help Kangobai or explain his condition to his fellow islanders. Kangobai grew up deaf in a world so inexperienced with deafness that the local people gave his silence a mythological explanation. Despite the fact that sign language was unknown on the island, Kangobai created one. Some of his fellow villagers learned Kangobai's signs and are able to communicate with him.[13] This example is probably as strong a one as we shall ever have to illustrate the natural tendency of the deaf to use signs even when no prior tradition for sign language exists.

Further evidence for this point comes from a study of deaf children aged one and a half to four whose parents refused to teach them sign language. The study found that the children create a sign language of their own anyway. Furthermore, the sign-language development follows the same process outlined in this book for speech development. The children begin with single gestures used in the same sorts of situations that evoke single words. As time passes, two of the gestures are combined into primitive sentences. Finally, more than two gestures are used together.[14]

Still more proof of the naturalness of sign language comes from observation of deaf children in special schools. It has been found that despite the teachers' emphasis on speech and lip reading, the children do have a sign language which they use among themselves.[15]

All of these examples make the same point. The deaf, like the hearing, need language because they have something to say. Since speech is denied them, they create sign languages by following the same process used by hearing children to create their first language. The fact of deafness certainly blocks speech, but it does not stunt the child's linguistic capacity.

Again and again the investigation of language and deafness leads away from doubts about the personal capacities of deaf children and moves toward questions about the social solutions to their predicament. The great difference in the development of deaf children comes at around age three, when hearing children put aside their first language in favor of an already established language. In the hearing world, this transition is routine and encouraged. If it does not take place, parents become concerned and we say the child's language is disordered; however, such transitions are frequently missed by the deaf. Instead of being abandoned, primitive sentences are expanded.

For Kangobai, of course, no transition was possible. He was the pioneer on his island. Elsewhere, however, the matter is not so straightforward. In the past there has been a great debate over whether or not the deaf should use a sign language. In the light of modern scientific findings, we can see that the question was poorly phrased. Deaf children will create and use a sign language whether or not adults approve. Put into the context of modern science, the education question is: should children be kept locked in the sign language of their own devising; or should they be allowed and even encouraged to replace their first language with an already established sign language such as Ameslan? Because this question deals with the purposes of education, science cannot provide an answer, but it can make two things clear. A decision to forbid the use of an established sign language is a decision to thwart individual potential far more deeply than was previously realized; a decision to introduce a child to a language like Ameslan opens doors to a culture that is much richer than formerly suspected.

The heritage and nature of sign language have recently been demonstrated in several good studies; the best one for parents of deaf children is probably R. B. Wilbur's book (listed in the bibliography). His account is technical, but the writing is clear, and parents of deaf children should find their own motivation is strong enough to let them read the book without difficulty. Wilbur's account of Ameslan overturns the old prejudice that sign language is just some crude situation-bound form of pantomime. It is a real language which uses grammar, expresses a point of view, and is varied enough to permit many different expressive styles.[16]

Ameslan is the fourth most widely used language in the USA (after English, Spanish, and Italian).[17] Like other established languages, it has generations of minds and experiences behind it, and they have shaped a distinct cultural outlook. Just as in the spoken languages, Ameslan has changed over time.[18]

Children who use Ameslan go through the same sort of development found in English-speaking children. The grammar is too complex and irregular for them to use all at once. Overgeneralization of grammatical practices is found in signing children, as in speaking ones.[19] Even the matter of proper pronunciation has its analogy. In sign language, good pronunciation means getting the shape of the hand right.[20] At first, children can make only a few of the shapes correctly, but they slowly improve. Once signing children get beyond the first-language period, we see the same sorts of social communication found in speaking children. They *tell* (not "act out") stories, and they shape the information they express as the context requires.[21]

Our clearer understanding of language—of what it is (an intermediary), of what it does (expresses nonlinguistic thought), and where it comes from (we create it ourselves)—combined with our new understanding of sign language makes it hard to sustain the old belief that the deaf have a language handicap. They certainly are at a social disadvantage and traditional American education has left the deaf in a linguistically stunted condition, but the failure to teach them to read seriously or to express themselves richly has not been the fault of the deaf. Parents can be confident that the new insights will permit a much richer personal and social development for today's children who are diagnosed as having a serious hearing difficulty.

Chapter 15
Judging Your Child's Speech

Perhaps the most remarkable idea to come out of the children's language revolution is this notion that there can be a "language disorder." Folk wisdom from untold ages has insisted that there is no such thing as a speech disorder. The child has just not learned to talk. Implied in that bit of lore is the judgment that either the parents have been unusually negligent teachers or the child is desperately backward. Moral condemnation of the child is sometimes part of the explanation. Lazy, stubborn, self-centered . . . these are some of the terms applied to children whose speech is not developing as expected.

The folk notions can no longer stand. The discovery that language development depends on biologically based powers and on maturation implies that there can be biologically based difficulties of development. Just as the physical development of some children does not follow the normal path, a few children (and I emphasize *few)* do not develop language as expected. These children are double victims. First, nature has given them an extra burden out of the starting gate, but that problem might not be so disastrous if it were not for all the extras society plops on them. Branded as retarded or morally unfit, they are often shunted into a box canyon before their life has barely begun. Thus, parents who are concerned about their child's speech should be alert to the possibility that some specific language disorder may be present.

The first task of a parent who suspects a language disorder is to get an idea of how serious the matter really is, so the rest of this chapter is devoted to helping parents make a judgment about the severity of the particular situation they have

212

encountered. Of course, a proper diagnosis can come only after an individual child has been professionally examined.

This chapter is structured quite differently from the previous ones. It presents some yes-or-no questions and then lists several conditions which, if met, permit a *yes* answer to the question. If, as you read these points, you realize that your own answer must be *no*, skip on down to the next question.

Question one: is your concern about a language delay? Since folk wisdom has denied the possibility of an actual disorder, the traditional response to parents who express concerns about language development has been, "Oh, she'll grow out of it." Often this prophecy turns out to be correct. In any process of maturation, some individuals are going to be slower than others, and a few will be at the tail end of the statistician's normal curve, but if we first assume that every problem is a simple delay, correct diagnosis of a disordered speaker may be postponed until the child is five or six. One study found that of 280 children brought into a speech clinic because of parental concern, 206, or almost three-quarters, had a diagnosable disorder they could not be hoped to outgrow.[1] Fortunately, there are things a parent can check for to see whether or not their child really is likely just to "grow out of it." Parents who want to know if their child's speech is delayed should keep these points in mind:

- *Delayed development follows the typical developmental stages; it just takes more time.* The description of language development given in Parts II and III of this book still holds true. The only point that is off is the age range. In delayed development, the precultural stage might continue to the second birthday, primitive sentences only appear at age three, and the transition to English does not get under way until the fourth birthday. This prolongation of the stages can sometimes show the details of development with great clarity and richness. For example, by the end of the second year the vocalizations of children who are not yet using words should be long, complex, and contain plenty of the rhythms of speech, even though the words are absent.[2] I urge parents whose child's speech is delayed to make a special point of maintaining the language diary in the back of this book. That way you will be able to see that even though the major milestones are far apart, progress is steady.

• *Delayed language development is a specific condition.* Progress in language is largely independent of the many other developmental processes which are going on at the same time. If other development is also delayed, there may be some more general problem at work. For example, if your child's language is slow in coming, if her walking is also not appearing when expected, and if she is not much interested in the various toys designed for children her age, the immaturity is probably too general to be a simple language delay.[3]

• *Delayed language development is a speaking problem, not a disorder or comprehension.* If a fifteen-month-old child does not respond to any words, there may be a variety of nonlanguage problems. Another troubling indication that a parent may be facing more than delayed production comes if a child doesn't seem to know her mother's voice.[4]

• *Delayed language development is not a general disorder of communication.* How does your child make her wants known? If she seems miraculously "well behaved," seldom crying, never making requests, something is awry. Do not complacently congratulate yourself for having an unusually good baby. If she understands gestures better than words but never gestures herself, much more than language delay is present.[5]

• *Delayed language development is not endlessly delayed.* Any child aged over thirty months who has not yet reached the single-word stage should be considered disordered, rather than delayed.

If the above points have not excluded your child, you can assume that while your child's language development may be slow, it is still within the normal range. Parents should understand that "slow" refers to slow development, not slow wit, slow thought processes, or slow anything else. "Slow" is not a code word for low intelligence and is not a predictor of future schoolwork or even of future language abilities. By the age of five, children with delayed language development should be speaking pretty much like other children. That is to say, even though their speech is delayed in coming, they catch up by the end of the time span covered by this book. Thus, there is no reason to expect any special trouble once regular school begins.[6]

The reaction of people outside the family, however, will not be universally enlightened. A three-year-old child who talks like many children only half her age is subject to teasing from other children, heavy-handed attempts at correction from nursery-school or day-care teachers, and occasional put-downs from adult friends. You don't want your child to come out of this stage with any serious doubts about either her own worth or her ultimate ability to use language. Parents of children whose language is delayed have to make a special effort to encourage those skills and interests which are developing rapidly, to listen with interest to what their child has to say, and to talk to her as a person, rather than a backward unfortunate.

Question two: if your concern may be about a disorder, is it a minimal disorder? Any parent who suspects a language disorder is going to be upset and anxious; it sounds ruinous, but, in fact, it is usually not a long-term problem. One survey of nearly a thousand children aged three and a half found that 19 percent of them had some form of language disorder.[7] Common sense tells us that nothing like that percentage of adults or even teenagers have a speech disorder, so the presence of one in early childhood obviously does not automatically foreshadow lifelong difficulties, or even long-term therapy.

As a general rule, the earlier a language disorder appears, the more serious it is. The difficulty with this rule of thumb is that the symptoms of the disorder may go unrecognized for a long time, so that an early-appearing disorder seems to have

developed late. Box 44 summarizes the mental powers necessary for the development of language and notes the result if
that power breaks down. Parents should remember that
symptoms are almost always ambiguous and require an examination for actual diagnosis. All we are trying to do here is
determine whether a disorder is alarming enough to demand
professional attention.

Box 44 MENTAL POWERS SUPPORTING LANGUAGE		
Power	*Role in language development*	*Symptom of breakdown*
Perceive situations	Fundamental. Language begins with awareness of the situation.	At its worst there is a complete lack of self-expression with either voice or gesture. In less severe cases precultural sounds may appear and even single words, but they do not progress, and primitive sentences are not spoken.
Perceive spoken language	Comprehension and, thus, speech depend on this power; however, the communicative use of gesture persists.	Requires a medical examination to be distinguished from deafness. Child generally behaves as though she were deaf.
Quotation	The use of English words and grammar comes from this power.	In the most severe cases English does not appear. Less severe cases may seem at first to be problems of articulation, but there is no transition from the first language to speaking English.

Power	Role in language development	Symptom of breakdown
Voluntary control of speech	Visible progress in speech development is dependent on this power.	Takes many forms; commonly diagnosed as "motor aphasia"—e.g., confusion or mixing of names, sounds, or sequences of sounds. Child may seem to want to speak but doesn't.
Imagination	Permits language to treat contexts larger than the objective situation of the moment.	Grammar progresses, but language is still tied to situation. Even playful talk requires the presence of specific objects.

Most language symptoms are false alarms. While a chart such as the one in Box 44 may seem to suggest there are many things that can go wrong, in reality these problems are terribly rare, especially the ones that threaten the roots of language. Most readers will be able to go through Box 44 and rule out any relevance to their child.

Readers can now try to answer question two by considering the following points:

- *Minimal disorders are not part of a general developmental problem.* If you decided the problem is too general to be just a delayed language development, the number of possible difficulties is too great to be ignored.
- *Minimal disorders are not acquired.* If language development seemed to be proceeding normally and then suddenly broke down, especially after an accident involving a blow to the head or after a serious infection, you should assume the problem is not minimal.[8] These acquired disorders most commonly involve the power to control

speech and not the more fundamental powers at the roots of language itself. Experience suggests that with proper therapy, speech will be recovered.

- *Minimal disorders do not arise in the powers supporting language.* If any of the problems identified in Box 44 seem to apply to your child, the disorder should not be considered minimal.
- *Minimal disorders do not persist.* If the disorder is still present on your child's third birthday, it can no longer be dismissed as minimal.

If none of the above points rule out your child, you can assume that if there is any disorder, it is not potentially severe. Keep in mind that a minimal disorder is still a disorder. It may have no connection with the child's intelligence (which can be normal, or even well above average in the language-disordered child), but its symptoms may disappear only to reappear in school under a new guise, as a reading problem. Since many teachers commonly treat reading problems as intelligence failures, it is important for a parent to be able to suspect that the problems lie elsewhere, in a minimal language disorder. I urge parents whose children may be minimally disordered to maintain the diary in the back of this book. This practice can, in part, help a parent determine how much progress the child is making and can also provide a record of any signs of the disorder. If new language difficulties turn up in school (problems in reading, spelling, or composition), parents will have some evidence of what may be disturbing the language.

Question three: if your concern is about a potentially serious disorder, what should you do? Quite simply, see a doctor! The great majority of readers will never have to consider question three. If you are in the minority, you must have a doctor examine the child in order to determine the precise nature of the problem. Box 45 lists important signs of a potentially serious language disorder. If any of them are present in your child, you should not fail to bring that fact to the doctor's notice.

Box 45
POTENTIALLY SERIOUS DISORDERS

- Infrequent or no vocalizing
- Cannot understand speech
- Never gestures
- Inability to associate name with thing
- Knows names but cannot speak them when asked
- After a promising beginning, speech has largely disappeared
- Child almost never initiates speech
- Words that sound alike or share similar definitions are frequently confused
- Most speech of more than one word is an inappropriate repetition of something heard before
- Primitive sentences do not appear
- Vocalizations are a meaningless noise, like a record playing too fast
- Behavioral problem is accompanied by disordered language
- Word order is severely jumbled
- Grammar is developing on schedule, but speech is still bound by the environment
- Primitive sentences are only growing longer, not grammatically more complex.
- Speech is extraordinarily literal.

Diagnosis means naming the problem, not explaining or understanding it in any physical detail. It is the tragedy of child-language studies that the *how* of language is not at all understood. This ignorance should not seem surprising to anyone who scans the first column in Box 44. Perception, apt quotation, imagination, voluntary control of behavior . . . these powers are the highest and most mysterious in humanity. Their effects are everywhere around us, yet their nature is as baffling to us as it was to the Greeks. Thus, treatment is seldom efficient; however, speech therapists have gained a lot of practical working experience at treating the problems, and many procedures are known to be effective, even though we don't know why they work.

PART V

FOR THOSE WHO WANT TO KNOW MORE

Chapter 16
Glossary of Language Disorders

Agnosia, the inability to perceive spoken language. This diagnosis is extremely rare. One British expert on speech therapy reported that in over twenty years of clinical practice she had seen only two cases.[1] Agnosia is a failure to perceive something, even though the sense organ is working perfectly well. In an agnosia which leads to language disorder, the ears are in working order but the child acts as though she were deaf. Sometimes there is a mild hearing impairment, but nothing severe enough to account for the profound inability to respond to words. One girl who recovered from it said later, "Well, I guess I heard, but everything sounded bla-bla-bla."[2] Other terms for this disorder are "receptive aphasia" or "word deafness."

In severe cases it is difficult to distinguish the responses of these children from the truly deaf, and it may be hard to distinguish their behavior from children with Kanner's Syndrome (discussed below). The most visible behavioral differences are that agnosia sufferers engage in much more imaginative play and use of gesture than do children with Kanner's Syndrome.[3]

In less severe cases a child will show an inability to name objects, an inability (or at best only a partial ability) to associate particular things with words spoken to her, and, if she vocalizes at all, a tendency to speak in "scribble speech." This latter speech is a confused or unintelligible jargon that sounds as though a record were running at high speed. Sometimes clear words are mixed in with this scribble speech. The speech is accompanied by expressive gestures and facial signals.[4]

Less severe agnosia may also be diagnosed as some form of emotional problem. In the past, many children with a language disorder and a behavioral problem have been diagnosed as having an emotional problem that affected speech. Now it is thought that at least some of these cases may have begun with a language disorder and then spilled over into the emotions.[5] A study of children with combined language and behavior disorders found that most of the children perceived no important difference between television programs with a clear soundtrack and programs with an unintelligible soundtrack.

The outlook in these cases depends, of course, on the severity, but also on the treatment and the age it is begun. Children almost never simply outgrow the problem.[6] Frightening as it is to hear, the presence of scribble speech is a promising sign, and the long-term outlook is good if treatment is begun early.[7]

Aphasia, the inability to voluntarily control one's speech; sometimes called "motor aphasia" to distinguish it from receptive aphasia or agnosia.[8] It can be hard to distinguish some aphasias from other problems of articulation. In some cases a parent may fear that the sounds being made are those of "scribble speech" in agnosia, but aphasia sufferers have no problems perceiving sounds. They can understand speech and they pay attention to sounds, but they have difficulty producing speech. Different aphasias lead to many different sorts of problems—e.g., cannot give names when asked; frequently confuses words that sound alike or which share similar meanings; constantly gets word order confused; words are unintelligible even though the child keeps up a steady chatter. Aphasias call for special therapy, but in children the outlook for proper language is good.

Blank's Syndrome, a disorder showing the kind of symptoms one would expect from a failure of the verbal imagination.[9] While developing Box 44 (Chapter 15), I had the feeling that although a failure of the imagination might be theoretically possible, it was unlikely to exist in reality. It seems hard to believe that the power of the imagination is really some separate power of the mind which can go awry by itself, but there is a case described by Marion Blank and her colleagues reporting exactly the kind of problem one would expect if this part of language development were blocked. At age three years five months, a boy, John, showed the grammatical development typical of a boy his age (as indicated in Box 26, Chapter 9). John's problem was not "pure" in the sense that there were no signs of a language difficulty before the transition to English. His first word was delayed and first primitive sentences were quite late; nevertheless, he appears to have caught up grammatically before he was three and a half. His language was astonishingly situation-bound. Blank reports that outside of play, his speech was "confined to ongoing or just-completed activities." His speech during play was much richer (apparently it was mostly straight quotation), but it still required the presence of some toy related to the playful talk. That is, he pretended to be driving a car only when a toy car was physically present. Apart from grammatical progress, the many developments described in Part III were entirely absent.

This condition is so rare that almost nothing is known about it or the likelihood of improvement.

Echolalia, a very rare trait that is a symptom rather than a separate disorder. It is so striking, however, that it may stand out even while other symptoms of a particular language disorder are unnoticed. Ordinary speech development includes a lot of immediate and delayed repetition (or quotation). This speech becomes echolalic if there is almost nothing else but simple and immediate repetition or delayed bizarre quotation. Echolalia appears if the normal power of quotation is unmodified by any perceptual insights which permit the breakdown and combination of quoted sentences. For example, one five-year-old boy used to say, "Don't throw the dog off the balcony," whenever he was tempted to throw something.[10] The sentence was an exact quotation (in word and intonation) of something his mother had said three years earlier when he had thrown a toy dog off a hotel balcony. Although there is a situational explanation for the quotation, there is no sense of context; the child's failure to break down any part of the sentence is clearly and profoundly disturbing.

One common feature of echolalia is incorrect use of pronouns; e.g., "You want cookie," when, "I want cookie," would be correct.[11] Although it is tempting to look for some psychological rejection of the self in this tendency, experiments have established that this explanation is overly profound.[12] Pronoun reversal is a simple result of echolalia. Echolalic children will use the word *I* if it is in the speech they echo.

The outlook for a particular echolalic child depends on the rest of her condition.

Kanner's Syndrome, the most mysterious of all language disorders. It is often associated with many other disabilities but in its "pure" form resembles the kind of problem expected for children who cannot perceive a situation. It is extremely rare (less than 1 per 2,000 grade-school-age children).[13]

It is hard to imagine a person who is conscious yet unable to perceive the situation at hand, but since language begins with an awareness of a situation, a theoretically conceivable language disorder could spring from an inability to integrate the separate sense perceptions into a portrait of the whole situation. It is well established that the different senses are perceived in different areas of the brain, so when we perceive the whole situation at once, some power of integration must be at work. If that power broke down, we would find a strange reversal of the old story about the five blind swamis who described an elephant on the basis of feeling its tail, or the trunk, or a foot, or its side. Here, one person looks at the elephant and knows what it looks like, what it smells like, what it sounds like, and what it feels like but does not unite all those separate perceptions into a whole. Such a person would be able to develop various abstract concepts of an elephant but never perceive the whole animal.

There is a language disorder that reveals just such symptoms. At its most severe level, of course, no language would appear at all, and over half of all children diagnosed with Kanner's Syndrome are mute.[14] So severe a language disorder must inevitably carry many side effects, and Kanner's Syndrome used to be considered some remarkable behavioral disorder. It is now agreed, however, that these children have a central disorder of language.[15] Present treatment is much more able to abolish the secondary symptoms (repetitive behavior, poor social relationships) than it is able to overcome the language disorder.[16]

Particularly striking is how even though the children cannot understand language, they can grasp abstract concepts which can be expressed without using language.[17] One observer reported, "Among the cleverer children, there is a marked preference for non-verbal languages such as mathematics or music. Some children with no visual handicap learn to read before they can talk."[18] Nonverbal languages are nonsituational languages. Reading, while not as abstract as math, is much less situation-oriented than speech. Because of this ability to think abstractly, Kanner's Syndrome does not automatically imply mental retardation. Memory too is often very good,[19] but any verbal recall is relatively independent of the word's meaning.[20] These characteristics are what we might expect of people who are intelligent and whose individual perceptual systems still work well, but not in unison.

Among children whose disorder is not so severe that they are mute, speech rarely gets beyond a single-word stage.[21] Echolalia is common. Gesture is rare. Words that are used are either very specific (e.g., a "bowl" will be only one kind of bowl) or extremely broad (e.g., "shoe" might be used for both a shoe and a sock). In neither case does the child show the kind of understanding that links the use of a particular word with certain recurring general situations.[22] The most advanced language users still show a strange tendency to take language quite literally. A typical answer to the question, "What would you do if you cut yourself?" is, "Bleed."[23]

One of the tragedies of this sort of disorder is that it commonly robs the child of all communication. All mammals use communication for social control. In humans, this natural system of signals has largely atrophied and been taken over by language. Thus, children with a disorder so severe that it attacks both speech and gesture are stuck without any way to express even their basic needs. The absence also makes it harder for parents to control the children. New teaching techniques involving sign language are helping parents gain control[24] over the children and enabling the children to express their wants.[25]

Menyuk's Syndrome, apparently a breakdown in the power of quotation.[26] This disorder is not discussed in the clinical literature but was studied in detail by an academic psycholinguist, Paul Menyuk. Even the single-word vocabulary depends on the power to quote, but if the problem is not drastically severe, it may not be recognized at first. It is hidden as language delay or poor pronunciation and only becomes apparent at the end of the typical primitive-sentence stage. The sentences get longer, but very little grammar using tense, preposition, and auxiliary verbs appears. The absence of helping verbs is striking. Since the appearance of these problems is so specifically a part of using English grammar, the matter is discussed more fully in Chapter 9.

Chapter 17
Bibliography

1. SUGGESTED READING

Abrahamsen, Adele A. *Child Language: An Interdisciplinary Guide to Theory and Research*. Baltimore: University Park Press, 1977.

Braine, Martin D. S. "Children's First Word Combinations," *Monographs of the Society for Research in Child Development*, 41 (1976), no. 1.

Brown, Roger. *A First Language: The Early Stages*. Cambridge: Harvard University Press, 1973.

Chomsky, Noam. "Review of 'Verbal Behavior,'" *Language*, 35 (1959), 26–58.

Cruttenden, Allen. *Language in Infancy and Childhood: A Linguistic Introduction to Language Acquisition*. Manchester: Manchester University Press, 1979.

Iwamura, Susan Grohs. *The Verbal Games of Pre-School Children*. New York: St. Martin's, 1980.

Lenneberg, Eric H. *Biological Foundations of Language*. New York: John Wiley & Sons, Inc., 1967.

Morley, Muriel F. *The Development and Disorders of Speech in Childhood*. Edinburgh: E & S Livingstone Ltd., 1957.

Pitcher, Evelyn Goodenough and Prelinger, Ernst. *Children Tell Stories: An Analysis of Fantasy*. New York: International Universities Press, 1963.

Steiner, George. *After Babel: Aspects of Language and Translation*. Oxford: Oxford University Press, 1975.

2. OTHER SOURCES

Aaronson, Doris and Rieber, Robert W., eds. "Developmental Psycholinguistics and Communication Disorders," *Annals of the New York Academy of Sciences*, 263 (1975).

Aimard, Paule. *Les Jeux de Mots de l'Enfant*. Villeurbonne: Simep Editions, 1975.

Allerton, D. J. "Early Phonotactic Development: Some Observations on a Child's Acquisition of Initial Consonant Clusters," *Journal of Child Language*, 3 (1976), 429–33.

Bettelheim, Bruno. *The Uses of Enchantment: The Uses and Importance of Fairy Tales*. New York: Alfred A. Knopf, 1976.

Blache, Stephen E. *The Acquisition of Distinctive Features*. Baltimore: University Park Press, 1978.

Blank, Marion; Gessner, Myron; and Esposito, Anita. "Language Without Communication; a case study," *Journal of Child Language,* 6 (1979), 329–52.

Bloom, Lois. *One Word at a Time: The Use of Single Word Utterances Before Syntax.* The Hague: Mouton, 1973.

———; Hood, Lois; and Lightblown, Penny. "Imitation in Language Development: if, when, and why?" *Cognitive Psychology,* 6 (1974), 380–420.

———; Rociassano, Lorranine; and Hood, Lois. "Adult-Child Discourse: Developmental Interaction Between Information Processing and Linguistic Knowledge," *Cognitive Psychology,* 8 (1976), 521–2.

Bokus, Barbara and Shugar, Grace Wales. "What Will a Three-Year-Old Say? An Experimental Study of Situational Variation," in Garnica and King.

Bolles, Edmund Blair. "Swahili Even Taxes Africans," *The Washington Post,* May 11, 1969.

———. "The Innate Grammar of Baby Talk," *Saturday Review of Science,* March 18, 1972.

Bowerman, Melissa. "Systematizing Semantic Knowledge: Changes Over Time in the Child's Organization of Meaning," *Child Development,* 49 (1978), 977–87.

Braine, Martin. "On What Might Constitute a Learnable Phonology," *Language,* 50 (1974), 270–99.

Brown, Roger; Fraser, Collin; and Bellugi, Ursula. "Control of Grammar in Imitation, Comprehension, and Production," *Journal of Verbal Learning and Verbal Behavior,* 2 (1963), 121–35.

Camaioni, Luigi. "Child-Adult and Child-Child Conversations: An Interactional Approach," in Ochs and Schieffelin.

Carmichael, Leonard, ed. *Manual of Child Psychology (2nd ed.).* New York: John Wiley & Sons, 1954.

Casey, La Deane Osler. "Development of Communicative Behavior in Autistic Children; A Parent Program Using Manual Signs," *Journal of Autism and Childhood Schizophrenia,* (1978), 45–59.

Charney, Rosalind. "The Comprehension of 'here' and 'there,'" *Journal of Child Language,* 6 (1979), 69–80.

Chomsky, Noam. *Syntactic Structures.* The Hague: Mouton, 1957.

Clark, Eve V. "Strategies for Communicating," *Child Development,* 49 (1978), 953–4.

Clark, Ruth. "Performing Without Competence," *Journal of Child Language,* 1 (1974), 1–10.

Clarke-Stewart, K. Allison. "Interactions Between Mothers and Their Young Children: Characteristics and Consequences," *Monographs of the Society for Research in Child Development,* 38 (1973), nos. 6–7.

Comrie, Bernard. *Aspect: An Introduction to the Study of Verbal Aspect and Related Problems.* Cambridge: Cambridge University Press, 1976.

Crystal, David. "Non-Segmental Phonology in Language Acquisition: A Review of the Issues," *Lingua,* 32 (1973), 1–45.

———. "The Analysis of Intonation in Young Children," in Minifie and Lloyd, 1978.

Damon, William. *The Social World of the Child.* San Francisco: Jossey-Bass Publishers, 1977.

Dore, John. "Holophrases, Speech Acts and Language Universals," *Journal of Child Language,* 2 (1975), 21–40.

———. "Variation in Preschool Children's Conversational Performances," in Keith Nelson, 1978.

———; Franklin, Margery B.; Miller, Robert T.; and Ramer, Andrya L. H. "Transitional Phenomena in Early Language Acquisition," *Journal of Child Language,* 3 (1976), 13–28.

Eliot, John, ed. *Human Development and Cognitive Processes.* New York: Holt, Rinehart and Winston, 1971.

Ervin-Tripp, Susan. "Children's Verbal Turn-Taking," in Ochs and Schieffelin.

——— and Miller, Wick. "Early Discourse: Some Questions about Questions," in Lewis and Rosenblum.

Ferguson, Charles A. "Learning to Pronounce: The Earliest Stages of Phonological Development in the Child," in Minifie and Lloyd, 1978.

——— and Slobin, Dan, eds. *Studies of Child Language Development.* New York: Holt, Rinehart and Winston, 1973.

———; Peizer, David B.; and Weeks, Thelma E. "Model-And-Replica Phonological Grammar of a Child's First Words," *Lingua,* 31 (1973), 35–65.

——— and Farwell, Carol B. "Words and Sounds in Early Language Acquisition," *Language,* 51 (1975), 419–39.

——— and Garnica, Olga K. "Theories of Phonological Development," in Lenneberg and Lenneberg, 1975.

Folger, Joseph P. and Chapman, Robin S. "A Pragmatic Analysis of Spontaneous Imitations," *Journal of Child Language,* 5 (1978), 25–38.

Fraser, G. M. and Blockley, J. *The Language Disordered Child: A New Look at Theory and Treatment.* Windsor, U.K.: NFE Publishing, 1973.

Friedlander, Bernard Z.; Wetstone, Harriet S.; and McPeek, Donna L. "Systematic Assessment of Selective Language Listening Deficit in Emotionally Disturbed Pre-School Children," *Journal of Child Psychology and Psychiatry,* 15 (1974), 1–12.

Gardner, Howard; Kircher, Mary; Winner, Ellen; and Perkins, David. "Children's Metaphoric Productions and Preferences," *Journal of Child Language,* 2 (1975), 125–41.

Garnica, Olga K. and King, Martha L. *Language, Children and Society: The Effect of Social Factors on Children Learning to Communicate.* London: Pergamon Press, 1979.

Garvey, Catherine. "Requests and Responses in Children's Speech," *Journal of Child Language,* 2 (1975), 41–63.

———. "The Contingent Query: A Dependent Act in Conversation," in Lewis and Rosenblum, 1977.

———. "Contingent Queries and Their Relations in Discourse," in Ochs and Schieffelin, 1979.

——— and Hogan, Robert. "Social Speech and Social Interaction: Egocentrism Revisited," *Child Development,* 44 (1973), 562–8.

Goldin-Meadow, Susan; Seligman, Martin E. P.; and Gelman, Rachel. "Language in the Two-Year-Old," *Cognition,* 4 (1976), 189–202.

Goldin-Meadow, Susan and Feldman, Heidi. "The Creation of a Communications System: A Study of Deaf Children of Hearing Parents," *Sign Language Studies,* 8 (1975), 225–34.

Greenfield, Patricia Marks and Smith, Joshua H. *The Structure of Communication in Early Language Development.* New York: Academic Press, 1976.

Gruendel, Janice M. "Referential Extension in Early Language Development," *Child Development,* 48 (1977), 1567–76.

Hale, Horatio. "The Origin of Languages and the Antiquity of Speaking Man," *Proceedings of the American Association for the Advancement of Science,* 35 (1886), 279–323.

Halliday, M. A. K. "Relevant Models of Language," *Educational Review,* 22 (1969), 26–37.

Harding, Carol Gibb and Golinkoff, Roberta Michnick. "The Origins of Intentional Vocalizations in Prelinguistic Infants," *Child Development,* 50 (1979), 33–40.

Hardy, William G. and Hardy, Miriam Pauls. *Essays on Communication and Communicative Disorders.* New York: Grune & Stratton, 1977.

Hinde, R. A. and Stevenson-Hinde, J. *Constraints on Learning: Limitations and Predispositions.* New York: Academic Press, 1973.

Ingram, David. "Transivity in Child Language," *Language,* 47 (1971), 888–910.

———. "Phonological Rules in Young Children," *Journal of Child Language,* 1 (1974a), 49–64.

———. "Fronting in Child Phonology," *Journal of Child Language,* 1 (1974b), 233–41.

———. *Phonological Disability in Children.* London: Edward Arnold, 1976a.

———. "Current Issues in Child Phonology," in Morehead and Morehead, 1976b.

———. "The Production of Word-Initial Fricatives and Affricatives by Normal and Linguistically Deviant Children," in Caramazza, Alfonso and Zurig, Edgar B., eds. *Language Acquisition and Language Breakdown: Parallels and Divergencies.* Baltimore: Johns Hopkins University Press, 1978.

Iscoe, Ira and Stevenson, Harold W., eds. *Personality Development in Children*. Austin: University of Texas Press, 1960.

Jakobson, Roman. *Child Language, Aphasia and Phonological Universals*. The Hague: Mouton, 1968.

Jespersen, Otto. *Language: Its Nature, Development and Origin*. London: Allen and Unwin, 1922.

Johnson, Wendell and Associates. *The Onset of Stuttering: Research Findings and Implications*. Minneapolis: University of Minnesota Press, 1959.

Kanner, Leo. "Irrelevant and Metaphorical Language in Early Infantile Autism," *The American Journal of Psychiatry*, 103 (1946), 242–45.

Kaplan, Eleanor and Kaplan, George. "The Prelinguistic Child," in Eliot.

Karlin, Isaac W.; Karlin, David B.; and Gurren, Louise. *Development and Disorders of Speech in Childhood*. Springfield, Ill.: Charles C. Thomas, 1965.

Keenan, Elinor O. "Conversation Competence in Children," *Journal of Child Language*, 1 (1974), 163–83.

Kendon, Adam. "The Sign Language of the Women of Yuendumu," *Sign Language Studies*, 27 (1980), 101–12.

Kuczaj II, Stan A. and Brannick, Nancy. "Children's Use of the *Wh* Question Modal Auxiliary Placement Rule," *Journal of Experimental Child Psychology*, 29 (1979), 43–67.

Kuschel, Rolf. "The Silent Inventor or: The Creation of a Sign Language by the Only Deaf-Mute on a Polynesian Island," *Sign Language Studies*, 3 (1973), 1–27.

Landau, Rikva. "Spontaneous and Elicited Smiles and Vocalizations of Infants in Four Israeli Environments," *Developmental Psychology*, 13 (1977), 389–400.

Lenneberg, Eric H. and Lenneberg, Elizabeth, eds. *Foundations of Language Development: A Multidisciplinary Approach* 2 vols. New York: Academic Press, 1975.

Leonard, Laurence B. *Meaning in Child Language: Issues in the Study of Early Semantic Development*. New York: Grune and Straton, 1976.

————; Schwartz, Richard G.; Folger, M. Karen; and Wolcox, Jeanne. "Some Aspects of Child Phonology in Imitative and Spontaneous Speech," *Journal of Child Language*, 5 (1978), 403–15.

————; Newhoff, Marilyn; and Fey, Marc E. "Some Instances of Word Usage in the Absence of Comprehension," *Journal of Child Language*, 7 (1980), 189–96.

Lewis, M. M. *Language, Thought and Personality in Infancy and Childhood*. New York: Basic Books, 1963.

Lewis, Michael and Rosenblum, Leonard A., eds. *Interaction, Conversation, and the Development of Language*. New York: John Wiley and Sons, 1977.

Macken, Marlys A. "Developmental Reorganization of Phonology: A

Hierarchy of Basic Units of Acquisition," *Lingua,* 49 (1979), 11–49.

——— and Barton, David. "The Acquisition of the Voicing Contrast in English: A Study of Voice Onset Time in Word-Initial Stop Consonants," *Journal of Child Language,* 7 (1980), 41–74.

McCarthy, Dorothea. "Language Development in Children," in Carmichael.

McGinnis, Mildred A. *Aphasic Children: Identification and Education by the Association Method.* Washington: Alexander Graham Bell Association for the Deaf, 1963.

McNeill, David and McNeill, N. "What Does a Child Mean When He Says No?" in Ferguson and Slobin, 1973.

Meissner, Martin and Philpott, Stuart B. "The Sign Language of Sawmill Workers in British Columbia," *Sign Language Studies,* 9 (1975), 291–308.

Menn, Lise. "Phonotactic Rules in Beginning Speech: A Study in the Development of English Discourse," *Lingua,* 26 (1971), 225–51.

Menyuk, Paula. *Sentences Children Use.* Cambridge: M.I.T. Press, 1969.

Minifie, Fred D. and Lloyd, Lyle L., eds. *Communicative and Cognitive Abilities—Early Behavioral Assessment.* Baltimore: University Park Press, 1978.

Morehead, Donald M. and Morehead, Anne E., eds. *Normal and Deficient Child Language.* Baltimore: University Park Press, 1976.

Moskowitz, Arlene I. "The Two-Year-Old Stage in the Acquisition of English Phonology," in Ferguson and Slobin.

Nakazima, Sei. "A Comparative Study of the Speech Development of Japanese and American English in Childhood," *Studia Phonologica,* 4 (1966), 38–55.

———. "Phonemicization and Symbolization in Language Development," in Lenneberg and Lenneberg, 1975.

Nelson, Katherine. "Structure and Strategy in Learning to Talk," *Monographs of the Society for Research in Child Development,* 38 (1973).

———. "Some Attributes of Adjectives Used by Young Children," *Cognition,* 4 (1976), 13–30.

———; Rescorla, Leslie; Gruendel, Janice; and Benedict, Helen. "Early Lexicons: What Do They Mean?" *Child Development,* 49 (1978), 960–8.

Nelson, Keith E. "Facilitating Children's Syntax Acquisition," *Developmental Psychology,* 13 (1977), 101–7.

———, ed. *Children's Language; Volume 1.* New York: Gardner Press, 1978.

———; Carskaddon, Gaye; and Bonvillian, John D. "Syntax Acquisition: Impact of Experimental Variation in Adult Verbal Interaction With the Child," *Child Development,* 44 (1973), 497–504.

——— and Bonvillian, John D. "Concepts and Words in the 18-Month Old:

Acquiring Concept Names Under Controlled Conditions," *Cognition,* 2 (1973), 435–50.

Newport, Elissa L.; Gleitman, Henry; and Gleitman, Lila R. "Mother, I'd Rather Do It Myself: Some Effects and Non-Effects of Maternal Speech Style," in Snow and Ferguson.

Ochs, Elinor and Schieffelin, Bambi B., eds. *Developmental Pragmatics.* New York: Academic Press, 1979.

Oller, D. Kimbrough; Wieman, Leslie A.; Doyle, William J.; and Ross, Carol. "Infant Babbling and Speech," *Journal of Child Language,* 3 (1976), 1–11.

Olmsted, D. L. *Out of the Mouth of Babes: Earliest Stages in Language Learning.* The Hague: Mouton, 1971.

Park, Clara Claiborne. "Review of 'Nadia,'" *Journal of Autism and Childhood Schizophrenia,* 8 (1978), 457–72.

Piaget, Jean. *Play, Dreams and Imitation in Childhood.* New York: Norton, 1951.

Potts, Marion; Carlson, Patricia; Cocking, Rodney; and Copple, Carol. *Structure and Development in Child Language: The Preschool Years.* Ithaca, 1979.

Ramer, Andrya L. H. "Syntactic Styles in Emerging Language," *Journal of Child Language,* 3 (1976a), 49–62.

———. "The Function of Imitation in Child Language," *Journal of Speech & Hearing Research,* 19 (1976b), 700–17.

Richards, Meredith M. "Sorting Out What's in a Word from What's Not: Evaluating Clark's Semantic Features Acquisition Theory," *Journal of Experimental Child Psychology,* 27 (1979), 1–47.

Rodgon, Maris Monitz. *Single-Word Usage, Cognitive Development, and the Beginnings of Combinatorial Speech: A Study of Ten English-Speaking Children.* Cambridge: Cambridge University Press, 1976.

———. "Knowing What to Say and Wanting to Say It: Some Communicative and Structural Aspects of Single-Word Responses to Questions," *Journal of Child Language,* 6 (1979), 81–90.

Rutter, Michael, ed. *Infantile Autism: Concepts, Characteristics and Treatment.* Edinburgh: Churchill Livingstone, 1971.

———. "Diagnosis and Definition of Childhood Autism," *Journal of Autism and Childhood Schizophrenia,* 8 (1978), 139–60.

———; Bartak, Lawrence; and Newman, Steven. "Autism—A Central Disorder of Cognition and Language?" in Rutter, 1971.

Ryan, Joanna. "Interpretation and Imitation in Early Language Development," in Hinde and Stevenson-Hinde.

Sachs, Jacqueline and Devin, Judith. "Young Children's Use of Age-Appropriate Speech Styles in Social Interaction and Role Playing," *Journal of Child Language,* 3 (1976), 81–98.

Savic, Svenka. "Mother-Child Verbal Interaction; the Functioning of

Completions in the Twin Situation," *Journal of Child Language,* 6 (1979), 153–8.

Schachter, Frances Fuchs; Kirshner, Kathryn; Klips, Bonnie; Friedricks, Martha; and Sanders, Karin. "Everyday Preschool Interpersonal Speech Usage: Methodological, Developmental, and Sociolinguistic Studies." With commentary by Courtney B. Cazden and Lois Bloom. *Monographs of the Society for Research in Child Development,* 39 (1974), no. 3.

Schaeffer, Benson; Kollinzas, George; Musil, Arlene; and McDowell, Peter. "Spontaneous Verbal Language for Autistic Children Through Signed Speech," *Sign Language Studies,* 17 (1977), 287–328.

Schwartz, Richard G.; Leonard, Laurence B.; Wilcox, M. Jeanne; and Folger, M. Karen. "Again and Again: Reduplication in Child Phonology," *Journal of Child Language,* 7 (1980), 75–87.

Sears, Robert R. "The Growth of Conscience," in Iscoe and Stevenson.

Shatz, Marilyn and Gelman, Rachel. "The Development of Communication Skills: Modifications in the Speech of Young Children as a Function of Listener," *Monographs of the Society for Research in Child Development,* 38 (1973), no. 5.

Shields, Maureen M. "Dialogue, Monologue and Egocentric Speech by Children in Nursery Schools," in Garnica and King.

Shirley, Mary. "Common Content in the Speech of Preschool Children," *Child Development,* 9 (1938), 333–46.

Silberg, Joyanna L. "The Development of Pronoun Usage in the Psychotic Child," *Journal of Autism and Childhood Schizophrenia,* 8 (1978), 413–25.

Singer, Dorothy G. and Singer, Jerome L. *Partners in Play: A Step-by-Step Guide to Imaginative Play in Children.* New York: Harper & Row, 1977.

Slobin, Dan I. "The More It Changes . . . On Understanding Language By Watching It Move Through Time," *Papers and Reports on Child Language Development,* 10 (Sept. 1975), 1–30.

Smith, Frank and Miller, George A., eds. *The Genesis of Language: A Psycholinguistic Approach.* Cambridge: M.I.T. Press, 1966.

Smith, Madorah Elizabeth. "An Investigation of the Development of the Sentence and the Extent of Vocabulary in Young Children," *University of Iowa Studies in Child Welfare,* 3 (1926), no. 5.

Smith, Neilson V. *The Acquisition of Phonology: A Case Study.* Cambridge: Cambridge University Press, 1973.

Snow, Catherine E. and Ferguson, Charles A., eds. *Talking to Children: Language Input and Acquisition.* Cambridge: Cambridge University Press, 1977.

Steffensen, Margaret S. "Satisfying Inquisitive Adults: Some Simple Methods of Answering Yes/No Questions," *Journal of Child Language,* 5 (1978), 221–36.

Templin, Mildred C. *Certain Language Skills in Children: Their Development and Interrelationships.* Institute of Child Welfare Monograph No. 25. Minneapolis: The University of Minnesota Press, 1957.

Tervoort, Bernard T. *Developmental Features of Visual Communication: A Psycholinguistic Analysis of Deaf Children's Growth in Communicative Competence.* Amsterdam: North Holland Publishing Co., 1975.

Tonkova-Yampol'skaya, R. V. "Development of Speech Intonation in Infants During First Two Years of Life," in Ferguson and Slobin.

Trantham, Carla Ross and Pedersen, Joan K. *Normal Language Development: the Key to Diagnosis and Therapy for Language-Disordered Children.* Baltimore: Williams & Wilkins, 1976.

Trow, Jr., George W. S. "Within the Context of No-Context," *The New Yorker,* Nov. 17, 1980, 63–171.

Tyack, Dorothy and Ingram, David. "Children's Production and Comprehension of Questions," *Journal of Child Language,* 4 (1977), 211–24.

Viham, Marilyn Man. "Consonant Harmony: Its Scope and Function in Child Language," in Joseph H. Greenberg, ed. *Universals of Human Language: vol. 2, Phonology.* Stanford: Stanford University Press, 1978.

von Raffler-Engle, Walburga. "An Example of Linguistic Consciousness in the Child," in Ferguson and Slobin.

Weiss, Curtis E. and Lillywhite, Harold S. *Communicative Disorders.* St. Louis: C. V. Mosby Co., 1976.

Wilbur, Ronnie Bring. *American Sign Language and Sign Systems.* Baltimore: University Park Press, 1979.

Wing, J. K. "Diagnosis, Epidemiology, Aetiology," in J. K. Wing, ed. *Early Childhood Autism: Clinical, Educational and Social Aspects.* Oxford: Pergamon Press, 1966.

Wing, Lorna. "Perceptual and Language Development in Autistic Children: A Comparative Study," in Rutter, 1971.

Chapter 18
Notes

Chapter 4: *Cries, Coos, and Syllables*

[1] Landau, Table 5
[2] Lenneberg, 276–7.
[3] Crystal (1973), 25.
[4] Ferguson, 279–80; Piaget, 19.
[5] Landau, Table 6.
[6] Ferguson, Peizer and Weeks, 41.
[7] Crystal (1973), 22.
[8] Tonkova-Yampol'skaya, 130.
[9] Crystal (1973), 13.
[10] Ferguson, 280.
[11] Tonkova-Yampol'skaya.
[12] Ferguson, Peizer and Weeks, 40.
[13] Harding and Golinkoff, 34.
[14] Ferguson, 280.
[15] Lenneberg, 140.
[16] Kaplan and Kaplan, 365.
[17] based on Nakazima (1975), 183.
[18] Ferguson, 278.
[19] Nakazima (1975), 183.
[20] Oller, Wieman, Doyle and Ross, 2.
[21] based on Kaplan and Kaplan, 364.
[22] Jakobson, 69.
[23] Ferguson, 279.
[24] Nakazima (1966).

Chapter 5: *The First Words*

[1] Katherine Nelson (1973), 20.
[2] McCarthy, 527.
[3] Goldin-Meadow, Seligman and Gelman, 191.
[4] Greenfield and Smith, 206.
[5] *Ibid.*, 87.
[6] *Ibid.*, 112.
[7] Nelson and Bonvillian, 443–4.
[8] Gruendel, 1574–5.
[9] Nelson and Bonvillian, 895.
[10] see Bloom, 70; Ingram (1971), 898; Greenfield and Smith, 205; and Katherine Nelson (1973), general thesis.

238

[11] Greenfield and Smith, 159; Rodgon (1976), 43.
[12] *Ibid.,* Table 9.
[13] Nelson and Bonvillian, 442.
[14] Bloom, 93–4.
[15] Greenfield and Smith, 21–108.
[16] Greenfield and Smith, 112–23.
[17] Bloom, 51.
[18] Greenfield and Smith, 81–3.
[19] Greenfield and Smith, 134–42.
[20] Leonard, 100.
[21] Bloom, 90–3.
[22] Greenfield and Smith, 95–103.
[23] Bloom, 33.
[24] Greenfield and Smith, 156–7.
[25] *Ibid.,* 52.
[26] Rodgon (1976), 12–3.
[27] Nelson, Rescorla, Gruendel and Benedict, 964.
[28] Bloom, 110.
[29] Nelson (1976), 15n.
[30] Bloom, 66.
[31] Greenfield and Smith, 91.
[32] Bloom, 73.
[33] Eve Clark, 954.
[34] Bloom, 72.
[35] Nelson, Rescorla, Gruendel and Benedict, 967.
[36] M. M. Lewis, 51.
[37] Nelson, Rescorla, Gruendel and Benedict, 961.

Chapter 6: *Beyond Words*

[1] Brown, 89.
[2] Newport et al., 131.
[3] Folger and Chapman, 36.
[4] Leonard, Schwartz et al., 404; Bloom, Hood and Lightblown; Ramer (1976b).
[5] Savic, 154.
[6] Newport et al., 133.
[7] *Ibid.,* 138.
[8] Dore et al., 21–2.
[9] Steffensen, 234.
[10] *Ibid.,* 229.
[11] Braine (1976), Table 1 (Andrew corpus).
[12] *Ibid.,* Table 11 (David I corpus).
[13] *Ibid.,* Table 12 (David II corpus).
[14] *Ibid.,* Table 3 (Kendall II corpus).
[15] *Ibid.,* Table 14 (Embla corpus).
[16] *Ibid.,* Table 3 (Kendall II corpus).
[17] Brown, 181.
[18] Braine (1976), Table 10, footnote (Odi corpus).

Chapter 7: *The Discovery of Tradition*
[1]Hale, thesis; Jespersen, 183–7.
[2]Aimard examples #1, 5, 12, 74, 115, 192, 220, 312, 376, 520.

Chapter 8: *The Secrets of Conversation*
[1]Schachter et al., Table 26.
[2]Iwamura, 25.
[3]Tyack and Ingram, 222.
[4]Schachter et al., 39.
[5]Picture-book game based on work of Bokus and Shugar.
[6]Blank and Esposito.
[7]Garvey (1975), 56.
[8]Schachter et al.; Keenan; and Halliday (1969).
[9]Garvey and Hogan.
[10]Development of translation is static, based on analysis of Schachter et al., Table 7.
[11]*Ibid.*
[12]*Ibid.*
[13]Garvey (1975), 60.
[14]Schachter et al., Table 7.
[15]Iwamura, 59.
[16]Dore (1975); Sachs and Devin; and Shatz and Gelman.
[17]Rarity in child-adult talk of form (1) child speaks (2) adult replies, (3) child replies: Bloom, Rocissano and Hood, 541.
[18]Leonard, Newhoff and Fey, 193.
[19]Sachs and Devin; and Shatz and Gelman.
[20]Iwamura, 23.
[21]Keenan, 168.
[22]Bloom, Rocissano and Hood, Table 1.
[23]*Ibid.,* 541.
[24]Sachs and Devin, thesis.
[25]Iwamura, 128.
[26]Shields, 255.
[27]Iwamura, 126.
[28]Keenan, 168.
[29]Shields, 255.
[30]Garvey and Hogan, 566.
[31]Iwamura, 64.
[32]Garvey (1975), 42.

Chapter 9: *Confronting Grammar*
[1]Menyuk cover.
[2]Brown; Potts, Carlson, Cocking and Copple; Tranthan and Pedersen.
[3]Puppet game based on Kuczaj and Brannick.
[4]Keith Nelson (1977); Keith Nelson, Carskaddon and Bonvillian, Table 1.
[5]Menyuk, 129.
[6]*Ibid.,* 137.
[7]Cruttenden, 66.

[8] Ruth Clark, 3.
[9] *Ibid.,* 4.
[10] Slobin, 7–8.
[11] Cruttenden, 62.
[12] Cruttenden, 59; Kuczaj and Brannick, 43.
[13] Comrie, 8.

Chapter 10: *The Emergence of Style*

[1] M. Smith; McCarthy; Camaioni.
[2] Ervin-Tripp, 410.
[3] Camaioni, 75–76.
[4] Garvey (1979), 366.
[5] Camaioni, 73.
[6] Garvey (1979), 368.
[7] Camaioni, 73.
[8] Garvey (1979), 369.
[9] Ervin-Tripp, 409.
[10] *Ibid.,* 406.
[11] Garvey (1979), 366–9.
[12] Shirley, 334.
[13] *Ibid.,* Table 2.
[14] Iwamura, 120–1.
[15] Ervin-Tripp and Miller, 13–4.
[16] Dore (1978), 425.
[17] Richards, 37–9.
[18] *Ibid.,* 6–7.
[19] Ervin-Tripp and Miller, 10–1.
[20] Camaioni, 331.
[21] Gardner et al., 135.

Chapter 11: *The Role of the Parent*

[1] Pitcher and Prelinger, 169.
[2] *Ibid.,* 29.
[3] *Ibid.,* 37.
[4] *Ibid.,* 31.
[5] *Ibid.,* 71.

Chapter 12: *Language and the Home*

[1] Damon, 179.
[2] Sears, 105.
[3] Bettelheim, 9.
[4] Singer and Singer, 11.
[5] *Ibid.,* 166–9.
[6] Clarke-Stewart, 93.

Chapter 13: *Pronouncing It Correctly*

[1] Moskowitz; Macken and Barton; Olmsted; Blache; Ingram (1978); Allerton; N. Smith; and Templin.

[2] Menn, 247.
[3] Macken and Barton technique for testing words.
[4] Ferguson and Farwell, 436.
[5] Ingram (1976a), 124.
[6] Morley, 232.
[7] Jakobson, 15.
[8] Ingram (1976a), 128.
[9] Jakobson, 23.
[10] N. Smith, 145, 149.
[11] Ingram (1974b), 236–7.
[12] Morley, 41–2.
[13] Johnson and associates, thesis.
[14] von Raffler-Engle, 156.
[15] Ferguson, 293.
[16] Schwartz et al., 80.
[17] Ingram (1974a), part of his theory.
[18] Schwartz et al., Table 2.
[19] *Ibid.,* 246.
[20] Menn, Table 1.
[21] Ferguson and Farwell, 436.
[22] N. Smith, 219.
[23] Ingram (1976b).
[24] Braine (1974), 283–4.
[25] Ferguson, Peizer and Weeks, 41.
[26] Ferguson and Farwell, 431–7.
[27] Menn, 226.
[28] Ferguson, Peizer and Weeks, 36.
[29] Macken; Ingram (1974a, 1974b, 1976b); Viham.

Chapter 14: *Hearing Difficulty*
[1] Morley, 81.
[2] *Ibid.,* 61.
[3] Weiss and Lillywhite, 65.
[4] Jakobson, 14.
[5] Morley, 152.
[6] Hardy and Hardy, 17.
[7] Morley, 61.
[8] *Ibid.,* 140.
[9] Fraser and Blockley, 8.
[10] Wilbur, 196.
[11] *Ibid.,* 230.
[12] Meissner and Philpott; Kendon.
[13] Kangobai story: Kuschel.
[14] Goldin-Meadow and Feldman.
[15] Tervoort, 1–2.
[16] Wilbur, 37.
[17] *Ibid.,* 1.
[18] *Ibid.,* 33.

[19] *Ibid.*, 170.
[20] *Ibid.*, 158.
[21] *Ibid.*, 162.

Chapter 15: *Judging Your Child's Speech*
[1] Morley, 125.
[2] Rutter (1978), 148.
[3] Morley, 141.
[4] L. Wing, Table 2.
[5] Rutter (1978), 148.
[6] Morley, 135.
[7] *Ibid.*, 29.
[8] Karlin et al., 148.

Chapter 16: *Glossary*
[1] Morley, 131.
[2] McGinnis, 53.
[3] Rutter, Bartak and Newman, Table 2.
[4] McGinnis, 42–3.
[5] Friedlander et al.
[6] Rutter, Bartak and Newman, 162.
[7] McGinnis, 43.
[8] McGinnis; L. Wing, Table 8.
[9] Blank et al.
[10] Kanner, 242.
[11] Rutter (1978), 148.
[12] Silberg, 405.
[13] J. K. Wing, 24.
[14] Rutter (1978), 148.
[15] Rutter, Bartak and Newman, 153–4.
[16] L. Wing, 189.
[17] L. Wing, 193.
[18] J. K. Wing, 10.
[19] Kanner, 242.
[20] Rutter, Bartak and Newman, 145.
[21] Park, 458.
[22] J. K. Wing, 9.
[23] *Ibid.*, 10.
[24] Casey, 54–6.
[25] Schaeffer et al., 293–5.
[26] Menyuk, 125–43.

PART SIX

A
LANGUAGE
DIARY
FOR

This diary provides two ways for parents to keep track of their child's particular development. On each page is a drawing of a tape measure. Instead of measuring the child's physical growth, this tape follows language growth. Some of the spaces in the tape include a description of a key development. Parents can write the date of this event in the rule markings at the top of the space. I suppose it will be a miracle if it works right every time, but in theory the tape milestones should be reached in the order given. (Entries marked with an asterisk have room for fuller remarks in the diary below.)

The rest of the page raises specific questions about development and allows room for a variety of comments. These entries are arranged according to specific stages. During the transition periods, parents are likely to find they are making entries in two sections simultaneously.

Dates form an essential part of any diary entry; however, even well-trained observers are hard put to swear when some linguistic event happens the first time. The date you first notice something is close enough.

```
  |     |     |     |     |     |     |     |
0   Birth          1                 2
  |                 |                 |
```

PRECULTURAL SOUNDS

BIRTH CRY: Was it during or after delivery? If after, how long? Any remarks on how it sounded?_____

_____

_____

ONE MONTH OLD: Can human voice ever calm crying? What sounds have appeared besides crying? Fake cry? _Uh_ sound?_____

_____

_____

_____

HEARING MILESTONES: Give baby's age when you first notice . . .
turns in general direction of sudden loud noise_____
turns with head and eyes towards speaker_____
always able to locate sound source on first glance_____
ignores sound that would have previously called for a look. _
How do these milestones compare with Box 43? _____

_____

COO TO YOU TOO: How do you induce the baby to make sounds at age two months—by smiling, talking? Are there any settings where it is most easily done? _____

_____

_____

246

| 3 | *Makes cooing sound when sees a familiar face.* | 4 | | | 5 | *Whole jaw moves while making sounds.* |

THREE MONTHS OLD: What sounds does the baby make during a bath?

_____

_____

TONES OF VOICE: What age do you first notice your baby expressing
contentment _____
delight _____
effort _____
insistence _____

FIVE MONTHS OLD: What sort of listener is the baby? _____

_____

_____

BABBLING: Begins by voicing a series of vowel sounds. When did you first notice this? What were the circumstances? _____

_____

At a later stage, syllables like *ga-ga* appear. When did this happen? Examples of first such sounds? _____

_____

FAVORITE SOUNDS: Do you notice any sounds used in particular situations? Date each entry. _____

_____

_____

6	*Makes sound indicating desire.*	7	*Makes sound imitating a parent's sound.*	8

PLAY CHITCHAT: Three stages of pretend conversations are described for babbling children. Note when each stage could be played and how.

Stage 1 _____

_____

Stage 2 _____

_____

Stage 3 _____

_____

TEN MONTHS OLD: Preferred situations for vocalizing? Sorts of sounds in bath? Good way to evoke sounds? _____

_____

_____

WALKING: What is the language development like when child first begins to walk by self? Date? _____

_____

_____

COMPREHENSION: * A great milestone is when the child actually obeys an instruction. What was the instruction and response?

_____

_____

9	10 *Obeys an instruction.**	11

FIRST BIRTHDAY: This date offers a good opportunity to summarize your child's communication developments; first describe what the linguistic development has seemed like from a parent's view. _____

_____

_____

_____

Communication: What sounds does child make? What kinds of things are communicated by the sounds? _____

_____

Gesture: What are some typical gestures at this point? What situations provoke them? _____

_____

_____

Comprehension: What are some words and phrases the child can understand and respond to, even though she does not yet say anything similar? _____

_____

_____

_____

| 12 | 13 | 14 |

SECOND-YEAR BABBLING: During this period, babbling sounds grow more intricate; a number of personally expressive inventions are used; often, babbling sounds disappear almost completely in favor of words. Chart this development by noting for different ages: relative amount of babbling; examples of typical sounds and situations; what the sounds seem to express.

14 months _____

_____

15 months _____

_____

16 months _____

_____

18 months _____

_____

20 months _____

22 months _____

_____

15	16	17

SECOND-YEAR COMPREHENSION: Words and phrases child can understand but does not use. If any of these listed are later used, add date of this later accomplishment.

Names of family and friends _____

_____
_____
_____
_____

Names of things _____

_____
_____
_____

Instructions _____

_____
_____

Special examples of good understanding or interesting confusions _____

_____
_____
_____
_____

18	19	20	*Tenth word listed.**

SINGLE WORD

FIRST TEN WORDS: For each give date, word, pronunciation, likely source. A "word" is any sound the child has taken from others.

1 _____

2 _____

3 _____

4 _____

5 _____

6 _____

7 _____

8 _____

9 _____

10* _____

21 *Says* no *(or yes) in order to reject something.**	**22** *Uses greeting word (*hi *or* hello*) when friend arrives.*	**23**

Are most of the first ten words names or action words? _____

NO: Use of this word goes through several stages. Note date when you first hear it used in the following ways:
while doing something forbidden _____
when resisting temptation _____
when rejecting something (might also say *yes* here)* _____
_____

PRONUNCIATION: Chapter 13 lists two approaches to pronunciation. One is to repeat sounds. List any words that seem to fit this class.

_____
_____

A second approach is to reduce word to a monosyllable. List any words that seem to fit this class. _____
_____

Some words during this period are pronounced unusually well. List any words child can say nearly perfectly. _____
_____

Give words and pronunciation of words that fit no class. ___
_____

Does child prefer to repeat sounds or use monosyllables?
_____

| 24 | 25 | *Uses word to name thing associated with something present.* * | 26 |

NAMING SITUATIONS: Give date, word, and general situation when you first notice a word used in each of these situations:

Sees thing and uses pointing word. _____

_____

Hears thing and says name. _____

_____

Remembers thing. _____

_____

Wants thing. _____

Associates thing named with something present.* _____

_____

Uses thing as object of action. _____

_____

Greetings (list people child greets by name). _____

_____

_____

DISAPPEARS: When something disappears, child is more likely to name the fact than the thing that disappeared—e.g., "allgone." Note date and word child uses. _____

254

| 27 | 28 *Speaks own name.* | 29 *Names action of somebody else.* |

MASTERING DEFINITIONS: Some words are used in wrong situations; defined too narrowly or broadly. Note examples, later changes.

1 _____

2 _____

3 _____

4 _____

5 _____

6 _____

Also note some words that seem to be used correctly and fully right from the beginning. _____

Are there any striking differences between the words with easy definitions and the especially troublesome words? _____

POINTING: Give date when you notice the child regularly points with a thrusting hand toward particular things. _____

Note date and describe sound when you note child has a favorite sound to make while pointing. _____

Note date when child first uses an English name of thing pointing at _____.

EIGHTEEN MONTHS OLD: This date is another good point to pause and summarize your child's language development.

Intonation: What are the variety of emotions, attitudes, and expectations expressed? _____

_____

Comprehension: What are the various signs of comprehension you notice? _____

_____

Typical speech-provoking situations: _____

_____.

What is the most advanced language noticed so far? _____

_____

Gesture: Describe sorts of gestures used. _____

_____

Is the child a chatterbox or tight-lipped? _____
Is the child's vocabulary mostly English or private? _____

256

REMARKABLE VOCABULARY: Children often surprise their parents with the words they know. Even single-word usages are striking. Note examples, dates, situations, possible sources.

1 _____

2 _____

3 _____

4 _____

5 _____

6 _____

7 _____

Is there a period when meaningless sounds are added to the front of words? _____

Give dates and examples when child seems uncertain which of two words to use. _____

_____

36	37 *Fourth original combination listed.**	38 *Fourth stock phrase listed.**

PRIMITIVE SENTENCES

STOCK PHRASES: * A major part of language development comes from the use of role phrases as clichés. List the first four noted, date.

1 _____

_____ _____

2 _____

_____

3 _____

_____

4 _____

_____

ORIGINAL COMBINATIONS: * At same time clichés arise, words are joined into original phrases invented by child. Give details.

1 _____

_____

2 _____

_____

3 _____

_____

4 _____

_____

Which list completed first, stock phrases or originals? _____

_____

258

PRONUNCIATION: Note date at which it seems to you the child can reliably pronounce the following sounds:

    p as in *pop* ————————————————————

    g as in *goes* ————————————————————

    w as in *weasel** ————————————————

    n as in *no.* —————————————————————

Are there any sounds the child seems to favor? (E.g., sounds stuck onto ends of words, used in substitutions.) —————

————————————————————————————

————————————————————————————

Are there any words the child seems to avoid saying because they are hard to pronounce? ——————————————

————————————————————————————

How does child respond to pronunciation correction?

    Early in primitive-sentence stage? ————————

————————————————————————————

    At end of stage? ——————————————————

————————————————————————————

————————————————————————————

FIRST GRAMMAR: * Give words, dates, and situations where you first notice the following relations expressed in two words.

Naming (e.g., *hi doggie*) _____

Desire (e.g., *want milk*) _____

Description (e.g., *big doggie*) _____

Association (e.g., *milk here*) _____

Action (e.g., *doggie run*) _____

NEGATIVES: Note date when *no* is used in combination with another word to indicate:

Rejection (e.g., *no push*) _____
Disappearance or absence (e.g., *no milk*) _____
What is child's preferred way of replying to yes/no questions?
Early in primitive-sentence stage? _____
_____

At end of stage? _____
_____
_____

45	46	47

CLEVER SENTENCES: Give examples of sentences that give striking insights into what child thinks or how child puts things.

1 _____

_____

2 _____

_____

3 _____

_____

4 _____

_____

GROPING: Give a few examples of any unstable word order you notice as child struggles to determine correct word order.

1 _____

_____

2 _____

_____

PRACTICE: Give examples of phase where one word is used in many sentences, once word order for that word is settled.

1 _____

_____

2 _____

_____

QUESTIONS: What kind of questions does child ask early in the primitive-sentence stage? _____

_____

Toward the end of the stage? _____

_____

_____

LONGER SENTENCES: Late in the stage, original combinations of three or more words appear. List some early examples and describe the situation.

1 _____

_____

2 _____

_____

3 _____

_____

ORIGINAL QUESTIONS: During this stage, stock questions like *what that?* are given a more original form, *what her say?* Give examples.

1 _____

_____

2 _____

_____

3 _____

_____

51 *Past tense indicated by adding -ed to word.*	**52** *Makes effort to clarify self.**	**53**

USING ENGLISH

STOCK SITUATIONS: By late primitive-sentence stage, there may be recurring situations that evoke recurring sentences. Examples:

1 _____

2 _____

3 _____

4 _____

BREAKDOWN: You may notice that some stock speech turns up in a novel situation with a slight change in the speech. List any.

1 _____

2 _____

3 _____

4 _____

5 _____

CONVERSATION: Note date, context when you first observe:
Makes effort to clarify self.* _____

_____

Uses speech to compare self with another. _____

_____

Uses speech to assert links with another. _____

_____

Expresses an idea sprung purely from imagination. _____

_____

Changes speech to take listener's needs into account. ____

_____

Suggests a mutual activity. _____

Resolves a dispute by relying on words.* _____

Able to converse with friend on telephone.* _____

_____

57	58 *Resolves a dispute through words.**	59

QUESTIONS: Questions provide interesting evidence of both a child's grammatical and intellectual state. List some questions that seem typical of child's interests. Date entries.

1 _____

_____

2 _____

_____

3 _____

_____

4 _____

_____

PRONUNCIATION: Note dates when following sounds are mastered:

oo as in b*oo*t _____

f as in *f*un _____

ng as in thi*ng* _____

ngk as in thi*nk* _____

kw as in *qu*ick _____

l as in *l*ion _____

r as in *r*oar _____

ch as in *ch*urch _____

sh as in *sh*ip _____

60	61	62	*Able t* *conver* *with* *friend* *tele-* *phone*

PUNS: From the late single-word stage on, you may observe your child consciously playing on words. Note examples and dates.

1 _____

2 _____

3 _____

4 _____

5 _____

6 _____

7 _____

8 _____

9 _____

10 _____

About the Author

EDMUND BLAIR BOLLES, born 1942 in Washington, D.C., studied language and literature at Washington University (St. Louis) and in graduate school. As a boy he lived in France for three years, and in this bilingual setting he first became interested in questions about the nature of language. After receiving an M.A. from the University of Pennsylvania, he entered the Peace Corps and was posted to a remote village in Tanzania, where he taught agriculture, science, and math at two primary schools. Eventually he was able to conduct all his classes in the Swahili language. This daily use of an African tongue led him to reconsider many of his assumptions about language. Returning to the United States in 1969, he published several articles about language and began to pursue a career as a writer. "The revolution in child-language studies became a passion of mine," he recalls. Indeed it did. So many child-language books appeared on the shelves in his home that guests sometimes assumed that before becoming a writer, he had been a professional linguist. He has previously published two books and many articles. His work has been translated into French and Italian.

Index